"The last thing Caden needs is to get caught in the middle," Zuri said.

Damon gave a wry smile.

"I think it's too late for that, but yeah, I don't even want to deal with telling my parents yet. Let's get through the holidays. Or wait until Caden brings it up. I'm sure once the idea of having me in his life sinks in, he'll realize through mere deduction that he has another set of grandparents."

He was implying that Caden was caught in the middle of the two of them, which meant he was still intending to take custody

"Damon, you want what's best for him, don't you? You wouldn't cause problems just to satisfy your need to stake your claim, would you?"

"Don't try and make me sound like the villain here. Guilt-tripping isn't going to work. What's best for him is having a father around. You wouldn't have come here if you didn't agree."

Dear Reader,

Whether it's retaking an exam or giving a heartfelt apology, second chances can open doors and change life's trajectory. But they can also range from simple to very complicated. After all, mental and emotional guards can be tough to crack.

In *Second Chance Christmas*, former navy SEAL Damon Woods isn't proud of his past. Not only had he caused unforgivable pain to the one friend he trusted in high school, he also had robbed himself of the first twelve years of his son's life. He's a changed man. He's faced death and suffering, but none of those challenges seem as impossible as earning back Zuri's trust...and heart.

Still mourning her sister's death, environmental chemist Dr. Zuri Habib knows introducing her nephew to his father is the right thing to do. But if she can't forgive the past, and Damon can't forgive himself, neither of them will ever get a second chance at love.

My door is open at rulasinara.com, where you'll find my newsletter sign-up, social media links, information on my books and more.

Wishing you love, peace and courage in life,

Rula Sinara

HEARTWARMING

Second Chance Christmas

Rula Sinara

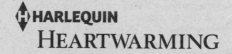

HARLEQUIN®
HEARTWARMING™

ISBN-13: 978-1-335-17973-9

Second Chance Christmas

Copyright © 2021 by Rula Sinara

Recycling programs for this product may not exist in your area.

This edition published by arrangement with Harlequin Books S.A.

For questions and comments about the quality of this book, please contact us at CustomerService@Harlequin.com.

Harlequin Enterprises ULC
22 Adelaide St. West, 40th Floor
Toronto, Ontario M5H 4E3, Canada
www.Harlequin.com

Printed in U.S.A.

Award-winning and *USA TODAY* bestselling author **Rula Sinara** lives in rural Virginia with her family and wild but endearing pets. She loves organic gardening, attracting wildlife to her yard, planting trees, raising backyard chickens and drinking more coffee than she'll ever admit to. Rula's writing has earned her a National Readers' Choice Award and a HOLT Medallion, among other honors. Her door is always open at rulasinara.com, where you can sign up for her newsletter, learn about her latest books and find links to her social media hangouts.

Books by Rula Sinara

Harlequin Heartwarming

From Kenya, with Love

The Promise of Rain
After the Silence
Through the Storm
Every Serengeti Sunrise
The Twin Test
The Marine's Return

Turtleback Beach

Almost a Bride
Caught by the Sheriff

A Heartwarming Thanksgiving
"The Sweetheart Tree"

Visit the Author Profile page
at Harlequin.com for more titles.

To Naya. You inspire me every day.

Acknowledgment

To Johanna Raisanen, fellow dog lover and amazing editor, for your expert guidance and patience. Thank you for helping me bring a stronger story to life.

CHAPTER ONE

ZURI HABIB USED to dream about jogging on a beach with windswept hair and Damon Woods—her high school friend and secret crush—running toward her with love in his eyes. It took a few years of brain development and maturity for her to realize that hormones and binging on the old seventies and eighties beach movies she'd found one summer in her grandmother's stash were to blame for those ridiculously naive teen fantasies.

Yet, here she was on Turtleback Beach more than a decade later, a few hundred yards from Damon with nothing but cool sand and a brisk breeze between them, failing miserably at squashing the unwelcomed butterflies in her stomach. *You're facing Damon of all people. They're not butterflies. Don't let him mess with your head.*

She sucked in a lungful of ocean air and

folded her arms. Damon Woods and all his mysterious broodiness was not going to get to her. She wasn't a teenager anymore. Her brains had earned her a PhD and she was building name recognition in the environmental research community. She knew how to stand her ground and earn respect amongst men in her field. She could certainly face Damon again.

For one thing, life had turned her into a realist. She'd given up long ago on ever looking like a hot ten from a beach flick. Those genes had gone to her older sister. But unlike young Zuri, the woman she was now had enough self-respect to not want to be anyone else. Which was why it bugged the heck out of her that she was suddenly feeling self-conscious for not changing out of her old jeans and her favorite sweatshirt with the recycling symbol on it and into something more…she wasn't sure. Attractive? Secondly, the look in Damon's eyes at the moment was dark and turbulent… but not in a good way. And lastly, it didn't help that the twelve-year-old at her side, whom he'd never met, looked just like him.

You've got this, Zuri. Everything will

turn out fine. His email reply was nice enough. Yeah, but only because she hadn't given him all the facts. Even from this distance, and with his moving through the surf, she could tell by the look in his eyes those facts were sinking in quickly. Unless he was merely struck by seeing her again after all these years. Bottom line was that some things warranted a face-to-face conversation. Coming down here in person also kept her in control of the situation. At least it made her *feel* like she was in control. After overhearing his mother mention where he was currently living and working, tracking down his work email online had been easy. The Turtleback Beach Ocean Rescue and Beach Patrol website had phone numbers, but she didn't dare call. Back when they were kids, Damon used to tell her he could hear it in her voice when something was up. Email put her in charge of that, too.

Zuri had kept it simple. She had mentioned that she was going to be in Turtleback over the holidays and that it would be nice to see him. She did say that she'd have a kid with her, but that the boy had been through a lot and she'd catch Damon up on her life when they had a chance to speak in private. She had to say that much so that he wouldn't react or ask questions in front of Caden. Damon didn't pry in the email. Clearly being in the military had taught him respect and manners. He simply said no problem—likely assuming the kid was hers and she was either a widow or divorcée—and then he let her know his schedule so that she could find him depending on when she arrived in Turtleback.

The sand beneath her sneakers gave way as she tried to stand a little taller. She fidgeted with the keys in her pocket. Angry as she was at him for enlisting in navy SEAL training out of high school and disappearing from her and her older sister's lives without a word, she had to admit he looked even better than he did back then, with shoulders built by years of SEAL operations and, later, water rescue experience. She'd never seen his hair so short either. The closest had been the tight coils he had senior year, but the short buzz cut he had now looked really good on him. The red windbreaker and matching uniform shorts helped his overall appeal, too. The man was at least a nine out of ten, which kind of irked her. Clearly too hot to be cold on a beach wearing shorts in December.

"Whoa. I never thought I'd see a live water rescue. That man saved him. Did you see him haul that guy out of the water, Aunt Zuri? Way cool!"

Caden pointed toward the man he had no idea was his father and the action underway down the stretch of beach. She had to admit, the Outer Banks of North Carolina made a stunning backdrop for the equally beautiful beach patrol group. This southern end of the two-hundred-mile-long string of islands, which formed the famous east coast barrier reef, was even more to her liking than the touristy northern tip. Hatteras Island, where the quaint town of Turtleback Beach lay between Avon and Rodanthe, harbored pristine beaches and marshes. Even Caden, who'd vehemently protested their Christmas vacation trip down here from Boston, had perked up at the sight of sand dunes, wildlife, sea turtle nesting grounds and picturesque lighthouses along their drive down Highway 12 toward their uncertain fate in Turtleback.

Damon looked their way again, as he exchanged a few last words with the man he'd just saved. This was it. She had to go through with her plan. She was essentially trapped at this point, in more ways than one. Ironically, the Outer Banks was flanked by water on both sides with basically one main road in and out. A part of her wanted to grab Caden's hand, turn around and run back to the B and B where she'd rented a room, but the anger and bitterness that had simmered all these years gave her strength. Her resolve to tell the truth and do what she knew to be right kept her grounded in place. As steady as she could be in sand. She'd face Damon, let Caden run off and play out of earshot, give Damon a brief and probably unwanted update on their lives…and mention that he's a father. Then her sister's secret and the truth that Zuri had been keeping from her nephew would be out and Damon could walk away if he wanted.

Just as he'd done before.

She took a deep breath and put a hand on Caden's shoulder.

"I saw. I wouldn't call it cool, though.

It's dangerous. That water is dangerous. Don't you dare go in without me present or without a lifeguard around while we're here. Got it?"

"I'm not stupid."

"I didn't say that you are. But swimming in an ocean is nothing like swimming in a pool."

She left out the part about him not being the strongest pool swimmer either. She'd been trying to build the boy's confidence, not tear it down. He was smart. Like his aunt. Athletic? Not so much. Again, much like his aunt. Plus, the kid had been extra sensitive lately, which was partly why she'd brought him down here. *Forced* him down here was more like it. Caden hadn't wanted to leave home. Getting him to go anywhere had been a struggle since his mom had lost her battle with cancer right after the school year had begun. But her sister had foreseen everything Zuri was dealing with and she had made Zuri promise that she'd take Caden on a vacation for the holidays…a time when she knew the boy would struggle more with his loss. What her sister hadn't intended was for Zuri to finally bring father and son together.

I'm so sorry, Vera, but I have to do this. For Caden. I love you, sis. Forgive me.

"I get it. I read the warning pamphlet in our room," Caden said. "Pretty sick stuff. I know all about undertows and riptides now, not that I'm planning on swimming. I didn't even bring my trunks. You didn't tell me it would be warmer down here than back home. December without snow. As if this Christmas wasn't ruined enough already."

"Caden, we talked about this. Please don't get started again. I get it. I really do. But we're here. Let's make the most of it." She was exhausted. Drained. She just wanted to get through the day.

He shrugged and looked away, kicking sand for good measure, then he challenged her, trudging closer to the surf, where the wet sand glistened in the midday sun. Just close enough for the salt water to skim the bottom of his sneakers. It wasn't exactly flip-flop weather and they'd packed light. Which meant no extra shoes and he knew it.

A massive black dog wearing an orange life vest emerged from the group where

Damon stood in the distance, barked in her direction, then made a beeline for her nephew.

"Caden! Get back here!" She ran, trying to put herself between the barking, bear-like beast and the kid.

"Duck! No! Leave it," Damon called out, as he sprinted after the dog.

It all registered in agonizingly slow motion… Damon closing the distance just as his dog bounded through the fizzling surf, drenching Zuri's jeans and most of Caden. "Duck" grabbed the hem of Caden's jacket and tugged him up onto dry sand. Then, just as Damon reached them, the dog shook the water out of his thick fur and all over Zuri. Clearly, Duck had been in the water for the rescue operation before spotting them and hadn't had a chance to dry out. Caden laughed and began petting the dog. Zuri closed her eyes for a moment, trying to will her cheeks not to turn red. It wasn't working. They only felt hotter. So much for feeling self-conscious *before* getting drenched. She pinched her wet sweatshirt away from her body and tried to wipe some of the water off her cheeks.

"Zuri."

His voice was deeper than she remembered. More commanding. She peered at him from beneath her lashes. *Come on. You're not in high school anymore.* She raised her chin and cleared her throat.

"Damon. Hi. I mean, tell me that's not your dog." She glanced over at Caden, who seemed preoccupied enough with Duck.

"She is. Sorry. I remember how you were about dogs. We live over there. Just the two of us," he said, as he took hold of Duck's collar and gently ordered her to stay by his side.

Just the two of them? Was he trying to tell her he was single? She hadn't asked. She wasn't interested, other than how anyone in his life would potentially impact her nephew. She'd been around single guys who threw status hints out in midconversation. Unless it was his way of saying he liked being left alone. Man and dog. *Stop. Focus.* She really needed to stop overthinking. Nerves always did this to her.

He motioned over to a beach house that stood closer to where she'd first spotted him. Its wood was weathered and gray, unlike many of the other cottages along the beach. Several others had been painted in pastels, from pink tones to blue and yellow. Some were simple in architecture, while a few, like a Victorian-style white one down the beach on the opposite side of the town's boardwalk, looked as though their owners had recently renovated them. All of them were built on stilts, lifting them over the short dunes that separated the town and road from the actual beach and protecting them, no doubt, from flooding.

"I'm okay with normal-sized dogs," she said. That was kind of a stretch. Dogs still made her a bit nervous, but she could handle most. This one was *not* a typical dog. Damon gave a lopsided grin and glanced at his girl, but the smile didn't reach his eyes. Zuri was thankful that he was sticking to what she'd requested in the email and holding any questions for later.

"Her name is Duck. Newfoundlands have water rescue in their genes. Down to her webbed feet. She'd live in the water if she could. Goes with her name. She believes she just saved you," he told Caden.

"That's awesome," Caden said, letting

the dog lick his face. "I don't mind getting wet. Did she help you save that man over there, too?"

Damon looked back over his shoulder and, this time, couldn't resist a full smile. Zuri's insides went to mush. His smile hadn't changed. It was the same one that used to break hearts and ruin lives. Only this time it was lit with pride. God, she hoped he'd be able to open his heart and show love and pride for his son, too, someday.

"Yes and no," Damon said. "What you saw wasn't a real rescue. It was a training session, both for her and for some new recruits on my team."

"Cool. Can she play fetch or is she still having a lesson?" Caden asked, picking up a small piece of driftwood.

"Wait," Zuri said. "We should get back to our room so we can get dried up. I don't want you getting sick. I'm sure you can see Duck again later."

"But it's a beach. You're supposed to get wet," Caden said.

"Not in the middle of winter. It's cold and you're a mess with all the sand sticking to your clothes."

"Oh, come on. Who cares?" Caden cocked his head in a way that laid on the guilt. Leave it to a kid to make her feel superficial and ridiculous.

"Yeah, who cares. It's just water and sand." Damon wasn't smiling anymore. He raised one brow in challenge. *He doesn't want to wait. He's trying to get the kid to go off so he can speak freely. You expected this. Postponing it won't make a difference.* She stood a little straighter and tugged the hem of her shirt.

"Okay. Just for a few minutes. If you're sure it's all right, her being a working dog and all," she added, turning to Damon.

"Duck can play. Just stay off the areas marked with those short reed fences. Those are sea turtle nesting grounds. And stay away from the water."

Caden threw the stick before Damon finished his sentence, then took off after Duck. Damon folded his arms and narrowed his eyes at Zuri.

"It's good to see you, Zuri. It really is. But why do I get the distinct feeling you didn't come to Turtleback for a vacation like your email implied?"

She shifted her feet in the sand and wrapped her arms around her waist. It was in the fifties, but the wet clothes and wind made her shiver. That and standing so close to Damon.

"True." She rubbed her forehead. "I mean, it is a vacation. Of sorts."

He nodded and narrowed his eyes in Duck and Caden's direction.

"You were always straight with me, Zuri. Who's the kid?"

She closed her eyes briefly, then glanced at her nephew to assure herself he was far enough not to hear.

"His name is Caden." She fished for the right words. How was she supposed to break it to him? It was obvious he suspected but putting it in words felt so conclusive. There'd be no more turning back. No more secrets or lies after so many years of keeping them. "He doesn't know—"

"That he's mine?" Damon's lips tightened and his eyes darkened as he scanned the horizon. "Is he? Mine?"

She looked down at the sand sticking to her wet sneakers and focused on the broken shell a few inches away.

"Yes." The weight that lifted off her chest with that simple word was instantly replaced with a heavier one as she held her breath and waited for his reaction.

He rubbed the back of his neck and top of his head. She could see his jaw clench and unclench.

"You and I never…which means—"

"I'm his aunt."

He was smart enough to conclude the rest. The creases around his eyes deepened, as though eroded by betrayal and questions. She remembered feeling lost and broken when he'd left Boston and never returned. Only she couldn't blame him right now. Her sister had kept the worst possible secret from him and Zuri's loyalty had been with Vera, not him. Vera was her sister and Zuri didn't believe in turning one's back on family. Damon stepped closer, his expression shifting from confusion and anger to worry, as he connected the dots.

"What happened, Zuri? What's wrong? Where's Vera?"

The rims of her eyes stung, and she pressed her fingers to her mouth to try and stop her chin from quivering. She needed to stay strong. For Vera. For Caden. She had always been the person they could lean on and she needed to keep being that person for her nephew. Father or not, Damon wasn't her responsibility. Caden was. She swallowed hard and looked up at Damon, her heart crumbling to pieces all over again as the words caught in her throat.

"Vera is dead."

DAMON FELT LIKE he'd had the air knocked out of him. Vera was dead? He was a father? He wasn't sure which fact was tripping him more. He glanced over at the boy playing with Duck. The kid reminded him so much of his late, younger brother it hurt. He looked a lot like Damon, too. He knew it. The second he saw the boy and Zuri he knew in his gut something was wrong. She'd mentioned bringing a kid along, but Damon had assumed that meant she'd had a child in the years since he last saw her. He'd assumed that maybe she had a recent breakup and needed to get away. Lots of people came to the Outer Banks as an escape. His chest felt numb. He was a father and had been for the past twelve years and the truth had been kept from him? He'd been slammed and pulled under by monstrous waves before, but none had left his lungs feeling as useless as right now.

Throughout his training as a SEAL, through every covert operation overseas, through the past four years here as head of Turtleback Beach's Ocean Rescue and Beach Patrol division...and all along he'd had a son. He muttered a curse and turned his back on her. He looked over the rough waters of the Atlantic, familiar with every square inch of the shoreline he lived on, yet fully aware that it never stayed the same. The ocean ebbed and flowed and changed its sands every day. He'd come to believe that he'd finally found stability in his life. What a lie. He should have known. He was trained to expect the unexpected. He just never thought it would involve a kid. Nor was he expecting it to involve the death of someone else from his past. He'd never quite gotten over the loss of his own brother. Or so many of his SEAL brothers in the line of duty.

"Are you sure?" The question sounded pathetic considering the boy's looks. He had Woods in him all right. Those dark eyes, full lashes and the way his lips quirked and revealed dimples when he smiled were how everyone could always tell that Damon, Leo, Shawn and Lucas were brothers.

"That you're the father? Absolutely. But you're free to get tested."

He might have to get tested if Vera didn't have him listed on the birth certificate, but the boy was definitely a younger version of him…or more so, Lucas. He looked so much like a Woods that the sight of him opened an old wound. Lucas couldn't have been much older than Caden when Damon had gotten word, while overseas, that he'd drowned. The memory still haunted him. Lucas had been the youngest of four. Damon, the oldest. And he still couldn't get past the belief that, had he not escaped his home life the first chance he had, he'd have been around to save his little brother.

A lump rose in his chest and he tried rubbing it away but it grew and hardened when he turned and caught Zuri wiping her cheeks. She'd lost her older sister. He knew the pain she had to be going through. He sucked in a breath of salty air and tucked his hands in the pockets of his windbreaker to keep himself from wrapping his arms around her. There was a time when doing so would have felt natural and expected, but not anymore.

"I'm sorry, Zuri. When? I don't mean the testing. I mean Vera. What happened? How long ago?"

Zuri closed her eyes briefly before answering.

"October 5. Her cancer had metastasized by the time they found it. It started as ovarian. She endured every treatment the doctors recommended and was so determined to be okay for him."

Damon muttered a curse under his breath. They were still in mourning. Still learning to cope. Zuri shivered and lifted her shoulders as a gust blew past them.

"Here." Damon took off his windbreaker and put it around her shoulders. "I'm really sorry. I don't know what to say. I'm sorry you lost your sister and furious all at once and I—I just don't know. I'm trying to process it all," he said, looking back at Caden as the boy took the stick from

Duck, then tried wiping the slobber it came with on his clothes. Duck was never short on drool. *Caden. Your son's name is Caden.* Damon's head pounded and he squeezed his temples between his thumb and fingers. Why hadn't either of his parents mentioned that an old classmate had died? His dad had moved out of state but his mother still lived on the same street as Zuri's family. Wouldn't they have heard? Then again, they knew any talk of funerals or loss never ended well with him. Their phone calls tended to be short as it was, so they learned to avoid talking about Lucas or anything that would cause an argument. That included visits during any major holiday. "You caught me off guard. I just need to let it sink in."

"Of course. I, um, have to ask you not to say anything just yet. To Caden. He's been through a lot and dealing with his mother dying has been hard on him, to say the least. He's asked about who his father is multiple times, especially since entering middle school, but I think we need to be sitting somewhere private and bring it up gently."

"Sure. I get that. And you should both go change and warm up. But first I need to know why she never told me."

"You left," she said, tugging his jacket across her chest, then reaching back to pull her long dark hair out from under it. There was a fierceness in her eyes he'd never seen before. She'd always been soft, from her brown eyes to her personality. Too insecure for the friends he hung around back then. She'd taken being an introvert to an extreme—a quintessential bookworm— and he…well, he'd been the opposite. He had been part of the popular crowd. The jocks and cheerleaders and otherwise "cool" students, including Vera.

"That's no excuse. You found me now. She could have if she had wanted to. You could have found me."

"Why in the world would I betray my sister? To you of all people? After what you did to me? You hurt me. Humiliated me and I couldn't even comprehend why. Vera asked me not to say anything and I agreed with her. Could you blame either of us? You know what our parents were like, Damon. Our moms never got along even prior to that lawsuit. Our dads might have been more reasonable—mine always commented on how smart and well-mannered your brothers were, but that you were another matter. You grated on his nerves. At least he understood that your mother had simply been doing her job as a lawyer when she took that medical liability case against my mother, but I doubt he would have been so levelheaded if he knew you were Caden's father. Could you imagine what would have happened had Vera told them that she'd lost her virginity to you? War would have broken out. My mother would have flipped, especially since that trial had just ended. You, the school's girl magnet. A player. God, how many times had they warned me about high school guys having one track minds? I should have listened. All you cared about was maintaining your image."

Damon's chest tightened. He knew exactly what she meant. Not just the way he was back then, but the heartless way he'd gone above and beyond to make sure Zuri—and every student who'd overheard her asking him out and started gossiping about it—understood that she wasn't his type. That he was out of her league. He'd come to really value the friendship they had that had grown so naturally out of the sessions where she helped him in a school-sponsored peer-tutoring clinic—a program where there was always a teacher on hand, but approved students with good grades could volunteer there for extra credit.

He never realized he'd given her the wrong impression. Or maybe he had but he liked the comfortable relationship they'd formed so much that he didn't want to let it go. He had thought his reputation was safe being around her under the excuse of homework tutoring. She'd caught him off guard when she asked him out and, instead of handling it well, he'd been a jerk. An immature idiot who'd scoffed at her, acted surprised, then by the next day, had asked her sister, Vera, a fellow senior, to prom. In retrospect, he couldn't excuse the behavior and the damage was done.

"Maybe you should have," he hissed, then pressed his fingers to his eyes. "Look. I'm sorry for what happened. I was a different person back then. A messed-up kid.

If I could go back, I'd handle it all differently, but I can't time travel. I'm not asking for forgiveness. I think we're both past that. But it has been over a decade since I took Vera to prom. You can't tell me that she was under your parents' rule all that time. That she cared so much about what they thought of me that she didn't try to find me."

"In some ways, yes, she cared. For the sake of keeping the peace and because she needed their help. The only people she could count on and trust were our parents and myself. You can't blame her for not believing she could count on you after the way you ignored her after prom then left town without a word. No goodbyes. No explanations or apologies. No visits. Even your social media went dark. And the fact was that, yes, you *were* a player. You couldn't even commit to a club at school or to future college plans. She didn't want someone like that being her son's role model. I couldn't disagree with her. Nor could I betray her. She didn't want you in the picture and it was her call. You couldn't possibly imagine how scared she was at first, finding herself pregnant at eighteen."

Damon couldn't move. He didn't have a right to move, to think, to feel. Zuri was right. He'd failed her. He'd failed her sister…and his brother. But he'd known at the time that he'd never live up to his own parents' expectations, let alone anyone else's. That was part of the reason why he'd left town. There was no way to right what he'd done or what had happened.

There were times he'd wanted to tell Zuri he had valued and cared for her beyond tutoring or friendship, but he didn't want to ruin how things were between them. And when she'd indicated she liked him as more, it had scared him. It had him running and throwing up every barrier he could think of. Zuri Woods, with her smooth olive skin and her warm brown eyes, had been the very picture of a soft-hearted girl who only entered meaningful, long-term relationships. He didn't believe in long term. He'd witnessed firsthand his parents' abysmal marriage. And as shallow as he'd acted at times in school, deep down he knew better than to drag someone like Zuri—someone he actually respected—into the circle of self-centered, popular kids he hung around with. Smart kids for sure, but also way too willing to push boundaries and test rules. Students her sister, who was way more of a rebel than Zuri, hung out with, too. Zuri wouldn't have been comfortable around them. In a way, he had been protecting her. He hadn't wanted to ruin Zuri's life, yet apparently, he had anyway. Hers and her sister's.

"You have me there. I know there's nothing I can say and no amount of apology can come close to fixing things. I'm sorry, Zuri. I know you won't believe it, but despite how I acted in high school, you were the one person I trusted. All those other kids I hung around didn't count. They were fun, but not people I could count on. I didn't realize all that until after I went on my first SEAL mission and understood what trusting another human being—putting your life on the line for them and trusting them with yours—really meant. I'm sorry Vera couldn't count on me. I'm sorry I hurt you. But that doesn't change the fact that I wasn't told I had a son. A *child*, Zuri. My making bad choices at eighteen doesn't mean I didn't have a right to know about something that important."

"Doesn't it? Did your choices really change after that? You didn't even come back for Lucas's funeral. Your own brother. Even my parents had the decency to attend."

"I was overseas on a mission!" He swallowed his next words, realizing his voice was carrying on the wind. He squeezed the bridge of his nose, then let his arms fall to his sides. He hadn't heard about Lucas until after he'd completed the military operation. It had been three days after the fact and the news had lengthened the mental and emotional recovery time before he was able to get cleared for another assignment. War had a way of twisting even the toughest person's mind, but for all the death he'd witnessed, nothing had hollowed him out and left him numb like being told his little brother had died. Damon had been the one risking his life in dangerous regions. Not Lucas. It wasn't fair. The sound of Caden laughing and Duck barking drew his attention. Life wasn't fair. "I did visit his grave when I had been given a few days' leave to do so," he said, lowering his voice.

"Wait a minute. You came to Boston?"

He'd never meant for anyone to find out. He had wanted to slip in, check on his other siblings and parents—who'd finally divorced by then—and get out of town.

"I didn't know I had a child. Had I known I would have gone to see him. Maybe I couldn't have been around every day, given my deployment, but I wouldn't have been MIA. But I wasn't given the chance to prove that. Was I?"

"Well, if you really care, you have the chance to prove it now. If we've learned anything from Vera's and Lucas's deaths it's that life's too short for lies. I couldn't go on lying to Caden when I know the truth. I don't expect anything from you, other than to stay in touch with him. He needs to know that he won't be alone. He'll always have me and his grandparents, but I wanted him to know he has a father, too. A living parent. I'm hoping that maybe it will give him a little hope while dealing with his mother's loss."

"You want me to introduce myself as

his dad, then send him on his merry way? That's supposed to make him feel better?"

Unbelievable.

"Yes, actually. I'm listed as his legal guardian and I won't have Caden uprooted at a fragile time in his life and sent to live with a man he doesn't even know. You don't know anything about him. I've been around him since he was born. I'm trying to do what's right here by telling you the truth, but wc have to do what's best for Caden. He needs stability in his life. He's had enough upheaval. Get to know him and stay in touch or spend vacations with him in the future, but please don't fight me on this. He'll be the one who ends up getting hurt."

That was it. Heat crawled up the back of his neck. Zuri wanted him to ignore or give up his rights? She didn't trust him with his own son but she wanted to trust him not to take custody? He shook his head but he wasn't sure which part he was disagreeing with.

Did he even trust himself? Maybe she was right. He didn't know the first thing about being a parent. His certainly hadn't been good role models.

He gave a two-finger whistle and slapped his thigh when Duck looked over. The dog circled Caden, then nudged and waited for him to follow, before bounding toward Zuri and Damon. Caden's eyes met his and Damon's mouth went dry.

You weren't there for me, but you can damn well be there for your son. Lucas's voice filled his ears. No. It was guilt speaking, taunting him with his brother's voice, as it had done for years in his dreams. Damon took a deep breath.

"Do what's best for Caden?" Damon said, before the kid got closer. "Is that what you and your sister did all these years by keeping him from me? I may not know how to be a father, but I can promise you one thing, Zuri. I won't be giving up my rights. Not to you or anyone else."

CHAPTER TWO

ZURI PULLED OUT a change of clothes from Caden's suitcase and set them by the bathroom door. The room wasn't that big but it was comfortable and she liked that it had its own bathroom. The only downside was that she and Caden had to share it. The other room available for rent was currently occupied. Even if it wasn't, rent for two rooms would have eaten up her Christmas shopping budget, plus the other room, she was told, only had access to a hallway bath. Apparently, the owner's granddaughter, who was visiting from out of town, was using it.

She glanced at the clock on the nightstand that separated the two twin-size beds. Thirty minutes had passed since he'd started his shower. Ten since the last time she'd knocked on the door and ordered him to wrap it up. She had reminded him to get his clothes out before showering, but it was just like him to only hear half of what he was told. Her sister used to blame it on teen hormones, even though he still had six months to go before officially becoming a teenager. Obviously, the hormonal mind suck wasn't something that happened overnight, but the mood swings that started over the summer, when they knew Vera's health wasn't going to improve, had made normal teenager behavior seem like a piece of cake.

She really couldn't blame Caden. He was dealing with what no child should have to, but at the same time, it was Zuri's job to give him structure. She stepped into her sister's shoes the day she died and she was in this for the long haul. If she had given in to the urge to coddle and spoil him out of sympathy, he would have never gone back to school after the funeral. She had to be his rock and source of normalcy. At the same time, she was afraid to be too strict. She didn't want to screw up and make his depression or mourning any worse than it already was.

A part of her feared her choice to bring

him to meet his father would backfire and make things worse instead of better. Here she was, used to relying on science and facts, yet all she had to go on at the moment was her gut instinct. Her moral compass. Why did life have to be so subjective? The last time she trusted her gut, Damon had rejected her in the worst possible way.

She yanked her own change of clothes out of her bag and tossed them on the bed closest to the window overlooking the beach, not caring if they wrinkled, then slumped into the wingback chair in the corner of the small room. She had barely slept last night, thinking about coming face-to-face with Damon after so many years. Anticipation anxiety had kept her awake. And now, after the fact, Damon's reaction down at the beach had her wishing she'd never come to Turtleback. But she knew that was selfish. At least he'd tried to apologize, not that words could erase the past. It wasn't even just about how he'd crushed her heart in high school anymore. It was also the fact that if her sister had been destined to get cancer and die, then maybe if she'd never gone to prom with

Damon she'd have had a freer life than the years she'd spent as a single mother out of high school. *Stop thinking like that. It's wrong. Vera loved Caden. She'd have given her life for him.* Zuri would, too. Her mother always said that everything happens for a reason. She wasn't sure she believed it though. She couldn't think of a good enough reason for her sister's life to end so soon.

The shower stopped running and she could hear faint singing coming from the bathroom. She hadn't even heard Caden so much as hum since the funeral. Maybe getting out of Boston had been a good idea after all. It could have been that dog down at the beach cheering him up, though she wasn't sure they could handle getting a puppy back home. She wasn't a dog person and she'd felt guilty when Caden's therapist had asked if they had any pets. She'd been told they could be quite therapeutic. Honestly? Dogs made her anxious and she was allergic to cats. Maybe finding out that the man he'd referred to as a cool hero on the beach was his father would make her nephew happy. No pet needed. Maybe it would make the difference between him spiraling into darkness, as his grief counselor had warned, versus pulling through.

"I hung your clothes on the doorknob," she called out. The bathroom door cracked open and a hefty cloud of steam filled the room. His hand reached out to grab his stuff.

"Thanks." The door closed. He had been irritated when he found out they weren't staying in a real hotel. She understood that teens liked their own space but he didn't know that they were here for other reasons and she had to go with what was available in the tiny town and make it work.

"You might want to turn the vent on," she called out.

There was no mistaking he'd obeyed this time. The exhaust fan motor roared to life. It was so loud and grumbly it had to be as old as the place itself. The Turtleback Bed & Breakfast was a two-story, pale yellow cottage on stilts, with a deck off the first floor. Stairs from the deck led visitors down onto a wooden, planked pathway, which in turn took them past tall reeds and short dunes, onto the beach itself. It was charming inside and out, especially with the holiday touches that had been added for the season. Evergreen boughs and lights spiraled along the deck railing and the main entrance was graced with a seaside-themed Christmas wreath and a Santa figure wearing sunglasses and holding a fishing rod.

The interior was decorated with antique furniture and marine-themed artwork, which the owner—Melanie Biddle—said her late husband had painted. In fact, she had explained that she had opened the house to guests only after his passing, as a way of earning enough income to cover seasonal repairs. And of course, Melanie had a Christmas tree in the main room downstairs. Several photos of her husband and of the two of them together hung proudly on it. The place was warm and homey. Even the bedroom they were renting included seasonal throws and decorative pillows in red and green. A regular hotel wouldn't have felt like a home away from home for the holidays.

Zuri wanted desperately to curl up on the matelassé bedspread and nap, but she needed to wash up, change and take Caden over to Damon's place—the gray, bleak house he'd pointed out from the beach. No holiday lights or decor to brighten it up. Nothing like the colorful homes and shops that made Turtleback the subject of one of the paintings downstairs. He'd insisted that she bring Caden over for dinner, so that they could tell the boy who he really was. Damon's place would offer them the most privacy and she sort of hoped that maybe having Duck around would help. The therapist must have known a thing or two. The boy and dog seemed to hit it off—a fact that made her feel guilty for resisting the whole pet idea.

"All yours," Caden said, finally emerging from the bathroom.

"Take another shower that long and Mrs. Biddle is going to kick us out or charge us double the rate," she quipped, gathering her clothes and walking past him.

"Maybe if I had a cell phone, I could set an alarm, so I don't lose track of time."

"Nice try, but your mom said you're supposed to get one for your thirteenth birthday."

"Everyone in my class already has one. Except Joey, but his was confiscated."

"Look at it this way. You can't have yours confiscated if you don't have one."

"But what if it's the only thing I put on my Christmas wish list?"

She gave him a pointed look and he huffed before propping up his pillow and lying on his bed with the copy of *The Lord of the Rings* she'd given him over the summer. He hadn't touched it until now. She closed the bathroom door and leaned against it. *Pick your battles.* He didn't know that she'd found his Christmas wish list—which Vera had encouraged him to start before she died, thinking it would give him things to look forward to. Zuri came across the list while cleaning. Finding his dad had been the second thing on it.

Zuri had moved in to her sister's place last summer to help care for him, since Vera had to spend so much time in treatment. Even when Vera was home, she had been too weak to do much. Zuri hadn't been snooping when she found the wish list. She'd been trying to pick up enough books and clothes to make the kid's bedroom less treacherous to navigate.

His list had broken her down. The first thing written on it had been for his mother to get well. The second had been to find his father. What had killed her was the thick black marker line drawn through number one. He'd given up hope that his mom would live. If a cell phone was truly the only thing he wanted now, it meant that he'd also given up hope of ever finding his father. Or maybe he was so angry at losing his mom that he didn't want another parent replacing her.

Zuri knew the power of hope and how devastating the loss of it could be. She'd seen how losing hope had once left Damon depressed and unmotivated when he realized his family was crumbling apart. It had been part of the reason his grades had plummeted and his teachers had sent him to the student assisted tutoring clinic at the school. Teenage and young adult depression, with all the life changes mixed in, could be deep and gouging…and grim. And she was terrified that if her nephew gave up on family, she might lose him, too.

DAMON FIDGETED WITH the buckle on his diver's watch, then with the collar of his sweatshirt. He still couldn't wrap his head around the fact that he had a son and Vera Habib was dead. He'd been shocked enough when he first got Zuri's email. Shocked…then excited for a fleeting moment. The sort of excitement you felt when you reconnected with a friend from the past. But then reality quickly set in. He knew seeing her after how he'd shunned her in front of their peers would be awkward. Then he had assumed, from her mention of a kid, that she'd found someone to start a family with and a strange, wistful feeling hit him. He didn't do wistful. He had no business feeling let down. No right to wish the past had been different between them. He'd missed their connection. Their friendship. And he couldn't blame anyone but himself. He'd thought of her a lot after leaving town. She had been his motivation without knowing it. He had become a navy SEAL in order to prove he'd be good enough for his parents and someone else like her someday. That he *could* live up to expectations and earn respect.

He sat down and scratched Duck behind the ear, as she lay resting in front of his old cracked leather couch. She raised one eyelid then, satisfied that he seemed all right, closed her eyes again. He snatched one of the rags he kept in a basket dedicated to drool mopping and wiped the floor directly under the corner of her mouth. They'd be here any minute now and keeping up with a Newfoundland's slobber trails was akin to picking up toys or laundry after a human child. He didn't usually think twice about it, but he had company on the way. First impressions were everything, especially when seeing Zuri again forced all his high school insecurities to resurface. She was the one person he wanted to show he'd gotten his act together. And then there was Caden. What if the boy ended up being disappointed in who his father was?

He rubbed the crick in his neck and went to the cottage's newly renovated galley kitchen to pull out plates and cups. The pizza he'd ordered had already arrived and he was keeping it warm in the oven. Kids liked pizza. Right? He figured it was a safe bet. He also had a tub of mint chocolate chip ice cream in the freezer—the only flavor he ever bought. He remembered that Zuri had never been fond of the flavor, but he didn't have time to run to the store. They didn't have to have dessert. He just kind of thought that maybe it was something a kid Caden's age would want or that ice cream would soften the blow.

He used to take Lucas out for the treat whenever his brother got a bad grade in school or got in trouble for missing curfew. Going to the ice cream shop down the street from their school in Boston had also been a tradition for celebrations. But Damon wasn't sure whether Caden would be feeling celebratory once he found out he was standing next to his father—a man who'd missed every milestone in the boy's life thus far. He'd know soon enough if today was going to be a celebration or a fu—no… *Not funeral*. He shook the inadvertent word choice from his head.

He got up and started setting plates out. He had to keep busy. His nerves were on fire and he was overthinking this whole Operation Parenthood.

Duck jumped up and barked once. The

girl had lungs on her, and the sound shook every cell in his body. Or maybe that was adrenaline. They were here.

He started for the door, then realized he had forgotten to lock up the room next to his and across from the hall bathroom. What if one of them accidentally entered the wrong room in search of the bathroom? He wasn't used to visitors. He let out a breath. Everything that had happened today had him thrown off. He needed to keep his wits about him. He swore at himself and hurried to the room, reached in and clicked the lock on the knob before pulling it shut and jogged back to the front door. He paused for a brief second to gather himself. *It's all good. They're not going to find out who you really are. At least not yet. Just open the front door before they think you're not home and leave, you idiot.*

"Back." Duck obeyed, giving him some clearance in the narrow entryway, but she kept wagging her tail. Clearly, he wasn't the only one anxious to see Zuri and Caden again.

He opened the door and gave them a casual I'm-in-control-and-unfazed welcome.

A sort of cross between the way he and his teammates used to psych themselves before a military op and a beach bum attitude. Zuri, standing there looking effortlessly beautiful, and Caden, looking up at him as though he'd met a superhero, tore at him. He was an imposter. Anything but a hero. Townsfolk and tourists using the term had no idea how uncomfortable it made him. He'd seen that same look in their eyes before.

"Hey. Come on in." He didn't sound as casual as he'd hoped but they didn't seem to notice. He stepped aside and Caden went straight for Duck, oblivious to the rest of the place. The kid had his priorities.

"Hey," Zuri said. She entered but stayed within a few feet of the door, clutching an oversize canvas purse. Her brow furrowed as she looked around.

"You don't have to stay by the door. Make yourself comfortable," he said, waving her into the living room area. Her cheeks flushed and she smoothed out her sweater. She looked anything but comfortable, but she gave a small, quick smile, set her bag on the wooden console and moved cautiously to where Duck and Caden sat in the middle of a dark red afghan rug patterned in traditional geometric designs. He'd gotten it during one of his deployments.

"This place is nice."

"Surprised? You thought the place would be a mess. Didn't you?" he asked. He hadn't been the neatest person during high school. In fact, she had helped him find lost assignments crumpled in the bottom of his backpack multiple times.

"No. I never said that."

"You didn't have to," he said, picking up one of Duck's fake bones and tossing it in her toy basket. He knew the beach cottage still needed a lot of work on the outside. He had been investing his time and effort on renovating it inside first. When he bought the place, he had planned on updating and making it livable before trying to keep up with the beating the homes along the Outer Banks endured from the weather. The outside had been in solid enough shape—no leaks or anything like that—and he wasn't as concerned with curb appeal as he was with the heart of the place. He couldn't see the outside when he spent evenings with his dog on the inside. Besides, he liked the fact that the drab exterior didn't draw attention during tourist season. And looks could be deceiving. His mother had always kept a tidy front yard and home, yet life inside had never been comfortable.

"It's very nice, Damon. Very…neat."

"Why don't you have any Christmas decorations up?" Caden asked.

"Caden!" Zuri shot her nephew a look, though Damon was pretty sure the boy was saying exactly what she'd really meant by "neat."

"Nah, it's fine," Damon said, laying his hand on her shoulder to guide her past the dog and to the armchair. He did it without thinking. He thought she wasn't sitting because Duck was blocking her way. He intended the gesture as reassurance, but she sucked in a soft breath at the contact and he quickly pulled away. He cleared his throat and went over to scratch Duck behind the ears with Caden. "I just haven't gotten around to decorating yet," he lied. He hadn't planned on it. And Christmas was just over a week away. Not that he ever went all out with his place. He was usually too busy with work or renovating. And then there was Duck. Last year, she knocked the tree at the ocean patrol office down twice. But she had still been in training back then.

"Sorry if I was rude," Caden said. His brow furrowed, and he nibbled at his lip. The poor kid embarrassed too easily.

"Like I said, no big deal. You hungry? I ordered pizza. I hope that's okay. If not, the restaurant on the boardwalk makes good frics and grilled fish. I assumed here would be better for—" Zuri glanced worriedly in Caden's direction when the boy looked up. She widened her eyes at Damon. "I mean better so that Duck can hang out with us," Damon clarified, before the boy could ask why. "She and restaurants don't mesh well together. Trust me on that." Zuri's shoulders relaxed, but only slightly. "You don't have allergies, do you?" Damon asked his son. He should have thought of that. Most parents would have known to ask.

"Oh. No, not to food. Dogs, I'm not sure. He's never owned one."

Caden gave his aunt an annoyed look. "I've been doing just fine."

Damon reached in the woven toy basket by the couch and pulled out a thick red-and-white rope with a rubber ball attached to the end. Duck's favorite toy. He tossed it to Caden.

"She's the biggest dog I've ever petted," Caden said. "I wish I had a dog."

Damon and Zuri exchanged glances. Technically, he now had one. He just didn't know it.

"You can play with Duck all you want while you're here. Except when she's training or on duty, of course," he said.

"Cool. Nix the cell phone idea, Aunt Zuri. I want one of these for Christmas. Will she ever have puppies?"

"Not anymore. She's been spayed. I adopted her almost a year ago. She had been abandoned and someone found her with her litter of puppies. Our town veterinarian stepped in and helped get them adopted. In fact, one, Shamu, now belongs to one of our police officers—and Duck came to live with me. She had been found in the town of Duck, but I named her because of her affinity for water. Not the town. Actually, it's really 'Mother Duck' because of all her pups, but everyone calls her Duck for short."

He was rambling. The boy asked about puppies and he was getting the dog's full medical history. *What's wrong with you, Damon? Since when do you get nerves?* He rubbed his palms together and rocked on his heels. Caden was so preoccupied with Duck he'd probably tuned out half of what Damon had said.

"That's sad that someone abandoned her," Zuri said, eyeing Caden on the floor. She sucked in the corner of her lip.

At least Zuri didn't seem to think he was talking too much. Maybe she had a heart for dogs after all.

"I promise she won't bite, Zuri." He hadn't forgotten the story she told him once about how a dog had bitten her when she was a kid. A bite that had left a scar on her ankle. But that dog hadn't been trained and everyone in their neighborhood knew his owner didn't deserve to keep animals. "She's a gentle giant. You can pet her if you want. I mean, look at how good she is with Caden," Damon said.

"I just…well, fine. Just one pet to feel her coat. She won't jump like earlier?"

"Duck, stay." Damon tipped his head toward his dog who put her head in the boy's lap as proof that she wasn't going anywhere. Zuri took a slow step toward her, reached down and ran her fingers through the dog's impressive coat, then stepped back as if not wanting to press her luck.

"Boy is her hair thick. I can't imagine brushing through that," Zuri said.

"She has a double coat. The real grooming happens a few times a year when she blows it. She's worth the trouble. She's an amazing dog."

"I don't understand why she was abandoned. I'm not a dog person and even I wouldn't have just left a pregnant pet somewhere and taken off. And not that it would matter to me, but aren't Newfoundland dogs expensive? You'd think her owner would have wanted to make money off the litter. Or they could have at least taken her to a shelter. It would have been better than abandonment. That's just cruel."

Abandonment. Was she trying to say more? Her attention was on Duck, so he was probably the only one drawing connections. His leaving Boston had more to do with himself than any intention of abandoning family and friends. And he couldn't be accused of abandoning a child he never knew he had.

"My guess is that they didn't know she was pregnant. A lot of people will go and get a puppy, not realizing how fast they grow or how much training and exercise they require. Especially a dog Duck's size. They just think all the fluff is cute and they get nostalgic over the character Nana in *Peter Pan* and they are totally unprepared for what ownership entails, including the cost of spaying or neutering. Puppyhood doesn't last as long as the teen years seem to."

He realized how that came out when Zuri raised her brow at him. Was everything going to be a Caden analogy from here on out?

"So, you rescued her. Just like you do with swimmers," Caden said. There was that hero implication again.

"I believe it's pets who rescue us," Damon deflected.

Zuri nibbled at her bottom lip the way she used to while helping him with math problems. He could see her mind churning, reading into what he said, but she had no way of understanding what he'd been through as a SEAL or how the loss of his brother still haunted him. She couldn't appreciate the impact Duck had had on his life in the short time since the adoption. How his dog's presence had helped him sleep better at night and focus during the day. How she'd lowered his anxiety level behind the mask of confidence he put on every morning.

"I'm starving. That pizza smells good," Caden said.

"Caden, you have to wait to be invited to the table," Zuri said.

"Sorry," Caden added.

"No need to apologize." Damon headed toward his kitchen and pulled the oven open. "I used to eat an entire roasted chicken by myself at your age. And I'd get hungry again within a couple of hours. I'd be upset if I ordered all this food and you weren't hungry. There's nothing formal about eating here. Let's dig in. Just don't give any to Duck. It makes her gassy. Oh, and there's chocolate chip mint ice cream if you want some afterward," he hedged, as he carried the warm pizza boxes over to a dining table right off the kitchen.

"No way! That's my absolute favorite flavor. Aunt Zuri thinks it's gross."

"You don't say." Damon chuckled and glanced at Zuri. She splayed her hands and tried not to smile. Maybe things hadn't changed so much after all. And maybe looks weren't the only thing his son had inherited from him.

The kid proved that he could eat as much as Damon ever had. Zuri, on the other hand, sitting right across from him at the table, didn't seem to have much of an appetite. She barely made it through one slice by the time Caden had finished his sixth. Maybe Damon asking the boy questions made her nervous, but he hadn't asked anything that didn't sound conversational. Eating in silence would have been weird. At least he'd gleaned a few stats on the kid between the boy's mouthfuls. He was twelve, made mostly As in school—until this year—and took piano lessons. No sports. Not one, other than the required physical education class at school. *That's gotta change*. Damon washed his last bite down with water and scooted his chair back.

"Coffee?" he offered.

"No thanks. I need to sleep tonight. I think we should…" She motioned her head toward Caden, who'd gone to use the restroom. "Unless you've changed your mind."

"Not a chance. I was just waiting for the right moment to tell him."

"Tell me what?" Caden asked, catching them off guard. Duck had instinctively followed the kid to the restroom and was escorting him back to the table. That dog's maternal instincts were strong.

"That Mother Duck seems to think you're her new puppy," Damon said. Caden chuckled.

"You're sure she's safe with kids? She never lashes out? Ever?" Zuri asked.

"I'm sure. She's well-trained and her breed in general is sweet-natured and protective. I know her size can be scary but trust me. Caden's in good paws."

Zuri rolled her eyes at his use of *paws* in the expression. Damon chuckled as he picked up the empty pizza boxes, folded them and put them in his recycling bin. Zuri cleared up their used napkins and cups, then joined Caden in the living room. Damon was glad he'd renovated with an open concept. With Duck, the space would have seemed cramped otherwise.

"Come sit down on the couch a sec." Damon motioned for Caden to park himself on the couch, while he and Zuri each took a chair to either side of the boy. Caden's face went from relaxed to suspicious. He narrowed his eyes at his aunt, then at Damon.

"What'd I do now?" Caden asked.

"Nothing at all," Damon and Zuri both chimed in a little too eagerly. Zuri grabbed the small pillow on the chair and hugged it.

"It's all good, Caden," she said. "I just didn't want you wondering how I know Mr. Woods. I mean, obviously I knew him before. We wouldn't be having dinner here with a total stranger we'd just met on the beach. You know never to go to a stranger's house, right? But this is different because well… Damon and I knew each other before."

She was the one rambling now. Nervous. She twisted her hands into the pillow as she spoke. He needed to jump in and rescue her but he didn't know where to start.

"Wait a minute. You two know each other? Like, before earlier on the beach? Aunt Zuri never dates, but I thought maybe you two hit it off. Like one of those love at first sight—"

"No! Nooo." Once again, Damon and Zuri had jumped in together, adamantly shaking their heads. Zuri waved her hands as if to clear the air of that notion. "God, no," Zuri added emphatically. Poor Caden scrunched his face and sat on his hands.

"Okay, okay. Chill," he said.

"You misunderstood," Damon said, softening his voice.

"Yeah, totally. That's not what happened. *At all*," Zuri insisted. Her cheeks were flushed. *Aunt Zuri never dates*. Interesting.

"Then what's up? You're both acting weird. Who are you, really?"

"Your aunt and I were just friends. A

long time ago. She used to help me out with homework once in a while." *Just friends*. The words pinched his chest. That's what he'd thought and he'd valued their friendship, but he'd ruined it. Sure, she was the one who'd messed up the way things were by asking him out, but his reaction and actions afterward had pushed things to a point of no return.

Caden frowned. Damon scrubbed at a day's worth of stubble. He usually shaved at night to save himself time with early morning work schedules and taking care of Duck's needs. Today had been akin to getting struck by lightning, but it would all work out. This was going to be all right. He knew how to handle an ambush. He was trained to deal with shock and the unexpected. He'd get things under control. The kid liked his dog and seemed to like him enough. They were getting along so far.

Don't overthink it.

"So, you were classmates?" Caden asked.

"I was a year behind him, but Damon knew your mom, too. They were in the same class. We all went to the same high school. The same one you'll go to after middle school," Zuri said.

"You knew my mom?"

"Yeah. I did." Damon looked over at Zuri for guidance. He couldn't read her face. He cleared his throat and studied the pattern in the rug for a moment. This was that moment…the seconds before an order came through from his commander. The brief instant where he told himself he could cheat death. Where there was no room for second-guessing or fear. He let out the breath he'd been holding and looked the kid straight in the eyes. "Caden, I'm your father."

The boy recoiled. His forehead wrinkled and his hands fisted in Duck's wavy coat. He glared at his aunt, confusion and shock swirling in his eyes.

Zuri leaned forward and put her hand gently on Caden's knee but he shrugged her off and got up. He looked like he wanted to punch something. The sweet kid from moments ago had all but disappeared.

"Caden, please sit down," Zuri begged. "You wanted to find your father. You've been asking questions and deserve all the answers, honey. I'm trying to do what's right. I thought you'd be happy to have your wish come true."

"No. I wished for Mom to get better. And when I wished I could find my dad, I swore I'd give anything to find him. But I didn't mean trading Mom for him. I didn't want her dying. I'd rather have her back than live with...with...you." He practically spat the word "you" at Damon, who'd clearly gone from cool to evil in a flash.

Caden stomped over to the other side of the coffee table, inhaling and exhaling in rapid fire. Damon stood, not wanting to scare him off, but aware that the boy's anxious breathing could lead to him hyperventilating. He'd seen it happen with parents on the beach during a child water rescue.

"Nothing is changing. We just want to talk." Damon winced at his own words. Nothing was changing? Too much had changed for the boy in the past few months. Caden took a step back, bumping into Duck, who stood her ground behind him like a solid wall.

"Stop treating me like some stupid kid!" Damon remembered yelling those same words at his parents once. He had felt help-less, ungrounded and desperate. He had hated the feeling that his life had been spi-raling out of control. The least he could do was spare his own son that pain.

"You're not stupid. That's not what's happening." Zuri tossed the pillow aside and shifted to face her nephew. She wiped her cheek with the back of her hand. Caden glared at her.

"This whole trip was a setup? You knew all along? I know what you're doing. You're trying to send me away already?" he ac-cused Zuri. "You promised Mom that you'd take care of me but you lied. You don't want to."

"That's not true," Zuri said.

"You guys are not making me move. Now I know why you've been acting so nice. You thought you could fool me, but I'm not an idiot. I don't need you," he told Damon. "I don't want anyone but Mom. If you're such a lifesaver, then maybe you should have saved hers. I want to go home."

Caden took off, slamming the front door behind him. Zuri shook her head at Damon when he started after him.

"Don't. Give him time. We can touch base tomorrow." She grabbed her purse and ran after her nephew. Duck whimpered and stomped her paws near the door, anxious to follow.

"Not this time, Duck. Zuri's right. I'm the last person he wants to see right now."

Less than twenty-four hours as a father and he'd already failed. Maybe Zuri was right.

Maybe his son would be better off with her.

CHAPTER THREE

ZURI WALKED PAST the B and B's patio doors for the third time that evening. She wasn't trying to spy on Caden. He seemed to be content sitting at a firepit with Melanie's granddaughter, who'd come to visit her grandmother for the holidays. The girl, Sara, was about Caden's age and quite pretty. She wore her long, red hair in a French braid that ended at her waist and had managed to put a shy smile on Caden's face for the first time since they'd gotten back from Damon's place. A smile that disappeared thirty minutes ago, when Zuri had offered to carry down the tray of marshmallows, chocolate and graham crackers Melanie had put together.

Caden was still angry with her. Heck, he was angry at the world. But somehow this Sara girl had him forgetting why they were in Turtleback. At least for the evening. It had taken a while for Zuri to convince him that there was no way for them to head back home to Boston this evening.

"Don't you want to join them? You could take these throws down with you, if you like. It's dropping into the mid-forties tonight. Even with the wind gone and that fire roaring, it's getting brisk." Melanie held a stack of handwoven blankets in her arms.

"I think I'll stay up here, if that's okay," she said, cradling her hot chocolate. She didn't want to ruin his mood any more than she already had. The two kids seemed to be doing all right on their own. She let the ocean air wash over her face when Melanie opened the door, then watched as she made her way down the deck steps and over to where four Adirondack chairs and the firepit were set up in the sand, right before the reed-dappled sand dunes and wood planked path that led to the beach. Sara wrapped a throw around her shoulders. Caden shook his head, presumably declining the offer. Melanie set the stack on one of the chairs and rejoined Zuri.

"He said he's not cold. I tried. I don't want anyone getting sick before Christmas."

Zuri thought of her sister enduring one chemo treatment after another until they knew she wouldn't make it to Christmas or the New Year. She still couldn't hear the word *sick* and merely think of the common cold.

"It's fine. He's used to chillier weather. Today's high of fifty-five felt like spring to us."

"How about more hot chocolate?" Melanie asked, as she headed for the kitchen.

"I'm good. Thanks."

Zuri glanced outside again. Everything would turn out all right. It had to. She needed to stay strong for him. Melanie returned with a plate of cookies and set it on the coffee table. Each one was a meticulously decorated Christmas tree. They almost didn't look real, but they smelled heavenly.

"You made those? I'm impressed."

"I wish I could bake like that. Savory meals are my specialty. Baked goods, not so much. I have a business deal with The Saltwater Sweetery to provide any breakfast goods or desserts for my guests. I don't know if you saw it when you came through town. Best bakery you'll ever visit. Darla, the owner, is gifted. She even made her own wedding cake this past Thanksgiving. Her wife, Nora, is a tech at the vet clinic but loves organic gardening, so she supplied real orange pansies for the cake instead of using fondant. It was divine. Did you know pansies are edible? I didn't."

"I knew roses were but I hadn't heard about pansies. Sweets are my downfall. I'll have to stop by the bakery while I'm in town."

"You definitely should. I have brochures from some of the other shops stacked on that console by the door. Feel free to browse or take any that interest you."

"Thanks." She wasn't sure how their visit would pan out or whether they'd have time for sightseeing. She had promised her sister that she'd take Caden on a vacation to help him cope, but right now, after their visit with Damon, everything seemed so heavy and serious. She simply couldn't wrap her head around more carefree activities like sightseeing. It didn't feel right, especially since her nephew already wanted to go home. Maybe she should have listened to her parents and taken him to spend the holidays with them, surrounded by family support. *But Damon is family to him.* She took a brochure to be polite.

"Sara knows the town well. I'm sure she won't mind being a tour guide, if you like." Melanie looked out the window and gave Zuri a knowing smile. "What I wouldn't give to be a teenager again. There's nothing as sweet as puppy love."

Sweet? If only Mrs. Biddle knew how painful puppy love could be. Zuri had been too much of a bookworm in middle school to tune into boys, but in high school Damon had been her first real crush and it didn't end well for her. All it did was convince her that the term *crush* referred to having your heart smashed to bits and stomped on. She was a late bloomer when it came to self-esteem and confidence, but several years of college and graduate school had done the trick. Maybe the secret was being surrounded by like minds, such as fellow STEM students.

Caden was studious, or he used to be. He

did seem to relax around Sara. She doubted it was puppy love but perhaps Melanie had more experience observing relationships. After all, she did get to observe the dynamic of her renters. But their hostess had no idea why Zuri and Caden were really in Turtleback, other than for a vacation.

She'd even assumed they were mother and son, before Caden corrected her at check-in. Zuri hadn't missed the worried look on Melanie's face at the time. Apparently, there was something about an aunt taking her nephew to the small beach town off-season that had sent off warning bells. It wasn't until they had returned from Damon's that Melanie had apologized for acting strangely. She had explained that only ten months ago, the sheriff's now fiancée had shown up in town after kidnapping her baby niece and posing as her mother. But one call to the sheriff earlier today, who had in turn checked in with his friend, Damon, after he was seen with Zuri and Caden, cleared things up and put Melanie at ease with her guests.

And here Zuri had assumed the only

danger in Turtleback Beach involved hurricanes, riptides and, perhaps, sharks.

"You miss being a teenager? You'd really want to deal with puberty again?" Zuri asked, trying to keep the conversation light.

"It would be better than menopause. Besides, Tom and I met when we were their age. We knew everything about each other—the good and the bad—and we grew to love each other more for all of it. No one knew me like he did."

"You must miss him." She couldn't help but think of how she and Damon had gotten along fine at that age. They'd grown up in the same neighborhood and had gone to the same schools from kindergarten on up. Even if he was a year ahead, they were often on the same playground or at the same community and school events, especially since her sister was in his class.

Their moms had been more civil with each other back then. It wasn't until after third and fourth grade that their irritation with each other grew. As a kid, she didn't really understand why. Now she understood that there was some sort of unspoken competitiveness between them. One was a lawyer and the other a doctor but how they each approached blending that with motherhood had been the crux of the problem.

Zuri's parents had hired a nanny. Damon's mother had more family support and she had been able to adjust her schedule so that she could volunteer in her kids' classrooms as much as possible. There was no right or wrong. Each had done what made sense for their families and careers. If only judgment and defensiveness hadn't come into play.

But even if Damon and Zuri didn't always hang around together because their families, who lived down the street from each other, weren't the best of friends, they knew each other well enough. She knew what he liked to get in the lunch line and he knew she hated catching balls or anything else flying at her face, but that she was also one of the few girls who wasn't afraid of spiders, lizards and grass snakes. Plus, she was pulled out of her reading class during fourth grade and spent that time with the fifth graders because she was advanced in that area.

They'd known and had accepted everything about each other and, although he'd become the stereotypical popular kid in high school, he still acted as though he respected her. He'd flat out asked to work with her in the tutoring clinic. But puppy love had ruined everything. A part of her missed the way things had been before the "crush."

"I miss him every day," Melanie said. "But it gets easier. Especially when you're surrounded by family and friends who love you. Around here, that includes just about the entire town."

Zuri swirled the last sip of cocoa in her mug. *It gets easier.* Would it? Would she ever adjust to not having Vera around anymore? Would it ever get easier for Caden? She thought about Damon losing Lucas and realized, of all the people she knew, he'd survived the kind of loss she was enduring. But what about Caden? Losing a parent at his age had to be horrible. Completely unimaginable. Vera had lined up a grief therapist for him before her passing and he'd been to a few sessions, but from what Zuri had witnessed, a connection was missing. The kid had refused to open up and talk.

She watched as he used a fork to push a marshmallow off his skewer and onto the graham cracker and chocolate Sara was holding. Funny how the most precious connections could come out of nowhere. And they couldn't be forced.

"Are Sara's parents not coming?" She didn't mean to pry but the question had slipped from her subconscious. All the confusion about kids and parenthood was clouding her better judgment. "I don't mean to be nosy. You don't have to answer."

"It's fine. They'll join us on Christmas Eve. I insisted that they take some time off together. It's the secret to having a marriage last as long as mine did. Besides, it gives me time to spoil her rotten before they come and start reinforcing rules." Her sly grin revealed a mischievous, sassy side.

Neither Zuri's paternal nor maternal grandparents had been spoilers or rule breakers. They were almost stricter than her parents had been, which was probably why her parents ended up becoming medical doctors who devoted long hours to their careers. Vera hadn't been nearly as strict, although Caden had a natural affinity for information gathering and didn't need to be prodded to do homework. Zuri was still trying to get a feel for where she fell on the spectrum of parenting, but she did believe structure was needed. She was just applying the science of entropy. Without putting energy into raising a kid, they'd inevitably become more disorderly. She glanced at her watch.

"I should probably get him to bed. Do you need help putting out the fire?"

"I've got it. I might spend a few minutes with Sara down there before dousing it." She opened the door and called Caden up for Zuri, then held up a finger. "Oh. Before I forget. Damon called and said he'd be joining us for breakfast tomorrow morning. And no, I don't know how you two know each other and I'm not asking for the story. I'm not a gossip. I will warn you, though, the grapevine is very ripe around here. Small towns have that reputation for a reason. It's not merely a cliché.

Anyhow, I thought I should let you know about breakfast."

Seriously? After what happened at dinner he wanted to show up for breakfast?

"Thank you."

It was the only response she could muster. Couldn't he have waited until lunch or until she and Caden could meet him somewhere other than where she was staying? Ripe grapevine and all. Couldn't he at least let her enjoy her cup of coffee before stirring up Caden's emotions again…and hers?

Caden opened the glass patio door and slipped past her without a word. No doubt he had overheard Melanie. His mood swings were going to give Zuri whiplash. She followed him upstairs and they took turns in the bathroom without a word.

She bit her tongue to give him whatever space he needed and crawled into her bed by the window with the latest issue of the research journal she subscribed to. He settled into his bed on the other side of the room, turned on his side, his back to her, and switched off his bedside lamp.

The sounds of the wind and shore made

her feel like they were camping. She never heard this much nature at her apartment in Boston, nor at her sister's house. No doubt he wished he was in his own room back home. She wished she was in hers as well, although she had to admit that having to share this space at the B and B allowed her to keep an eye on him.

Everything happens for a reason. His therapist had warned her about signs of worsening depression, including running away or self-harm or worse. It was hard enough to sleep and relax away from home. Being able to hear his soft, rhythmic breathing while he slept was reassuring. But she didn't want him to go to sleep upset.

She started counting in her head. If he didn't say something within sixty seconds, she'd turn off her light and let it all go until morning. She could hear the waves scrambling ashore. The sound would have soothed her under any other circumstances. Thirty seconds…twenty-nine…

"Are you leaving me here, Aunt Zuri?"

Bless his heart. She tossed her reading

material on the foot of the bed and pulled her knees up to her chest.

"Why would you think that?"

"You didn't pack as much as you made me pack. And I just found out my father lives here." He still kept his back to her.

"Do you really think I'd let you spend Christmas without me? Honestly, I had considered leaving you here but only for a week or so, once I made sure things would be okay. And only so that I can get work done at the lab. But not forever. No way, kiddo."

He rolled over in bed and faced her, twisting his lips as if deciding whether or not to believe her.

"How long have you known?" he asked. *Oh, boy.*

"Long enough. It wasn't my place to say anything."

"How long?"

"Since the beginning." She couldn't lie to him anymore. The least she could do was to tell the truth. Not that it would make up for all the years he'd lost with his dad.

Would Caden still be the same Caden had Damon been around? The two liked the same ice cream flavor and had similar mannerisms, all without ever having met each other. But would Caden have grown to like sports more had Damon been around? Or was that idea rooted in sexism?

Damon's little brother Lucas, as well as his other brothers, Leo and Shawn, hadn't pursued athletics to the same degree Damon had. As far as she'd gathered from social media, Leo and Shawn had followed in their parents' footsteps and had gone into law. Would Caden have been influenced by his uncles the way he was so much like his aunt? Or would his father have had more of an influence? Unless none of it mattered as much as behavioral genetics.

There she was falling back on science again and coming up with nothing. Kids were an enigma. Surely having his dad around would have changed things one way or another. Maybe her nephew would have gotten the puppy he never had. Vera had avoided having pets because of the added work and expense. Zuri fell along the same lines. Would having had a dog made a difference in terms of his confidence and social skills? Had they deprived him of a nonjudgmental, loyal friend? She remembered Damon and his brothers had a dog when they were kids. Damon had never needed help with confidence. Or at least he didn't seem to.

She thought about how different Damon was after his years as a SEAL and living on his own. The man had changed. He was actually organized and neat. He came off as more humble than he used to be. Reliable, too, judging from his heading the Turtleback Beach Ocean Rescue and Beach Patrol. But that didn't necessarily translate into being a good father. She didn't trust Damon not to drop the ball and disappear from his son's life when things got tough. It would be more than a grieving child could handle.

Caden was a wonderful kid. Vera had been a good mother and role model. She shouldn't wonder about how a different life would have changed him. Life was unpredictable at best and changes affected everyone. For better or for worse.

"You lied to me. You *and* Mom. All those times I asked and no one told me. All lies."

"I'm so sorry, Caden. Sometimes parents and family members don't make the right decisions. All we can do is make the best decisions we can at the time. Your mom loved you more than anything in the world. So do I. We never wanted to hurt you."

He turned his back again.

"I don't care anymore. I don't care about anything. I just want to go home."

"We can't leave yet. Damon—your dad—wants a chance to get to know you."

"Maybe I don't want to know him. I thought I did, but not if it means you might leave me here. You say you won't, but you've lied before. And I'm old enough to know he can probably take me away from you 'cause he's my dad. I don't want to be here. I want to be close to Mom."

She understood he meant that he wanted to remain near his mother's grave. Close enough to visit as often as he wanted. He was trying to hang on. It wasn't fair. A child being forced to think and plan their future on where their parent's grave lay. Her chest ached and her eyes burned. She fought the urge to sniff because she didn't want him questioning her strength and ability to be there for him. She needed to be the strong one. His rock. His guiding lighthouse, like the one that anchored the town.

"Listen to me, Caden. I will always be in your life. I'm not leaving you."

A tree outside their window rustled its branches against the pane and the sound of the ocean grew louder as the wind picked up again. Caden sniffled and pulled his covers up over his head.

"Mom said the same thing to me once. She lied about that, too."

THE MORNING SUN struck Caden's eyelids when he rolled over in bed. He yanked the covers over his face, then flipped his pillow over his head. He didn't want to see the light of day. He didn't want to see anyone, especially not his aunt or da—that…that man. Damon, as his aunt called him? Mr. Woods? Dad? The word stung his brain and he squeezed his eyes tighter and fisted his hair. Life sucked. It made no sense. It wasn't worth it. Why did people bother?

A gull screeched as it flew past the bedroom window. It didn't sound free and joyful like the sound of gulls on the beach yesterday, when he was tossing driftwood to Duck. Or maybe it was all about perception and positive versus negative thinking and all that crap his therapist kept talking about. There wasn't anything positive about having your mother die and then finding out she'd lied to you your entire life. Kept the worst kind of secret from you.

He just wanted to soar like that seabird and scream at the top of his lungs while pulling his hair…but it would freak his aunt out. Plus, it would make everyone come running to check on him and the last thing he wanted was attention. He wanted everyone to leave him the heck alone. Maybe staying underwater like a fish, where human voices would be muffled, until some bird swooped down and swallowed him whole, would be better. He had waited in bed, still as prey, until he heard his aunt head downstairs for breakfast fifteen minutes ago. He could smell coffee and bacon wafting through the vents. His stomach growled.

He surfaced from the suffocating covers and took a deep breath. *You lied, Mom. How could you? I hate you for doing this to me. I hate you for leaving...for lying. For not getting better.* No. No, he didn't hate her. He used the corner of his sheet to dry his face. He missed her. He loved her so much it hurt. Guilt cramped his entire chest. He was an awful person. How could he be angry at his mom? She'd done everything for him. He knew she had loved him. She was the best mother he could have had. Which is why he was an ungrateful, terrible example of a human being. But he was so confused. Life felt like it had been turned inside out and Aunt Zuri, who had sworn she'd make everything okay, had kept the truth from him, too. He had no one left to trust.

The softness of Duck's fur between his fingers and her soulful eyes came back to him, but he brushed away the memory. She wasn't his dog. He wasn't the one she was loyal to.

He threw off the covers and sat up. Did his…father…know before yesterday or did he just find out, too? He didn't act like he knew when they first met on the beach. Had he been lied to, as well? Or what if he knew all these years but didn't want to have anything to do with him? Was Aunt Zuri forcing him into their lives? Or was she being honest when she said his mom had kept her from saying anything and now that his mom was gone, she wanted to make things right. But that made his mom the bad guy and every time that notion pounded at his brain it came with gnawing guilt. He couldn't help but wonder if his mom would have ever told him. Did his grandparents know?

He got out of bed and went to the restroom, not because he wanted to face the world but because nature was calling. He half intended to crawl back under the sheets and he could have ignored his hunger pangs forever—well, maybe not forever—but Sara's warm laughter filled the halls of the house. An odd, bubbly feeling swirled in his stomach that had nothing to do with needing breakfast. It was the same feeling that had him fumbling for words last night at the firepit. The sound of her voice seemed to magically erase the gloom and replace all the dark places in his mind with light. She was cool. Chill. Pretty. He kind of liked the way the firelight made her red hair brighter. She was a good listener and he'd needed someone to listen.

He had mentioned his mom passing, but nothing about the whole vacation trick revolving around a father he'd never heard a word about until that day. He had wanted to. Sara came off as less judgy than the kids at his school up north. But she knew folks in Turtleback and, surely, she knew Mr. Woods and probably liked him. Just like with the dog, Sara's loyalties probably lay with his father and the other town residents…not some geeky new kid she'd only known a few hours. Still, he couldn't help but want to see her again. She was the only person his age he'd met around here. And he really liked the way she smiled at him.

He rummaged through his small suitcase and quickly tucked a clip-on reading light and book three of his favorite thriller series under his pillow so that his aunt wouldn't see it. He'd only just discovered the series this past year and it was incredible, but he was afraid his aunt would freak out if she knew he was reading something geared for grown-ups. It wasn't like there was anything nasty in it. That would be gross. But it was seriously suspenseful. The kind of story that got his heart pumping and made him feel like he could do all of those things the star of the series could do, fighting evil and saving innocents. Standing up to bullies.

He wasn't that strong in real life. He knew that. In fact, he hated gym class because being around all the athletic kids made him feel small and inept. But he could pretend when he was reading. He could escape and see himself as someone others would look up to. Maybe he'd finish the book tonight after his aunt fell asleep.

He changed into clean jeans and a green pullover sweater. His mom liked him in green and used to always say that this sweater looked good against his darker complexion. Plus, it worked for the holiday season and all…but he was more interested in looking good right now. He stood in front of the mirror that hung over a three-drawer wooden dresser on the wall adjacent to the bathroom. *You look like him. You look like your dad.* The realization hit him like a wave crashing on shore. He'd always thought that his complexion and curly hair had come from his maternal grandparents' Jordanian and Mexican heritages, and obviously that was part of him, but not all. He had decided that someday he'd do one of those genetic tests to see if he could find out more about his dad's side—in fact he had almost asked for one for his last birthday but decided not to stress his mom out at the time—but now he knew.

He took a deep breath and the pressure in his chest felt good…like he was being pumped with relief and pride and a sense of belonging. It felt like he'd somehow never been able to stand up for himself because a sneering voice in his head kept telling him that he didn't even know who he was. He'd had classmates ask if he was Black before and he'd hated giving the same answer every time. That he didn't know. But now he did. He had another proud history to add to all his grandma and grandpa had taught him about their side of the family. He mattered. He somehow felt a little stronger. Sort of…complete. If his aunt had never brought him here, he would have never known he was part African American. He didn't want to stay in the Outer Banks, but at least now he knew who his father was, where he was…and that he was alive.

DAMON CARRIED THREE boxes of pastries up the front steps of The Turtleback Bed-and-Breakfast. It was more than Melanie had ordered from the bakery, but he couldn't resist adding in some of his favorites, just in case Caden liked them, too. He had offered to deliver the order, since he had planned on showing up for breakfast at the B and B. He hoped the extra sugar would help win Caden over. A peace offering of sorts. He also hadn't forgotten that Zuri had a powerful sweet tooth and couldn't say no to anything that involved strawberries.

He balanced the boxes in one hand and rapped at the door before letting himself in.

"Good morning," he said.

Melanie was setting up for breakfast with Sara's help. He almost thought Zuri and Caden had slept in—maybe to avoid him—but she stepped out from behind the wall that separated the kitchen from the rest of the living space. Melanie shifted her gaze between them but didn't say a word.

"Hi." Her tone was flat. "Caden's still upstairs."

"Okay."

He was second-guessing the breakfast strategy. Had she told Melanie what the relationship was between them? Because he hadn't. He did explain it to the sheriff, but Carlos Ryker wasn't a talker. Carlos and the town veterinarian, Grayson Zale, were two of his closest friends. Carlos had served in the air force and Gray had completed vet school through the army, though he'd also worked in the navy's marine mammal program before ending up in witness protection. If Carlos had been able to keep Gray's identity a secret until the threat on his life had been neutralized, then he could be trusted with Damon's recent paternity news.

"You brought my favorite! Thanks, Mr. Woods," Sara said, opening the first box full of almond croissants.

"I can't take credit. Your grandma ordered those. I take it, just for you." Sara skipped over to her grandmother and planted a kiss on her cheek. "This box here has what I picked out," Damon said.

He set the box on the table where Melanie was putting everything on antique china. She claimed that if she ever served guests out of boxes, her late husband would roll in his grave. Zuri's lips parted when she peered into the box.

"Strawberry shortcakes?" She narrowed her eyes at him. He smiled.

"Darla actually calls them Strawberry Seacakes. Most of her items at the bakery are given ocean-related names. Like "Crab Claws" instead of "Bear Claws." It's part of her marketing."

The stairs creaked and Caden appeared. He was walking differently or something. Did he look taller? Older? Overnight?

"Good morning," Damon said.

"Yeah. Whatever." Caden shrugged without making eye contact.

"Hungry?" Zuri asked. Damon noticed she didn't call the boy out on rudeness. At least she understood the boy probably needed food the way she needed coffee first thing. What teenager didn't wake up famished?

"Hey. You've gotta try these," Sara said.

The corner of Caden's mouth lifted and he was at the table in seconds. Right by Sara's side. *So that's how it is.* He took the piece of almond croissant Sara had ripped off of hers and held out and he popped it in his mouth, nodding in approval. But then he reached for a Crab Claw pastry. Damon's favorite. Something akin to pride and awe, or maybe it was validation, filled his chest.

Damon stepped behind the chair where Zuri sat, closing her eyes with every bite of Strawberry Seacake, and grabbed a Crab Claw for himself. He took a bite and wiped the corner of his mouth with the back of his hand—freezing for a second when he noticed Caden doing the same thing at the same time. Even Zuri paused midbite when she caught them in the act. It had to be a coincidence. Granted, he'd read about behavioral genetics and all, but really? Zuri wiped her lips with a napkin.

"This is so good. Thank you," she said, taking a sip of the fresh coffee Melanie had just poured in her cup.

"I'm going to need your help later, Caden. If you don't mind and if it's okay with your aunt," Damon said.

The boy frowned and stopped chewing.

"Why?" he asked, before swallowing.

"It's Duck. I couldn't get her to leave the house this morning for a jog on the beach. I think it's her way of insisting that she'd rather play fetch with you."

Okay, so it was a white lie. Duck would live in the wet sand if she could and it had taken some effort to get her back inside after a quick potty break, instead of resuming their usual morning routine of a run and some training. He never had trouble getting her outside. Inside was another matter. But the fact was, she loved kids as much as Gray's rough collie, Laddie, who helped with story time at Castaway Books, the town's used bookshop. "She needs a lot of exercise or she'll start acting like a bear on sugar and caffeine."

Caden rolled his eyes at him.

"You can't tri—"

"I'll go with you," Sara chimed in.

"—trick a smart dog into walking if she doesn't want to. But, okay. Sure. I'll try." Caden gave Sara a side-glance.

Smooth save, kid. Damon cleared his throat to mask a chuckle. The power of a girl and dog. Understanding psychology was something he'd learned through his military training, not that Caden was an adversary, but he did want to get through to the boy.

"Can I, Gram? If I help clean up?" Sara asked.

"Of course," Mrs. Biddle said. "If it's all right with Mr. Woods."

"Absolutely," Damon said.

Zuri took another bite of her pastry and closed her eyes. She took another, then caught him watching her. She wiped the whipped cream off her upper lip and took another sip of coffee, pretending to ignore him. She was making up for not eating much dinner last night. Watching her brought a flood of memories from when she'd insisted he needed extra help with science outside of the school homework clinic and he would sneak snacks into the public library where they'd meet. It really made her nervous about breaking rules when he did that, but she never could resist a sweet treat. He sat down in a chair right next to her at the table.

"I know a bribe when I see one. It's not working, but thank you for remembering about strawberries," she whispered, when Melanie went into the kitchen and Sara and Caden took their breakfast out on the deck, while talking about some new television series.

"I don't know what you're talking about." He finished off his claw and reached for a blueberry muffin. "I think we should try dinner at my place again. Tonight."

He knew it sounded like he was asking her out, but he meant for Caden. She took another bite.

"No way. Have you forgotten his reaction last night? It's too soon. And he wants me to take him home, so I don't even know how long I can hold out."

"Tonight's a whole day away. You saw how he agreed to walk the dog and he seems to have made a friend. I bet he'll change his mind."

"I don't doubt it. He changes it every hour about everything. But dinner with you again is a whole different matter."

"I have a plan and I'm betting he won't want to leave so fast."

"What is it?" She folded her arms and lowered her chin.

"You don't trust me?"

She raised one brow at him and gave a look that he'd only ever seen from his mother and a few teachers. It wasn't really a question, so much as a statement, but she was making it clear that she didn't. She was just waiting for him to mess up.

"Never mind. But I think my place tonight is a good idea. I already have the Crock-Pot going. Pot roast."

"I don't know. I'll think about it. Let's see how your Duck trick works first and how the rest of the day goes."

"Fine. Dinner will be waiting. Oh, and I ordered a strawberry cheesecake for dessert. I hope that's okay."

"You're evil. Downright dangerous."

"Guess that depends on perception and whose side you're on. If I recall correctly, you didn't mind my willingness to take risks when it meant cookies and candy bars in the library."

Her cheeks turned beet red. She was still easy to fluster. Only he used to be too immature to understand how mean it was to flirt with her when they were teens. Mean, yes, but on some level that he had refused to acknowledge and tried to hide, it had been genuine. He had needed her in his life. His other friends had hung around him because they knew his family was well-off and he could afford to pay their way whenever they wanted to go to the theater or out to eat or any other entertainment. When he had cut himself off from family for a year or so, trying to figure life out, those friends had disappeared.

Real friends didn't care if you were popular or had money. Real friends were the ones who supported you and stuck with you when the going got tough. Like his SEAL mates. Like Carlos and Gray and his other friends in Turtleback Beach.

Like Zuri back in high school when his family struggles had caused his grades to plummet and threaten his position on the school's cross-country team.

And here she was right back in his life doing what she thought was right. He didn't deserve to have her in his life. He didn't have a right to fluster or tease her. But he loved seeing her blush. She'd always been the kind of girl who was pretty but didn't know it. It was refreshing. He was just trying to reminisce. He wasn't trying to be mean or misleading.

"Some things were a little too scary, even for big brave guys like you," she quipped. He nodded and couldn't hide his smile. Wow, she really had changed. Timid Zuri Woods had it in her after all. Standing up for herself like that. Confidence looked good on her. And she was right. He had been scared to death of falling for a girl like her back then. Of commitment.

He leaned in.

"Fear is a primal emotion that works like a survival instinct. It keeps us safe. Warns us to protect ourselves."

Something shifted in her face. She brushed

her hands clean of crumbs and scooted her chair back. He took the hint and gave her space. He regretted what had happened in high school. He regretted making her mad right now. He wasn't perfect, but he wanted her to understand where he was coming from. That he was being sincere. That he'd learned a thing or two in life, just as she had. They weren't kids anymore.

"Self-preservation. Spoken like a man who understands science."

"I understand a lot of things."

She glanced up at Caden and Sara as they came back inside to refill their plates, then head back out.

"We'll see about that."

She got up and followed her nephew out onto the deck. *Self-preservation.* It took an exorbitant amount of trust and courage to overcome fear. He knew that trust was almost impossible to earn once broken. Chances were that Zuri would never trust him again. He wasn't even sure if he'd ever earn his son's trust. However, he had faced worse odds. The kind where he had been one hundred percent certain he wouldn't come out of a mission alive. Yet he was still living and breathing. The only sure way to fail at something was to give up without trying. He had to at least try to make things right—make up for the past—for the kid's sake. The boy didn't need to put up with a father and aunt who didn't get along. Damon knew family arguments could really take their toll.

"I like her," Melanie said, as if Damon needed a second opinion. He shrugged noncommittally.

"Sara seems glad to have someone her age around," Damon said.

Melanie refilled his coffee mug and sat at the table next to him.

"She does. As much as I hate to admit it, hanging with Granny twenty-four-seven can't be all that fun. I bet that boy is just as happy as Sara to have a friend around. It takes some burden off Zuri, too. It can't be easy raising a tween boy on her own."

Damon cradled his mug and stared outside. Melanie didn't know the half of it. Vera had been a single mom. He took a swig of coffee but it suddenly tasted bitter. The anger he'd felt earlier bubbled up in his chest.

"No, I guess it's not."

The fact that Vera had been a single mother with no financial support from him—a fact he would remedy as soon as possible—and news of her passing were devastating. And he was furious that Zuri, who used to be the one person he could count on when homelife during his high school years had been so unstable, hadn't told him the truth all these years. But he did understand sister loyalty and he had to give her credit for being here now. For telling him the truth. Yes, he had regrets about the past and Vera, but he had a son for it and he wasn't going to let anyone take him out of his life again…even if he wasn't sure how to let anyone into a life that revolved around a secret he'd worked so hard to keep. All he knew right now was that he was a father and if it weren't for Caden, who knew if he'd have ever seen Zuri again. Maybe Caden wasn't the only person here he needed to get through to. There was Zuri, standing next to his son in the morning light, looking more serious and beautiful than he remembered. If what she said was true that everything in life was supposed to happen for a reason, then maybe…just maybe…he was being handed a second chance.

CHAPTER FOUR

Zuri hated leaving all her research and grant applications on hold, but she couldn't be two places at once and her nephew had to come first. She had explained her situation to the university's chemistry department head more than once and had cleared her vacation time, yet here he was sending her emails reiterating grant deadlines and the department's upcoming considerations for tenure track—a department that was notoriously male-dominated. In fact, the two other candidates were guys. She was the only female professor whose research had her being considered for tenure track and, as politically correct as the department head, Dr. Farthan, always was, the sexist undercurrent, as well as racial microaggressions, were always there.

Having grown up with mixed Jordanian-Mexican heritage, she was used to it—a fact that said a lot about how things that were so wrong in life could become wrongfully normalized. She hated it, along with the fact that, although Caden didn't have to deal with the sexist part, she'd witnessed his mom having to caution him because he was a minority.

Vera had never mentioned to him that he had African American heritage as well, though, a choice Zuri had disagreed with and had implored her to change her mind about, but Vera had been afraid he'd start narrowing down people from town or photos in yearbooks. As far as Zuri was concerned, it was wrong. Caden deserved to know. He needed to know, so that he could embrace his heritage from both sides. She knew it went against Vera's wishes, but Zuri wanted him to feel empowered and proud and to understand why the recent Black Lives Matter movement he was seeing on the news was so important. The bottom line was that no kid should have to be careful or fearful because of their DNA. It was sick. Not right. She wanted a better world for Caden. All kids deserved better.

And adults did, as well. Dealing with

work politics and dynamics was exhausting but necessary.

Zuri's mother had always said that it was up to her to stake her claim on who she was and who she wanted to be in life and how she wanted to be perceived, before anyone decided for her or labeled her. She had to demand respect in this world. That's why success and this tenure path were so important to her. It was why her parents had been driven to earn the utmost respect in their medical fields and why they'd always insisted that their daughters put their education first. They had been torn apart when they had learned about their eldest's pregnancy, but Zuri had to give them credit for coming to terms with it quickly and for supporting Vera all the way.

They'd all helped with Caden after he was born, so that Vera could earn her degree in special education. They'd all stepped in when illness had ended her career. Zuri had done whatever she could to help. Their parents, unable to be there in person, still assisted financially and came to visit when they could. That's what family was about.

She couldn't let herself get pressured into scrambling her priorities. She slapped her laptop shut. Forget emailing Farthan back. She grabbed her cell and hit his contact number. One thing she'd learned was that Dr. Farthan tended to be annoyingly bolder in emails, but when he was put on the spot, either verbally or face-to-face, he tended to pull back.

"Hello. Zuri?" Clearly he had her in his contacts, too.

"Hi, Dr. Farthan. Sor—" She almost apologized for bothering him but cut herself off. Why did women do that? Feel the need to say sorry all the time? Zuri used to be awful about it. Not that she was rude now. There was a time for politeness, but not with a man who had proven time and time again that he took it as a sign of weakness. *Be bold. Stand your ground.* "I got your email."

"Ah, yes. I wanted to be sure you hadn't forgotten dates and that we're good on the schedule. I didn't mean to intrude on your family time. I didn't call because I knew email could be set aside for your convenience."

The backing off. The semi-sincere consideration. Ugh. It was a good thing he couldn't see the look on her face. It had only been a couple of days since she got off work…giving herself extra time to pack and travel.

"Yes, I'm fully aware. It was made clear in our last meeting and in my written request for time off, as well as in your first email of the last three. I assure you, it's on my calendar and in my cell phone 'reminders.' That's why I'm calling instead of replying to your mail. I wanted to be sure there wasn't any misunderstanding over my time off for family. I will be back at work as planned."

"Good. Good. I figure it doesn't hurt to confirm."

Seriously? Why did it feel like he was setting things up so that he'd look like he'd given her extra chances and wasn't playing favorites if a man ended up getting the position?

"No problem. I just wanted to be clear that I'm still on schedule for the grant deadline and still interested in the tenure track position."

"Got it. You take care. I'll see you when you're back." Farthan hung up quickly. The man needed to busy himself with research more and spend less time on bureaucracy. Why did his email and tone make her feel harassed even without him doing so directly?

She tossed her phone aside. Even though she'd put in for vacation time, she'd originally planned to still pop back into the lab during her time off, if Caden and his dad hit it off and wanted to spend time together, but now that she was here in Turtleback and had seen Caden's reaction to meeting his father, she couldn't imagine leaving him alone with Damon, even for a few days. If things got complicated and she ended up having to extend her absence beyond what had been approved, she'd be out of the running for sure. Why was it that women were forced to juggle family and career in a way most men didn't understand? There were exceptions, of course, just not that often.

She glanced at her watch and jumped up. They'd all be done with breakfast by now. She had escaped, giving the excuse that she had to check mail, because Damon had left her frazzled. Maybe all the sugar in the strawberry shortcake—or seacake or whatever it was called—had gotten to her, but all her senses had fired up. The taste of strawberries and cream that transported her back to high school, the way he studied her as she ate, his freshly showered scent and, most of all, the way his hand accidentally brushed hers when they both reached for a napkin…and his talk of fear and survival. It had all been too much. Too engulfing. Dangerous. Coming upstairs had been an act of survival all right, but now she had to go back down and steel herself against all the emotions he triggered.

You're not naive anymore, Zuri. You swore you'd never put your heart on the line again. Don't let him get to you. He's just being nice because of Caden.

Besides, was he seriously trying to say that he had left her mortified and humiliated in front of other students because he had been afraid of her liking him? What in the world? What kind of convoluted excuse was that? Did men ever make sense?

It didn't matter, really. She was here

and she had a mission. Her nephew was the focus, not her. Her mother's exchange with Damon's mother, Mary, at the funeral came back to her.

"Caden's our priority now. We have to make sure he'll be okay."

"Absolutely," Damon's mom had replied. "Please let me know if you need anything. If there's any way I can help."

Funny how it always seemed to take death to get their parents to act kindly toward one another, even if temporarily. Even if they were just being polite and sympathetic. Their dads were better at putting the past behind them—but their moms and the ongoing judgmental and defensive attitude between them that had grown from when their kids were in grade school had really hit a peak when they sat on opposite sides of a table trying to negotiate a settlement.

That "unforgivable" lawsuit that pitted his mom against hers had taken Mary's judgment of Lucia's parenting skills to a whole new level. Lucia took her oath not to harm and her career as a doctor beyond seriously. It had been an attack on her morality and character. Lucia still hadn't let it go, even if she'd gotten an apology and explanation as to why the case had been taken on and how it wasn't meant to be anything personal.

Despite all of it, Damon's parents had appeared at Vera's funeral, separately due to their divorce, to pay respects, just as her parents had when the Woods family had lost Lucas. Everyone had been civil, too, because for some incomprehensible reason it always seems to take tragedy to bring people together in this world.

When asked about their grown children, Zuri had overheard Damon's mom mentioning that he now lived on a beach in North Carolina. Tracking him down after that had been easy after she heard the Outer Banks mentioned and Zuri had known immediately that she had to confront Damon for Caden's sake. For Damon's, too.

And she knew it would be difficult, but she never quite imagined just how hard being near him would be. Seeing him again made everything surface, from the wishful thinking and longing she felt when she tutored him in high school, to the bitterness and disillusionment she felt when he took her sister to prom—just to rub in the fact that Zuri wasn't the hot, with-it Habib sister—and to having the wind knocked out of her when she found out that Vera was pregnant.

What had she expected? Zuri, the simple, slightly geeky girl who was nothing like the popular, cheerleader types who used to flirt with him constantly. She had been dreaming. Well, she wasn't a dreamer anymore. She was a scientist. A PhD. A master of facts and evidence. And she didn't care what anyone thought of her, least of all, Damon.

You don't need to pine over some guy who abandoned your friendship and now spends his days on a beach. The female attention he got in school is probably nothing compared to the bikini babe groupies he probably has during summer vacation. He toyed with you once and he's at it again.

She needed to listen to herself. This whole father-son introduction would be over soon, and she and Caden would be getting back to their life in Boston after the holidays. She'd be back at work. The kid needed to get back to school and his therapist appointments whether Damon liked it or not. They'd have a new normal, because routines or not, nothing would ever be the same.

She got up and went to the mirror that hung over the dresser. She gave herself a quick look over. *Don't care. Don't care. Don't—* Darn it. She couldn't help but care a little. She grabbed her lip gloss and coated her lips. *It's just for moisture. Winter air and all.* She dabbed her mouth with a tissue. *Stop lying to yourself.* She let out a huff and pinched her cheeks then fluffed her hair. *Enough. It doesn't matter what he thinks of you. He hates you and Vera for keeping Caden from him. He plans to fight you for custody. Keep your head on, girl.*

When she first confronted him on the beach and told him he was a father, Damon had insisted he wouldn't be giving up his rights. Shè wanted him to be a part of the boy's life, that's why she was here, but no way was she going to let him take Caden away from her. Summer breaks, maybe, but the school year and everyday life? No way. He didn't know the kid like she did and she had promised her sister that she would raise Caden. She'd give her own life before breaking that promise to Vera, especially since she had already broken the one about never telling Damon he had a son.

She tried to head down the stairs quietly, hoping to catch some of the conversation in the living room. She didn't want to eavesdrop. She just wanted to see how things were going between father and son, but the third step creaked and the fifth step groaned, giving her away.

Melanie was consolidating all the leftover pastries in one box. Sara was showing Caden a collection of music CDs and it looked like they were picking out all of the holiday tracks. Caden barely looked up when Zuri walked past them on her way to the kitchen. Damon wasn't around.

"There you are," Melanie said. "I wanted to double-check with you about dinner. Damon said you'd be out and that I shouldn't bother. I realize lunch is usually up to our guests to grab in town, but dinner is included in your stay, you know."

"I do. Thank you. But, yes, we'll be out,

so don't worry about it. Unless you have other guests, of course."

"Not today. How about I have lunch ready instead, then? I'll have sandwiches made and I'll keep them in the fridge, that way you don't have to be here at a specific time."

"Sounds great, thanks. Um, did he leave? I thought he needed help with his dog."

"Oh, he's still here. He went around the side of the house to carry some wood to the firepit for me. I told him not to, but he never takes no for an answer. Always doing things and helping out, that one."

The patio door opened and Damon entered, wiping his hands off on his jeans.

"All done. Told you it wouldn't take long," he said.

"Thank you, my dear. You'll have to actually enjoy a fire with us one of these days."

Damon just smiled and seemed relieved that the sudden blare of music set too loud saved him from committing. The cheery beat of "Jingle Bell Rock" filled the place and Sara quickly adjusted the volume to a more enjoyable level. She moved her shoulders and hips to the beat, while Caden stood awkwardly, not daring to move. Zuri suddenly recalled her sister once saying the boy needed dance lessons if he was ever going to survive high school. She'd said it nonchalantly, without realizing she'd inadvertently poked fun at Zuri, too. Zuri had never been a great dancer in high school. She crinkled her nose. Maybe that's why they'd always gotten along so well.

"Ready, guys?" Damon asked. Caden shrugged. Poor kid had dancing or Damon to choose from and he clearly wasn't comfortable with either.

"Maybe they'd rather stay here and relax on the beach," Zuri suggested, trying to give her nephew an out. She still thought Damon was moving too fast with Caden.

"We're ready!" Sara called out over the music. She skipped toward the door, never questioning whether Caden agreed with her response. He followed her out without bothering to look at Zuri or Damon. Apparently, he was indeed ready to go. As long as Sara was.

"Are you joining us?" Damon asked.

"Of course, I am. I'm his aunt. What else would I do?"

"He's old enough not to get lost and you can trust he'd be safe with me. You could stroll through town? Shop?"

"That's sexist."

"What?" Damon gave her a baffled look. "Really? Everyone's out there shopping for the holidays. I wasn't trying to imply anything sexist or stereotypical. You've never been typical."

"Oh?"

Damon held up a finger and shook his head.

"That didn't come out right. What I meant was that you've always been smart and accomplished and not materialistic or the kind of person who goes after the latest fad. That's what I liked about you."

Liked about her? He liked that she wasn't typical? She looked nervously toward Melanie, who kept a straight face as she filled the dishwasher, but Zuri was sure she'd overheard the conversation.

"I don't need to shop right now and I know I can trust you with his safety. I mean, that's what you do every day. Save people and keep them safe. But I'd like to tag along and see what this idea of yours is all about." She was more worried about Caden's emotions. Not physical safety.

"After you," he said, waving her toward the door. "Catch you later, Melanie. Just text me if there's anything you need me to pick up before dropping Sara back here."

"Will do. You guys have fun," Melanie said.

Sara and Caden were drawing designs in the sand along the side of the driveway as they waited. They looked up and tossed their sticks aside.

"So, are we taking Duck for a walk or what?" Caden asked, in a clipped tone. He dug the toe of his sneaker in the sand and stuffed his hands in his pockets. Zuri could tell he was more interested in spending time with Sara than with adults, but since Sara seemed interested in doing whatever Damon suggested, he was reluctantly going along with it.

"More than just a walk. I'm going to have you two help with a training session and you'll get a tour of our ORBP headquarters. Ocean Rescue and Beach Patrol," Damon said.

"Way cool," Sara said.

"You guys hop in and we'll stop at my place to get Duck. We can walk to the station from there." He opened the passenger front and back doors of his red pickup truck and waited for Zuri to climb up front and the kids to get in the back. He'd caught her off guard with the chivalry. It was nice, but she just wasn't used to it. If anything, up in Boston at the university, she made a point of opening her own doors and not expecting anything from male colleagues, just because she felt the need to show that she could pull her own. She didn't want to give anyone a reason to act put out or condescending.

But somehow Damon opening the truck doors was different. He did it so casually and unassumingly. Something about that made her feel cared for and respected. She didn't really recall him being that chivalrous when he was younger. She was getting glimpses of the Damon who'd trained in the navy and had served on one of their elite teams. She was informed enough to know a person didn't go through all that and not come out changed.

A part of her wondered why he had quit. Was he injured? Not all injuries showed. Invisible things like PTSD and depression could eat away at someone from the inside, much like the cancer that had taken Vera. No one could see *it* until it was too late.

Damon revved the engine, backed out and headed from where the bed-and-breakfast stood on the north edge of the town, not far from a black-and-white lighthouse and a few other beach houses, and drove them down the only road that led through Turtleback. The distance was walkable, maybe within five or ten minutes, but there was still a chill in the air and he needed to get his truck back to his place on the south side of town. Zuri couldn't think of anything to say and was glad that, instead, Damon played tour guide by pointing out the beach town's main attractions.

The main street of town was lined with shops that looked like colorful rows of small cottages raised on short stilts and connected by wooden walkways and a boardwalk. He pointed out The Saltwater Sweetery bakery, where he'd gotten the pastries they'd enjoyed, a yoga studio with a law office above it, a gift shop and a used bookstore called Castaway Books. The town ended with a boardwalk restaurant that overlooked the beach. Every shop had holiday lights and wreaths on their windows and doors and, though Zuri was sure it was probably much busier in the summer, there were plenty of townsfolk bustling along the walkway and ducking into shops.

Holiday shopping. Christmas. Her chest ached and tears stung the rims of her eyes. She hated how her eyes would sting every single time she thought of her sister being gone. It would be their first Christmas without her. Caden's first without his mom. Zuri had promised her parents they'd visit closer to New Year's, but she had decided Christmas would be too much for Caden. She had worried that her parents would spend their visit breaking out in tears or upset, which would in turn only depress Caden more. At least here things were new and distracting—an understatement for meeting his father for the first time.

"You might want to take Caden to Castaway Books at some point, Sara. Maybe when Laddie's there for reading time." He glanced over his shoulder at Caden. "Laddie's the town veterinarian's rough collie. Gray Zale is a friend of mine and his dog loves sitting with kids during reading time. The reading time is geared for younger kids, but I'm betting you'd like Laddie. Great dog." Damon passed the town and drove down a back road that ran parallel to the beach. When Zuri and Caden had gone to Damon's place for dinner, they'd simply walked down the beach from the B and B. This road, she assumed, would lead up to the front of his place. They passed a yellow cottage with a blue door and one that was white with a fenced yard, before coming to Damon's weathered, gray house.

"All right. Give me a sec and I'll bring Duck out. Just take that path along the side of the house and I'll meet you on the beach."

They all exited the truck and started for the path he'd pointed out, which was merely a break in the tall reed grasses that grew in clumps along the dunes that separated his home and the road from the beach.

"Come on," Zuri said, leading the way. Sara and Caden ran ahead of her and disappeared beyond the reeds. She was so glad he was making a friend here. His therapist always made a point of asking whether he was still hanging out with classmates at school or on weekends. Friends mattered and provided a support system, and Caden had the few he hung out with at school, but weekends hadn't been getting any easier. He tended to hole up in his bedroom not wanting to do anything but read all day. He hadn't even bothered to practice his piano in the past few weeks and that had been something he loved. Thirteen or not, a cell phone might have helped him stay connected through texts. Although that went against everything she'd read about phones, social media, and increased anxiety and depression in teens. Man, she had a newfound appreciation for all her parents—and other parents including Damon's—went through to raise a family.

No college degree could really prep a person for that.

A gust of wind met her head-on, as if to jolt her out of her worries. She inhaled deeply and cleared the top of the low sand dune. Damon was already closing his back-patio door behind him as Duck bounded down the wooden steps leading off his deck. Zuri stiffened and stood still. That much she'd learned about dogs and being chased. Duck ran toward the kids, who were picking up shells. Damon let out a whistle and Duck stopped obediently in her tracks, looked back at him, then at Caden and Sara. Ah, choices. Distractions.

"I think she's shifting loyalties," Zuri called out.

"She's got her priorities," Damon said, as he came down the steps. "Go on, Duck." The dog, relieved that she didn't have to choose, ran over to the kids. "See that brown-and-beige house with the red flag? That's where we're headed," Damon called out to the kids. Zuri headed in the same direction and he joined her.

"He doesn't seem as upset today,"

Damon said, slowing his pace slightly so that they wouldn't be in earshot.

Zuri shook her head and put her hands in her pockets when the back of his hand accidentally brushed hers. He didn't seem to notice.

"You don't see it. I do. Sara is a distraction, but she won't be around all the time. You weren't there last night when he couldn't get to sleep. His world has been torn apart, Damon. I was hoping that meeting you would give him hope or some comfort in the fact that if something happened to me, he wouldn't be alone. Of course my parents adore him but they're always so busy. I'm not so sure coming here was the best idea. At least not yet. Maybe he wasn't ready."

"Maybe you're overthinking it. Give him a chance to adjust. He just found out." Damon scrubbed the stubble along his jaw. "Oh, man. My parents. My siblings. I don't see them that much, but they have a right to know, too. Why do I feel like a can of worms has been opened?"

"Who knows, maybe it won't be so bad. Maybe sharing a grandson will give our mothers a reason to get along in the same room. They'd finally have something in common."

"Or something concrete to fight over."

Zuri picked up a piece of sea glass and rubbed it between her fingers as she walked.

"Or a mutual understanding of what it's like to lose a child. Please, don't tell them just yet. The last thing Caden needs is to get caught in the middle."

Damon looked over at her and gave a wry smile.

"I think it's too late for that, but yeah, *I* don't even want to deal with telling them yet. Let's get through the holidays. Or wait until Caden brings it up. I'm sure once the idea of having me in his life sinks in, he'll realize through mere deduction that he has another set of grandparents."

He was implying that Caden was caught in the middle of the two of them, which meant he was still thinking about custody.

"Damon, you want what's best for him, don't you? You wouldn't cause problems just to satisfy your need to stake your claim at his expense, would you?"

"Don't try and make me sound like the villain here. Guilt-tripping isn't going to work. What's best for him is having a father around. You wouldn't have come here if you didn't agree on that." He cut off the conversation as they neared the rescue station.

"Duck. Come!"

The dog ran toward them, causing Zuri to stop in her tracks, then back up a few steps.

"She won't bite you or jump up with me standing next to you. She just got a bit excited yesterday. I think she gets an adrenaline rush when she's been in the water for a rescue, staged for training or not. Plus, she's dry this time," Damon said, giving Duck a good rub.

"Her size is intimidating," Zuri said.

"Duck, sit." The dog obeyed Damon, then he reached out and took Zuri's hand. His touch felt more personal to her than it probably did to him. He didn't seem fazed by it, but she couldn't stop the rush of energy that zipped up her arm and through her chest. She dredged up how he'd made her feel years ago and the energy was abruptly extinguished. Damon placed her hand on Duck's head and let go, keeping his dog in a seated position. "See. Just like last night. Harmless. She loves a good ear scratch."

Zuri scrunched her fingers through the dog's thick, wavy hair. Duck looked up at her with soulful eyes and panted.

"You're right. I've got this. I'm really not quite as afraid of dogs as I used to be. I know it doesn't look like it, but I'm just cautious. I believe I recently heard someone say something about how a bit of fear serves to protect us. Hmm? I don't think I've ever been near any breed this size."

"I remember how you were about dogs. You used to cross the street to the opposite sidewalk whenever our German shepherd came out to greet me or my brothers on the walk home from school."

"Yeah, I did do that."

"I remember a lot of things. Don't worry. I'll stay near you when she's around."

Zuri sucked at the corner of her lip for no reason other than she needed a reminder that she was the one who'd had a crush on him, not the other way around. All he was saying was that he was a responsible person now. That's the message he had been trying to get across. He was a protector. He could be trusted with Caden and he was proving it by using her as an example.

"Well, thanks, I guess. But see, I'm totally fine now." No protecting needed. She faced Duck full on and started petting her with both hands, giving her that big old scratch behind the ears and on top of her head and—

"I wouldn't do tha—"

Too late. Her hand was already under Duck's chin. She thought dogs were supposed to like chin scratches. She'd seen her elderly neighbor doing so with her miniature poodle at the end of every walk and right before a treat. Apparently, it wasn't the best place to touch a Newfoundland. She grimaced and looked at her hands. She'd been slimed.

"Sorry," Damon said. She knew by the way a cough escaped him and he cleared his throat that he was choking back laughter. "I tried to warn you. This breed drools quite a bit. Not all the time, but if they're expecting food or treats or just excited, it happens."

"Great." She splayed her hands. She was not about to wipe them on her jeans. Damon whipped a rag out from his pocket.

"Here. This hasn't been used yet. I keep a towel on hand—no pun intended—for when she drools. Some folks even use dog bibs. I don't think that look suits a rescue heroine. There's a bathroom at the station you can use to wash up if you want."

Zuri took the cloth and wiped her hands.

"You won't have to remind me." A small laugh escaped her. "This isn't funny. It's gross." Yet another chuckle blurted from her lips.

"Could have fooled me."

She really didn't think it was and didn't mean to laugh. It had to be nerves or some sort of stress release.

"Caden, you might want to avoid petting Duck under her mouth. Just saying," Zuri said, as they approached the two kids.

"Everyone knows that," her nephew said. "Some dogs drool a lot."

Had he been researching dogs? He'd mentioned wanting one once, but with his mom sick and Zuri working and not being exactly a dog person, she'd always dismissed the notion. Man. This was looking better for Damon than it was for her.

"Follow me." Damon led the way up the steps and held the back door to the station open for them. The place was really just a converted beach house, much simpler than some of the quainter ones on the other end of town. This one had a deck overlooking the stretch of sand and gave the team a good vantage point of the ocean.

"Yo, Damon. You bring friends." A guy who was almost as tall as Damon's six feet but had narrower shoulders and more of a lanky build greeted Duck and waved to Caden and Sara. "I'm Joe." He held out a hand to shake Zuri's but she held up her palms.

"You probably don't want to touch these. They were covered in drool."

"Nah, that doesn't bother me," Joe said, extending his offer and shaking her hand.

"Zuri. And this is my nephew, Caden, and his friend Sara."

Caden was wide-eyed and taking in everything in the place from the radio setup to a radar station, to a wall where red rescue buoys, flags, air horns, megaphones, first aid kits and other equipment were either hung or were organized on shelves. A giant board with grids and schedules written in hung on the wall adjacent to the door. But what stood out to her the most was that, unlike Damon's house, this place was decked out for the holidays. There were evergreen boughs framing each window, an artificial tree set up in the far corner and decorated with a surfing theme—so unlike anything she'd seen up North—and a giant cardboard box filled with wrapped and labeled gifts.

"Nice to meet you, Caden. I know Sara from swim lessons last summer and the beach party her grandma hosts every year."

"Hi, Mr. Joe," Sara said.

Damon pointed around the room.

"That there is Brad, Mark, Sanjay and Kiko. We have others, but the staff rotates and is bigger in the busier months. Some like Mark and Kiko also volunteer as EMTs, so they're not always here." Everyone gave a wave as their name was called and went back to what they were doing.

Duck headed for an oversize dog pillow in the corner of the room and plopped down.

"What do you do when no one is on the beach?" Caden asked.

"We have to keep an eye on the weather and water conditions, help warn people if the currents and undertow or waves are too rough. We have four-wheelers we use to comb the beach for litter, set up flags— red for 'stay out of the water it's too dangerous,' orange for caution and green for calm—and if we see anyone disturbing the sea turtle nesting sites that you'll see marked off by reed fences along the dunes, we'll step in or report them to the sheriff's department. And of course, we're also notified if any suspicious boats or activity is spotted in the area."

"What's with the box of toys?" Sara asked.

"A toy drive for Christmas. We do it every year," Brad said. "In fact—" Zuri caught Damon giving him a subtle headshake and Brad acknowledging the signal with nothing more than a twitch of his brow "—you two could donate something if you'd like. Books, toys, whatever. Even gently used items are fine. They get taken to women and children's shelters along the Outer Banks right before Christmas and some are handed out during the Christmas Day Parade," Brad said.

"Sure. We could do that. Right, Caden?" Sara asked. He hunched his shoulders slightly.

"Yeah. That would be cool. Except that I might be leaving, so I don't know if I can," Caden said. Sara's enthusiasm dimmed.

"Oh. Well, maybe we can find stuff today," she suggested.

Was Caden already regretting his earlier demand to leave town right away? Last night he wanted to leave immediately. But then he lasted through breakfast. Here they were, still in town at 9:30 a.m.

"You know, Caden, I'm sure we can stay as planned, if you want. I haven't changed anything at work yet, so it's up to you. Why don't we take it a day at a time? If you two don't find something to donate today, you can always look tomorrow," Zuri hedged.

Duck sat up as if she understood what had just been said and Sara gave Caden an elbow nudge and whispered something in his ear. He stood a little straighter and scratched his cheek.

"Sure. Why not. We can do that," he said. "So, what's the deal with helping you with your dog?"

"Yes. I haven't forgotten," Damon said, holding up a finger. "It's too cold this morning for any water training, but I need you two to serve as targets for Duck."

"What? Whoa. Targets?" Zuri asked. Damon kept his focus on the kids.

"As you learned yesterday, Duck has a tendency to want to pull people out of the water—especially kids—even if they're just swimming. This was a bit of a problem last summer, so we kept her on a leash, and we've been working with her on knowing when to rescue and when to 'leave it.' Yesterday, we did some water rescue drills, since it was relatively warm, and Mark here volunteered to be the victim. He hails from the Ice Age and has no sense of what's cold to the rest of the world." That earned a giggle from Sara and Caden and a few grins from the team. "But all I need you two to do is stand near the water…not too close…so that I can work with Duck to keep her with me. The goal is to only let her go round you up once I've given her the command. You up for it?"

"Yes!" Both kids answered.

"Okay, then. Put these on. Just a precaution," he added for Zuri's benefit, as he took two small life vests off a rack and tossed them to Sara and Caden. Sara had clearly put one on before. Caden fumbled with the strap, looking to see which direction it needed to go around his waist before buckling. Zuri started to step forward to help, but Damon put his hand on her arm to hold her back. Sure enough, Caden took one glance over at what Sara had done and strapped the vest on properly. Damon was right to stop Zuri. Had she stepped in, the boy would have been mortified and probably would have asked to drive out of town that minute, never to show his face again. Zuri linked her fingers behind her back and stood aside to make room for Damon and his dog to lead the way out.

"Nice to meet you all," she said to his team.

"We'll see you around. Enjoy Turtleback Beach," Sanjay said, before turning back to what looked like a radio system. They were near a lighthouse. She wouldn't be surprised if they listened for any boat distress calls offshore and worked with local law enforcement. What Damon did here wasn't just the type of lifeguard job college kids got. Turtleback Beach's ORBP was a full-fledged search and rescue operation and he was in charge of it. And his son had barely had enough swim lessons in a regular swimming pool.

She hurried after Damon, but he was already jogging toward Duck and calling out to the kids, telling them where to stand. She waited until he blew his whistle, signaling for the dog to go get them.

"Damon, you need to know something about Caden. He's not some super athlete like you always were. He's not a strong swimmer. He hasn't had enough lessons and started late because he used to be afraid of the water when he was younger." She braced her hands on her knees and stopped to catch her breath.

Damon's jaw hardened. He took off his sunglasses and, for a moment, didn't look at her. And from the dark look in his eyes when he finally faced her, she kind of wished he had kept his gaze on his dog.

"Not enough lessons? I don't care if he was afraid. Do you not understand how important learning to swim is? Learning to survive in the water, at least? How could you not have made swim lessons a priority?"

His tone was harsh and sliced right through her. She closed her eyes briefly. *His brother Lucas. His brother drowned. You hit a nerve.*

"I wasn't his mother. I helped out with him, but I didn't set his schedule. It didn't occur to me to press the issue with Vera."

"Didn't occur to you? Do you have any idea how many times it doesn't occur to people until it's too late?"

"Why do you think I just told you? So that you can be careful with all this," she said, waving toward the dog as she tugged Caden toward them. The boy was laughing hysterically. Zuri gave him a fake smile. She didn't want him hearing the argument or ruining the moment for him. He hadn't laughed like that in months.

"Good job," Damon told Caden. "You can go rejoin Sara. Duck, sit. Stay." He waited until Caden was far enough, made sure Duck stayed put, then blew his whistle and let her go. "It amazes me, you know?"

"What?"

"How all this time you and your sister kept him from me because you thought I wasn't reliable or responsible enough."

With that, he left her standing there and went to join his son.

DAMON PRESSED HIS fingers to his eyes for a moment, as he walked toward the water's edge. He tried to wash away the memory of Lucas's grave. He tried holding on to the way his brother looked the last time he'd seen him alive. The sound of Caden's voice brought him to the present. Caden—his son—held up his hand to try and get Duck to sit. She actually obeyed him, and the boy got a compliment from Sara.

He'd snapped at Zuri, but it wasn't just about the swimming, was it? Maybe it was. He wasn't sure. Or perhaps he had just needed a reason to release some of the shock and anger he had been trying hard to push to the back of his mind since yesterday. He knew he couldn't blame Zuri for everything. He'd heard her reasoning and, of all people, he understood how complicated life could be, but seeing Lucas in Caden pushed his self-doubt about being an instant father to the surface. Yes, he told Zuri he wasn't going to walk away, and he wasn't. But a part of him was scared. And something about learning that Caden couldn't swim made that fear grip him by the throat.

Fear is a protective mechanism. It warns you. You weren't with Lucas. You're here with Caden and you had him put on a life vest. He's fine. You save people for a living. You'll teach him to swim. He'll be okay.

But would he be? What about at other times or if he was in Boston and Damon was down here? What if he wasn't in Damon's sight? What if…what if…

"How was that? How many times do we repeat?" Sara asked.

"You two are doing great. Now for a switch. Take this whistle." He pulled the chain holding the whistle from his neck and put it over his son's head. "This time, you two go stand up on the beach where your aunt is, and I'll be the victim."

CHAPTER FIVE

CADEN FOLLOWED SARA off the beach, down the boardwalk and into town. His da—Mr. Woods—had taken Duck home and said that he had work to do. Aunt Zuri was trailing behind Sara and him and said that she wanted to stop in at the gift shop to look around. He and Sara were headed for the used bookstore. The place looked way cool, even from the outside. The rickety driftwood sign over the door had a palm tree overhanging a washed-up boat full of books carved into it. It made him think of pirate movies and shipwrecks. Castaway Books. The used books were castaways. He got it. Pretty funny.

"You'll love this place. I always come here when I visit my Granny Mel," Sara said. "If you like bookstores and libraries, you'll never want to leave this place."

"Yeah? I like those places. And books.

This place looks chill." God, he hoped that he wasn't coming off as nerdy. But she said she liked books first, right? So it was probably okay. He hated it when some of the kids back at school teased him for taking piano lessons and always hanging out in the library instead of at a sports practice. He hated team sports. He tried them once—basketball and then soccer—and usually got left out by the more skilled players, who just passed to each other, especially during a game.

With music and books, he could disappear into a rhythm or world that was so different from the one he had to live in. He could escape his mother's illness and bullies and not knowing his father. There were no exams and quizzes or homework projects in books, although he was generally okay with writing book reports.

They reached the storefront and he quickly pulled the door open for Sara. His English teacher once had his class talking about what chivalry was and whether it was dead or alive. That was the first time he'd understood why some guys opened doors. His teacher had been in the army and had always insisted on good manners in class.

"Thanks," Sara said. Her cheeks were redder than when they'd left the beach. Probably from the chilly air outside, although he wasn't that cold. In fact, he was sort of sweating a little.

A chime made of shells and bells dangling from the top of the door announced their entrance. *Whoa.* The place was amazing. It was basically a converted old house with scuffed wood floors and a narrow staircase that looked a bit crooked. It kind of felt like he'd stepped into a shop along Diagon Alley in *Harry Potter*, one of his favorite series. There was an old wooden checkout counter to his right and a main room off to the left that was lined with bookshelves, sprinkled with bean bag chairs, and had a centered rug and a comfy chair currently occupied by a woman reading a book out loud. A bunch of toddlers and grade-schoolers with their eyes glued on her sat on the floor in front of her. A couple of moms huddled around, looking just as mesmerized. Paper stars and fairies dangled from the ceiling above them and each wall had a decorative theme ranging from dragons and wizards to dragonflies, butterflies and fairies.

One wall was obviously seasonal, since it had reindeer, a Santa and sleigh, elves, and fake snow on top of the shelves. The wall behind had pictures and colors celebrating all the different holidays for the month, including Hanukah and Kwanzaa, and even had "Happy New Year" written all over a poster in every language possible, such as Swahili and Arabic, French and Portuguese, and a bunch of others.

But best of all, right next to the lady doing the reading sat a dog with long white and sable hair. It had to be the rough collie, Laddie, he was told about. The dog didn't jump up and run over the way Duck tended to do. Instead, he stayed put, watching the kids, while listening to the book. Or at least he looked like he really understood the story. This town had a lot of dogs. Boy, did he wish he could have one back home.

"You're right. This bookstore rocks," he said, keeping his voice down.

"Told ya," Sara said. "Follow me." She

gave the woman a quick wave and the woman winked back.

"You know her?"

"Miss Eve? She owns the place. She's super nice. Loves to decorate and lets me help if I'm around when she's changing things up. You should have seen how she had it decorated this past Halloween. The main room was really fun with pumpkins and all, but mostly cute stuff because of not scaring little kids. Upstairs and the back rooms were a little more haunted looking, since that's where the grown-up and older kid books are. Then right before Thanksgiving, she had decked the place out all wedding-like because she and Jordan, one of the local cops, got married. She wanted a small, private ceremony and she wanted it here because she said the books here were full of fairy-tale endings and she got hers. I wasn't here but I heard about it and saw pics. It sounded so romantic."

Caden just nodded. He had no clue how to respond to romance talk. His mom was never romantic. If anything, she used to get in a bad mood every time she came home from a date her friends set her up on. And when she thought Caden was up-stairs, he could overhear her venting to his aunt about how awful and ridiculous guys could be. He didn't want to be that kind of guy. He didn't want to grow up and be someone his mom thought of as bad. That's why he took all the good manners tips that his teacher mentioned to heart. And still, he always felt awkward.

"Shouldn't we buy books to donate from the kid section?" Caden asked, as he followed her past the staircase and to a back room. This room had movie posters depicting famous works of fiction hanging on the walls.

"After story time is over. It's almost done. But we can look for ourselves while we wait. Oooh, look!" She reached overhead and retrieved a book from the top shelf. "The second book in the Denali Dames series."

"Never heard of it."

"It's historical fiction that centers around women mountain climbers around the world. I love mountains. They're the one place where you can really be on top of the world. What do you read?"

Would she think his favorite series was stupid? How would it reflect on him? He could play it safe and go with books everyone liked. The one he was into was a bestseller, but he didn't think that many kids his age read it. But she liked mountain climbers so maybe she was into adventure.

"Well, there's this series I started that has a guy who's an ex–special agent, but he still keeps getting caught up in missions saving people and the world. It's like his gift and calling and he can't turn his back on doing what's right."

Sara's eyes lit up.

"The Chase Falcon books? I LOVE those!"

"You do? I mean, yeah. They're good. I mean, I'm only on the third one. Almost finished. I think number four came out this past summer."

"I won't give spoilers. I don't have my copies here at my grandma's, or I'd have loaned the fourth to you. But wait…"

She scurried over to the far shelf that, with one glance at all the spines, Caden knew was full of adventure and mystery books. He joined her and scanned the author names. Some of the books were in great shape and others had minor cover tears and wrinkles in the spines from being opened and read so much. He ran his fingertips along the shelf with all the *D*s.

"Here! D. L. Dylan…book two…book four! Oh, man. Seriously, no spoilers."

"Absolutely not. Spoiler people are the worst." Sara zipped her lips with her finger and thumb and twisted them in a locking fashion.

"This is cheap."

"They're used books, so they're great for kids on a limited budget. Great catch, finding that book."

"I wouldn't have thought to look for it here. Thanks."

"Sure thing. What's your favorite part about it?" she asked, peering over his shoulder, as he read the back cover. Her shampoo smelled fruity. Like gummy fruit snacks or milkshakes or something. He hoped it was close to lunchtime.

"I guess the way Chase can kick butt. I mean, he's like a black belt, special ops hero and superhero mixed all in one. And the suspense, too. Scary enough and edge-of-your-seat, but you know it'll all be okay in the end."

"Falcon is one hot hero, for sure."

Ew. Hot? Was that what she got from it? Clearly, they liked it for very, *very* different reasons. He flipped the book over and glanced at the cover. Okay, so the cover model was good-looking and very muscular. Caden wished he could look like that someday. He stepped away from Sara and pretended to check out another book on the shelf that he had no interest in. He just didn't like the twinge of…he wasn't sure what it was. What was wrong with him? Jealousy? Because Sara liked some made-up character? Or because he'd never be a Chase Falcon or the kind of guy his mom could have been proud of. As for his father, he probably thought Caden was a wimp. Maybe Sara did, too. And Caden wasn't sure if he could change that about himself, even if Aunt Zuri always told him that he could be anything he wanted to be, so long as he approached life with a fearless attitude. Chase Falcon never shied away from danger. He was fearless. He took risks. So did Damon Woods. Maybe it was time Caden did, too.

ZURI REMOVED THE receipt from one of the two gift bags she carried and stuffed the strip of paper in her purse as she headed toward the bookstore. She had only intended to browse, but when she saw the handblown glass ornaments made by a local artist in the gift shop, she knew it would make a nice thank-you gift for Melanie. Sure, she was paying to stay at the bed-and-breakfast, but still. Melanie was being extra nice and going out of her way to make them feel welcome, especially since she knew that Zuri had just lost her sister and Caden had lost his mother. Plus, she was so grateful that Sara was hanging out with Caden. Zuri really wanted to get them both something for Christmas.

She knew she was heading in the direction of the bakery before she even saw the sign for The Saltwater Sweetery, the place Damon had mentioned. She was so tempted to slip in there for a cup of coffee and more sugar. She crossed the street quickly before giving in. Castaway Books was right across from the bakery. She noticed a few grown-ups heading out of the bookstore with small kids. She loved how the town had one main street with shops lining either side. It was so easy to look around and pick the places to go.

A two-story yellow building at the far end of town had a sign indicating a yoga studio on the bottom floor. Maybe she'd try it out during her stay, not only to de-stress, but to burn off the baked goods she'd gorged on. A sign on the second floor read Law Office of Joel Burkitt. She had barely registered the sign when Damon walked out of the building.

She almost tripped over a pot of artificial poinsettias flanking an iron bench. Well, he sure wasn't wasting time. She mustered up every bad word she could think of, but swallowed them before they reached her mouth. What was this? Bait and switch? Mad yesterday afternoon, then nice at breakfast, then straight for the lawyer? Her jaw ached. She took a deep breath and resumed course, trying to ignore him.

"Hey, Zuri," he called out, raising his hand to get her attention. She stopped outside Castaway Books but didn't open the door. If they were going to have it out, she preferred that Caden be inside where he couldn't hear. She knew she was glaring at Damon because she could feel the heat behind her eyes. She'd tried to play nice and she totally understood his rights, but this wasn't about his rights. It was about what was best for her nephew.

"Damon. You're efficient. You can tell your lawyer that I'll be contacting mine as soon as possible."

Damon scowled and looked back at the law office, then at Zuri. He gave an irritated huff and braced his hands on his waist.

"You can do whatever you like," he said.

"You couldn't so much as wait until after Christmas? It didn't occur to you that I'm the one who brought him here so maybe you should trust *me* a little and let this play out longer? Give him time to adjust?"

"You're talking about filing for custody? What makes you think I did that?"

She raised her brow and nodded at the law office, then cocked her head and waited. Damon nodded.

"Nice place isn't it? It used to be the original Turtleback Beach fire station before it got moved to an updated building."

"Don't stall. Caden and Sara are buying

books and I don't want to talk about this in front of them. I deserve fair warning if you've gone and filed papers or taken legal action."

Damon took a step closer.

"Fair warning, Zuri."

"How could you?"

"How could I have my lawyer write up a living will to include Caden and set up a trust with enough to cover all that Vera should have and would have gotten from me since his birth? I don't need custody papers for getting that done. My job isn't always safe, Zuri. I respect the ocean enough to know that no one can predict tomorrow or even hours from now. I wanted to make sure I got that taken care of right away. If I get hit by lightning or swept out to sea a moment from now, at least I'll leave this life knowing that a kid by the name of Caden Habib will get everything. And when we get his name changed to mine, I'll make sure that Caden Woods or Habib-Woods or whatever we agree on is reflected in all the legal documents."

Zuri felt like her breath was stuck in her chest. She was caught between name changes and the fact that Damon had been doing something good and generous and she'd gone and assumed that he had been trying to take Caden away. But he still planned to, didn't he?

She tried to block what Damon standing so close did to her. His scent, energy and presence scrambled her mind and she needed to think. His taking steps to make sure Caden was financially taken care of had her heart in a twist. She closed her eyes briefly and shook her head.

"I'm sorry. I just thought—"

"You thought the worst of me. I don't blame you."

"You don't?"

"We have a history that I tried to apologize for. You're being protective of your nephew. I can't hold that against you when it's exactly how someone who cares should be feeling. I'm feeling it, too, Zuri. But I'm trying to do the right thing. It'd be nice not to have my every move judged."

"I just don't want to take any chances on his happiness and emotional recovery."

"You think I'd risk that? Look, of all people, I know about taking chances.

There's a place and time. Just because I served on dangerous missions in the past and work in rescue now doesn't mean I'm reckless. Far from it. Every action I take is well planned, thought out and carried out. The more dangerous a situation, the more important it is to be careful."

Was that a warning or an assurance? Because the way her pulse skittered and raced whenever he stood so close felt pretty dangerous. She would not let herself feel anything for him. Not again. She promised herself that all those years ago and reminded herself of that resolution before she came to Turtleback Beach. She was still very likely not his type. And she still couldn't get over the fact that he had actually taken her sister out to prove a point. She had closed her heart down then and there. She'd managed to control her anger over the situation for her sister's sake, but some wounds were too deep to heal.

She had tried a couple of relationships during college but neither lasted more than a few months. And after that she'd suffered through a few blind dates Vera and some coworkers had set up, but nothing came of them. Life in the lab was so much easier to take than experimenting with relationships. At least her water pollution test results weren't wishy-washy. She could read and interpret them far more easily than figuring out men.

But it didn't take analyzing data to figure out that the odds were pretty good that a criminally good-looking former navy SEAL in charge of an ocean rescue and living on a beach with plenty of bikini babes wouldn't have issues with dating. He had always been an extrovert. Wouldn't having a kid around cramp his style? Could he handle the added responsibility of a son?

Apparently so. She'd underestimated him. He'd just drawn up a will because of Caden. The Damon she knew as a kid had never been so methodical and reliable. A good friend, yes. But responsible? Not so much. If he had been, he wouldn't have left his family behind without a word until after he'd joined the navy. She should be happy that he was acting responsibly with his son, but could she trust him not to have something up his sleeve? He said he planned things carefully. Why did that make her feel so on guard?

"Promise me you won't take him from me. Promise that we'll sit and talk this out with his best interest at heart."

"His best interest is my first priority. I can promise you that," Damon said. His words were evasive. Cryptic. She didn't like it, but Caden and Sara exited the store with a young woman whose eyes literally twinkled when she smiled at Damon. Go figure.

DAMON TRIED TO shake off his irritation with Zuri. He immediately ended the conversation when Caden and Sara stepped out of Castaway Books. Eve followed, along with Laddie and Clara with her toddler, Nim. Clara had only been in Turtleback since last March. She'd moved down here with her identical twin sister, Faye, now Sheriff Ryker's fiancée, after finally escaping an abusive husband who had threatened her life and had her hidden where no one could find her. Faye, who had kidnapped her niece in order to protect her, had brought the little girl to Turtleback

Beach, where she tried to hide out with the help of her old friend Eve. Nim's birth name was Mia, but everyone in town had gotten to know her under her alias, Nim, and it stuck as her nickname. Clara was looking a lot more relaxed and at peace than she did nine months ago.

"Hey, Eve. Clara." Damon motioned toward Zuri. "This is an old friend of mine, Zuri. Zuri, this is Clara and her daughter, Nim. Clara has an identical twin around town, just so you don't get confused. Eve, here, owns the bookstore."

"Hi. Nice to meet you," Zuri said, shaking hands. "Nim is absolutely adorable."

"Thank you," Clara said, scooping the girl up and bouncing her on her hip. "It's nice to meet you. Sorry to run, but she'll get cranky if she doesn't get lunch and a nap."

"I'm no cracker," Nim said, pinching her mother's nose.

"Nope." Eve poked playfully at Nim's belly. "You're a cutie patootie."

Zuri laughed and waved as Clara left. He liked her laugh. He kind of missed it and had forgotten how happy it made him feel.

"That's a gorgeous dog you have. I'm not a huge dog person, but he's really calm," Zuri said. Caden and Sara were fawning all over the dog.

"Oh, he's not mine. This here is Laddie. He helps me with reading time. The kids love him, and he helps make them interested in books. It's a win-win. He belongs to our town vet, Gray. I'm just waiting for him to swing by and pick him up."

"Actually, I did hear about the reading time dog," Zuri said.

"Duck is a little too much dog for her." Damon grinned at the look on Zuri's face when she saw a Newfoundland bounding down the street with Jordan holding tight to his leash.

"I thought you took Duck home," Zuri said.

"That's Shamu. Duck's pup. He's not quite full-grown but he's getting there. Jordan here works for the sheriff's department. He adopted Shamu after I adopted, or rescued, Duck and she gave birth to her litter."

"Hey," Jordan said. "Shamu, sit." The dog

obeyed but enjoyed sniffing noses with Laddie. Jordan gave Eve a peck on the lips.

"Jordan, this is Zuri. Jordan and Eve are newlyweds, if you couldn't tell." Damon chuckled and patted Jordan on the shoulder.

Gray, Carlos and his deputy Jordan were his closest friends. Between the three of them they had the air force, army and navy covered. Carlos had lost both parents—his father shot by a fellow officer. No one in town had known who Gray really was until just under two years ago, when his witness protection cover was blown and he and his now wife were almost killed. They understood how fragile life was.

Carlos, Gray and Damon had all connected right away. They knew what it was like to be deployed and then to try and fit into civilian life afterward. And Jordan, who was like a younger brother to Carlos, fit right in, too. But they were all married or engaged now, which meant they didn't have as much time to hang out. Just the guys. Single guys.

Zuri exchanged hellos and added another when Gray showed up to pick up

Laddie. Gray had to leave pretty quickly, but Jordan lingered with Shamu.

"What books did you two get?" Jordan asked. Caden and Sara were each carrying three books. Sara held hers up one by one.

"One about women mountaineers, one about a lighthouse mystery—those two are for me—and one for the toy drive that's a dragon fantasy adventure."

"What about you, Caden?" Damon asked. The boy was sort of holding the books turned over and halfway behind him.

"Just a couple for the toy drive, the usual Christmas stories, and one other." He didn't show them off the way Sara had, but one slipped out of his pile and hit the ground. He hurried to pick it up.

"Wait, I recognize that one," Zuri said. "Isn't that the series they're talking about turning into a show because it hit all the lists? I'm not sure it's for your age group. Can I see?"

Damon knew exactly which books she was talking about. Sure, they were geared toward adults, but they weren't that bad for teens or even preteens, were they? Then again, he wasn't a parent. Or he was but he wasn't experienced at it. Caden's face tensed and he bit at his lower lip, but he held his shoulders back defiantly.

"Yeah, that's the one. I've already read the first two and a half, so what difference does it make. They're adventurous, Aunt Zuri. There's nothing that bad in them. They're not any scarier or violent than the *Lord of the Rings* you got me."

"But that's fantasy. This one's realistic. Isn't it? Have any of you read it? Do you know if it's okay for a twelve-year-old?" Zuri asked.

"I've read them," Sara offered.

Zuri gave her a sympathetic smile, then turned to the grownups. She obviously didn't trust teenage opinions on the matter.

Damon felt sorry for Caden. His aunt may have had more experience with taking care of him, but she sure was oblivious to how much she was embarrassing him. Just like when she had almost helped him with his life vest earlier. Damon could see that embarrassment all over Caden's face and in his body language. Reading people was something he was trained to do. It helped with interrogations and split-second decisions.

"Book choices are so personal. I usually don't interfere with parent rules and decisions on them," Eve said. "But personally, I think it depends on the kid. I think it's okay if he's not prone to bad dreams."

"I don't scare easily. I'm not some wimp."

"I think it's awesome. One of my favorites. Especially book two," Jordan said. He grinned at Damon. Damon gave him a look that warned him to shut up and stay out of it. Eve was right. What Caden was allowed to read or not read was personal.

Zuri nodded, as if to concede, but she frowned and kept glancing at the book. The boy looked like he wanted to crawl in a hole. He'd seen that look plenty of times on his younger brothers' faces, including Lucas's, when their parents had put them on the spot in public. They had been so particular about appearances and family reputation and they had expected Damon, being the oldest, to set a good example. That only made them blame him if his siblings did anything that remotely looked like something he might have put them up to or had set a bad example for.

Sometimes he thought that his parents were simply so annoyed with each other and frustrated with parenting that they needed someone to blame. They loved their kids. He didn't doubt that. However, they didn't love one another and that bled through the entire family. Being the oldest wasn't easy. Damon had covered for his siblings plenty of times, but no one had ever covered for him. But that's what a person was supposed to do. Have the back of those who were counting on them. Help those in need. Zuri had been that way.

"It's fine, in my opinion. Let him read it. It's no big deal. There's nothing raunchy in it. Just action," Damon said.

Zuri looked taken aback by him putting his foot down and making a decision as the boy's father. He wasn't trying to make her uncomfortable. He was trying to smooth things over for Caden. For crying out loud, the boy was twelve and standing next to a girl his age. Zuri had to clue in.

"All right. It's fine. I guess." She sounded

defeated and uncertain. Maybe she needed to read the books for herself.

"Like I said, I was going to read it anyway. I have the first ones. You can't stop me from reading books," Caden said.

Zuri's eyes were starting to glisten.

"Hey. No need to take that tone. Your aunt is just looking out for you," Damon said. "How about apologizing and then take this—" he reached in his wallet and pulled out a few bills to help change the subject. He handed Caden the money "—and take Sara over to the bakery. Get some hot chocolate and lunch." Damon gave him a look that said, in no uncertain terms, that apologizing wasn't optional. He was giving the boy a way out. Caden scowled at him, but took the money.

"Sorry," Caden mumbled. "And thanks," he added for Damon.

"Thanks, Mr. Woods," Sara said. "Come on."

She practically ushered Caden across the street, whispering something to him and glancing over her shoulder a time or two at the grown-ups. Zuri sighed.

"I'm sorry you witnessed that," she told Jordan and Eve.

"Nonsense. I watch parents and kids interact all the time. It gets pretty wild in the summer when lots of families from out of town visit. Trust me, this was nothing. I actually love watching families and learning from them," she said, exchanging looks with her husband.

Were those two planning to start soon?

"Well, I have to run. I need to get Shamu home and head in for my shift. I'll see you around, Zuri," Jordan said.

"And I need to get back to work. Stop by sometime. Grab something to read while you're here. On the house," Eve said.

"You don't have to do that."

"First book free for family and friends. A friend of Damon's is a friend of mine." Eve smiled and ducked back into her shop.

The minute they were alone, Zuri's smile disappeared and life seemed to fade from her eyes and her dark, thick lashes lowered like shields.

"Zuri, the stuff we were talking about before—"

"You know what? I'm feeling tired. I don't want to get into it now."

"Okay. I can give you and the kids a ride."

She shook her head and adjusted her purse strap on her shoulder.

"No, thank you. I'll get them and we'll walk back to the B and B." She started to cross the street.

"Are you sure? I don't mind giving you a ride. Zuri, look, you're overthinking things again. You always do that."

Zuri turned on her heel and looked right at him. Her eyes were full of fire.

"Do I? Always, huh? Because you've been around me so much in the past twelve years, you'd know. Right? Don't be condescending, Damon. Especially not now."

Her eyes watered. Her words may have dripped with sarcasm to some, but he knew it was her way of protecting herself. He couldn't blame her for feeling threatened, but he had rights, too. He was trying to come to terms with everything, too. He held up his palms and stepped back.

"Fine. Enjoy your stroll. I'm outta here." He shoved his hands in his pockets and walked away, just like he'd done after he'd graduated high school. Only this time, she was the one who had the power to leave and never come back. Maybe it was time he experienced what that felt like. She wouldn't be able to keep him from his son, but she could throw up an impenetrable, permanent wall between her and Damon. And now that she was back in his life, he wasn't sure he could handle her walking away.

CHAPTER SIX

DINNER AT DAMON'S didn't happen. He had left a message with Melanie to pass on to her that something had come up. That something had to be him realizing that she was right. He was moving too fast. She was relieved when she got the message because she had intended to get out of the plans anyway.

A part of her wanted to pack up and leave, just as Caden had been insisting on yesterday, only now he was the one who'd settled in. He and Sara were eating popcorn while watching a movie. Melanie was bustling around the kitchen and providing an endless supply of snacks for them. A hint of vanilla, cinnamon and ginger permeated the cottage as tray after tray of gingerbread cookies were set out to cool. And Melanie claimed she couldn't bake? Zuri had already eaten three with a cup of decaf coffee, which she was now cradling outside by the firepit—alone. The kids were supposed to have fun decorating the rest of the gingerbread people and filling tins for neighbors.

Her grandmother used to do that…giving baked goods as gifts. Her mom never did though. Being a doctor kept her so busy that she typically shopped online for gifts late at night. In fact, no one in their neighborhood up in Boston exchanged baked goods anymore. Everything started with an *e*, from e-cards to e-gifts sent directly from the seller. Maybe baked gifts were becoming too old-fashioned, but Zuri liked it. There was a warmth and hominess to the scents and sounds that filled Melanie's place. The kind of comfort that had been missing in Vera's house since her death.

Zuri had given up her apartment and had moved into her sister's house, under the advice that it would be easier for Caden. His home would be the constant in a life that was so variable. Just like in an experiment. Life was just one massive laboratory, wasn't it? In this case, she wasn't so sure the hypothesis had been proven. Or maybe it hadn't been set up right to begin with. Nothing felt constant…or solid and secure…at Vera's house. If anything, the void was cold and everything there was a reminder of their loss.

The fire popped and crackled and Zuri tugged the afghan Melanie had provided around her shoulders. She could smell the cookies from out here, mingling with the earthy aroma of woodsmoke and ocean mist. Laughter emanated from the living room where the movie was playing.

She looked up through the patio doors and could see Caden hugging his belly as he caught his breath. It was good to see him laugh like that. Such a relief. She could see Melanie through the smaller kitchen window setting trays out to cool. It was like looking into the perfect world of a snow globe. And she was on the outside. She was the one who had to keep the glass from breaking. She was the one who knew it was all an illusion and that life was far from perfect and never would be. But, as always, it was up to her to make it as perfect and safe as possible for Caden and she wasn't about to let him down. She needed to hold herself together. She came here so that he could meet and spend time with his father and that wasn't going to happen if she let her emotions, past or present, get in the way.

Her cell phone vibrated, jolting her and causing a few drops of coffee to slosh onto her jeans. The screen read Mom. Oh, geez. Did she have it in her to talk to her mom right now? Her parents knew she was taking Caden on a vacation for the holidays, but they didn't know about Damon.

She considered not answering but, knowing her mom, if she didn't pick up there would be numerous call attempts back-to-back and her mom would worry. She used to always tell Vera and her that if they didn't pick up, she'd send a search party out after them. Zuri didn't have location tracking turned on on her cell phone, but she wouldn't put it past her mom to track her down anyway. She so didn't need her parents showing up in Turtleback. Had Damon told his parents yet? What if his mother told her mother and that's why she was calling?

Zuri's head was about to explode. She took a breath and answered.

"Hi, Mama."

"*Mija.* How are things? I just wanted to check in on you and Caden. Is he doing all right? Is everything okay? I wish you would call or text more, just to let me know you're okay. You know how I worry. I just need to hear your voice."

Zuri waited for the well-intentioned onslaught of questions her mom always started calls with to be over. She used to try to get a word in, but soon learned it was easier to wait for.

"Zuri, can you hear me? Are you there?"

That was her opening. Every time. It was kind of funny that her mom still had no clue that she had this pattern of conversation and everyone had to wait their turn.

"I'm here. How are you and Baba?"

"Good. He has a cold, but nothing serious."

"It's not a cold." Her dad's voice carried through the receiver. Her dad had a tendency to overhear and join phone conversations even when they weren't on speaker. "Your mother thinks I'm one of her patients. Trust me, I'm fine. You take care of yourself, *habibti*," he called out.

"Love you, Baba. Feel better," Zuri said, a little louder to be sure her voice carried. She heard some coughing in the background.

"She said she loves you and to feel better," her mom repeated. "Please, Ali, go breathe some steam and drink the tea I made you so the cold doesn't settle in your chest."

"Are you sure he's okay?"

"Well, he was negative for flu and everything else I tested for. I'm sure it's just a cold but he's so stubborn and hates taking anything. Not that we want you catching it, but we wish you two were spending Christmas here, *mija*. He'll be better by then. This feels so wrong. Why don't you reconsider. Unless, of course, Caden is having a good time. He comes first, but the holidays aren't the same without you."

"Thanks. We miss you, but yeah, I think he's having fun. This is good for him. I don't want him wallowing around."

She didn't comment on the fact that neither she nor Caden really enjoyed the slightly formal holiday parties her mom always threw. Too many pretentious colleagues. Too much small talk.

"Where are you exactly? You never said."

Zuri scrunched her face. She had been hoping her mom wouldn't ask until after they returned.

"A beach. We're staying at a bed-and-breakfast and enjoying the beach. Nice and simple. There are other kids around and he's hanging out with a friend, so that's good."

"What beach? Are you up at Martha's Vineyard? That place we stayed at once? They have beautiful light displays during the holidays. Cold but cozy. Or are you closer at Carson Beach or one of the others around there? We could join you. It wouldn't be that long of a drive. Once I get through the party tomorrow night and the one after that, we could stop by for a day before the medical conference in Rome."

Oh, heaven help her.

"Um…no, we're not close enough. Sorry. We're down South. And everything is booked solid so you wouldn't have a place to stay." She didn't know about places to stay in nearby towns, but she knew that Melanie's B and B only had a few rooms, so between Sara, Caden and herself, it was full. It wasn't a total lie. "Besides, I'm getting work done on my laptop while he hangs with other kids." More lies. Harmless lies were okay, sometimes, weren't they? Until they got out of control. Like the one she told to cover for her sister going to prom with the son of her mother's adversary. Their parents had no idea Damon had been Vera's date. As far as they knew, Vera had gone with a group of girlfriends as a sort of feminist statement.

As upset as Zuri had been, she and Vera had a pact to always cover for each other. Vera hadn't heard about how Damon had shunned her until after prom and she had been so excited about him asking her out that Zuri had kept quiet. She had been too embarrassed to even tell her sister how stupid she had been, thinking Damon actually liked her.

Vera, the rebel and popular girl, would have thought Zuri's move was laughable. Maybe she wouldn't have accepted Damon's invite, because she was a good big sis in general, but at the time Zuri couldn't handle getting mocked by her own sister. It would have added insult to injury. She also never expected Damon to go ask Vera out so giving her sister a heads-up never occurred to her.

After Vera heard about what happened with Zuri, who had confessed after Vera came to her terrified about missing a period, she had insisted that Damon wasn't going to be involved in either of their lives. So of course, given how strict their parents were and how their moms didn't get along and in the name of world peace, neither Zuri nor Vera had ever revealed the father to their parents or anyone else. If Vera had, she'd have never been able to keep him out of their lives. Especially with the whole lawyer versus doctor lawsuit history. Vera didn't want to bring custody issues into play. Zuri was the one who'd be dealing with all that now. She knew she and Damon would have to bring their parents into the picture at some point, but she wasn't ready to deal with that just yet.

"Where down South?"

She hated the fishing. It had taken a year for her mom to stop prodding Vera on paternity before she gave up. But it wasn't like her mom had time to travel this far. A little truth wouldn't matter.

"North Carolina, but I promise we'll come visit you after we get back. It'll give me the chance to get him out of the house again. It really works best that way."

There was a moment of silence on the other end before her mom sighed loudly.

"Okay. If you insist. But I'm holding you to that promise. Oh, guess who I saw in the grocery store yesterday? She saw me, too, but she acted as if she didn't recognize me. Mary Woods."

Oh, boy.

"Well, it's not like you two hang out. Maybe she needs glasses or wasn't wearing hers or something and couldn't see your face clearly. Don't make a big deal of it, Mama. It's not like you would have wanted her talking to you."

"She was at Vera's funeral for goodness' sake. A simple hello or nod wouldn't have been a conversation, but it would have been decent. She was avoiding me for some reason."

"Mama, please let it go. This thing between you two. It's petty."

"No, it's not. You may not remember her attitude toward me when you were kids, but I do. I worked hard to pursue my education and career and just because I needed a babysitter and nanny to help out when I couldn't be home, she had the audacity to criticize working mothers in front of me and the other parents during that school open house, just because I couldn't volunteer the way she did. It spoke to her character, talking like that. Thinking she was a better parent. She's judgmental. Anyway, I won't get into it again. It's just that something about the expression on her face brought it all back."

Zuri still thought it was petty. She'd seen how they'd exchanged hugs at the funeral and the sympathy and gratitude had been genuine. If it hadn't been for the mothers not getting along, both families would have probably hung out at school barbecues.

"You know, Mama, Mary went to law school and she has a sister who is a hugely successful lawyer and a working mother, from what I hear, as are two of her sons. It's in the family. I'm sure if she had any issue with you having a full-time career versus her choice to only work part-time for a while, it had nothing to do with you personally. Mary had other things going on when we were in school. Marriage trouble, as you now know from the divorce. It wasn't all about you. Trust me, just let it go."

She'd gleaned enough from her conversations with Damon back then to put it all together. Mary had been juggling kids and volunteer work while suffering through a bad marriage—one that had impacted Damon, too. And Lucia had always fallen into easy guilt trips from her own mom for not being a full-time mother.

Zuri thought about her work at the lab and how her schedule had shifted to accommodate taking her nephew under her wing. She wasn't his mother, but as his guardian and aunt, she'd pretty much taken on that role. Was she going to be just like her mom, working all the time? Or more like Damon's or some cross in between?

How would she figure it out and make it work? Would she and Damon end up arguing all the time, as his parents had? Or would they get along like hers, who were madly in love?

Stop right there. Who said anything about love? And don't compare Damon and yourself to married couples. Get your head back on straight.

She was losing it. She really needed better sleep tonight. She and Damon were not a couple. Their situation was…complicated.

"I don't know. Maybe. She did seem sincere at the funeral. I don't know. I can't think about it now because your father is calling me. I'm telling you, the man is getting a fever but he's too stubborn to listen to me. Doctors really do make the worst patients. I have to go. But don't forget your promise."

"I won't. Go take care of him and don't catch whatever it is. Love you."

"Love you, too."

She stuffed her phone back into her pocket and held her hands up to the flickering flames to warm them.

At some point, she'd have to come clean. Right now, it was clear her mom had no idea Zuri was visiting Mary's son. How would she react when she found out that she and Mary shared a grandson?

Talk about shattering a snow globe. Real life could be so impossible.

DAMON LEANED IN his chair and rubbed the back of his neck. God help him, he couldn't think straight. He'd been sitting at his desk for a full hour and had barely gotten anything done. The office wasn't big, but it overlooked the Atlantic. He didn't care that the cottage needed a lot of work when he had bought it because it was beachfront and that was priceless to him. He'd watched plenty of hurricanes and tropical storms on their approach from here. Each time, the rough waters and dark skies served as a reminder that life could take on the worst maelstrom, but he always made it through. He'd watched every spectacular sunrise, too.

This room, converted into a private office space after he'd bought the run-down house, had been the one place where he could focus and zero in on the details of his work—work that not a lot of people knew about. Only his close buddies, Carlos, Gray and Jordan, and immediate family, who he'd told about two years prior, knew.

It was a matter of trust and knowing real friends from users. It was a matter of people respecting him for who he really was as a person and not some image they had of him. He'd had enough of false friends in high school and for some time after that, as well. Life-or-death situations during special ops had a way of showing a person what and who really mattered.

Zuri might have thought that he hadn't matured or learned a thing or two since senior year in high school, but he had learned his life lessons—especially about people—hard and fast.

He picked up a pen and tapped it against the notepad lying on the extra wide table that served as a workstation. Two large computer screens faced him but nothing on them fully registered. Nothing but a blur of words.

His mind was elsewhere, on Zuri and Caden. On his life getting turned upside down. Damon had locked the room door easily enough when they had come over for dinner, but what if Caden actually stayed here? How would he know if the boy snooped around while Damon was on search and rescue duty? Messed with his stuff. Posted something online to show off to other kids?

One person was all it took to blow an alias. He knew this from his experience working with operatives as a SEAL. He'd seen it happen firsthand to Gray in this very town when his witness protection cover had been blown. Not that his situation was of the same caliber, but Damon had his reasons for keeping his life as private as possible.

For one thing, the whole keeping toxic relationships and false friends out of his life and not having anyone pretend to like him for his money. And secondly, because writing under a pseudonym kept anyone dangerous from making the connection between who he had been and the missions he'd been on in real life and the adventures Chase Falcon experienced in his books.

Sure, if an old enemy or enemy associate wanted to track him down or any of the members of his SEAL team, a pseudonym wouldn't stop them, but other standard military precautions had been followed while he was serving and right now, lying low was just an extra barrier and smart move in his mind. He had been a part of several high-profile special ops missions. He was using that experience to bring Chase Falcon to life, but he also needed to be careful. The last thing he wanted was to endanger family or friends, and there were people in the world who would potentially seek revenge if they figured out who he really was and who he had been.

He also knew from Gray's experience in witness protection that even with the utmost care to hide one's identity, there was always a risk of getting discovered. Low tides uncovered the ocean's secrets and letting one's guard down could do the same. He didn't even use author photos but did play to readers with caricatures of Chase. That seemed to satisfy them so far, although he knew that once the books hit the big screen, lying low might prove harder. *What about Caden? Your son is apparently one of your fans. But doesn't he deserve more than the rest?*

He looked around the room. The only decor consisted of a wall with photos of his friends from the navy and his brothers. There was one of him and Lucas, when his brother had just started middle school. He stared at his brother's face, seeing the resemblance between Lucas and Caden and himself. He needed to add a photo of his son on that wall.

Duck grumbled as she shifted on her extra-large dog pillow in the corner of the room. The wall to her right was decorated with a dried wad of slobber that had flown and stuck in place when she had shaken her head earlier. He needed to clean it up but didn't have it in him right now. It wasn't like anyone else would see it.

There was a reason he worked on updating the interior but not the exterior of his home. He didn't want to stand out. He wanted the graying wood and unkempt appearance to convey someone penniless, uncaring and not worth the chase.

Chase. He'd chosen the character name because it literally meant "the hunt" and to him that embodied what it meant to be out on a mission looking for the bad guys—something he understood firsthand—as well as what social networking could be like. Dating. People always wanted to know what you did for a living and how much you had in the bank. Sure, the information wasn't typically asked for up front, but it was always on a checklist. No matter what most people claimed, people drew conclusions and stereotyped a person based on their job and how much money they made, just like they did based on race, gender and any other minority group. He'd seen it all over the world. And being Black, he'd experienced it in micro and macro ways. It had taught him how precious good friends were. It had taught the rebel teenager he'd been to value family...the people you surrounded yourself with who always have your back. *Teach your son. Guide him.*

His cell rang and he checked the ID. Carlos.

"Hey, what's up?" Damon asked, turning his chair away from the computer.

"Nothing. Just checking on you. Jordan

said you seemed tense at the bookstore. Woman problems?" Carlos asked.

"What? Nah," Damon scoffed. Carlos chuckled. "He was messing with me back there. I'm good. I'm just on a deadline."

"Well, if you say so. Maybe we can grab a beer. I'm dropping off some stuff for the toy drive when my shift ends. Faye went out of her way shopping for it."

Carlos had someone in his life now. His place was no longer a bachelor pad. Faye had put her touch on it. She'd softened the sheriff up somewhat as well. Damon's bros were all pairing up and starting families. Except for him. At least not in the traditional sense.

"Sounds good. Later, man."

"Later."

He scooted his chair back and went to sit cross-legged on the floor next to Duck.

"It'll be fine. Right, girl?"

He wasn't sure but Duck's tongue lolled. She didn't seem concerned. He looked around. The comforts and upgrades he'd done to the interior had always been for him and his dog. No one else.

Except that now, Zuri and Caden had

entered his life. They'd seen his place, but not this room. They didn't know about his pseudonym and he wasn't ready to tell them. Here he was bitter at Zuri for keeping secrets from him, yet he had stood right there in front of Castaway Books and didn't come out with the truth.

How was he supposed to tell her he was D. L. Dylan, the author of the Chase Falcon series when she was standing there thinking his books were inappropriate and a bad influence on Caden? His own son, who they were already at odds about. A kid who obviously didn't like Damon Woods but apparently loved D. L. Dylan and Chase Falcon.

Granted, the boy hardly knew his father and needed time, but Damon didn't want the kid deciding to like him just because he'd written the books. He didn't want Zuri forgiving or trusting him because he was a famous author. He wanted her to really understand and value who simple Damon Woods was.

He pinched the bridge of his nose, then rubbed his eyes. He wasn't getting any work done. If he didn't get his act together soon, he'd be hearing about it from his agent. As if her ears were burning, a message popped up on his phone from The General. It was his nickname for Scarlett because she kept him on schedule and helped maintain that identity bubble around him. She, of course, had no clue he'd listed her in his contacts as such. She'd be pissed at him if she did.

He ignored the email. He didn't feel like dealing with her or anyone else right now. All that mattered and all he could think about was what to do about being a father and how to keep his son—and Zuri—from finding out too much too soon. He needed to know that he would matter to them even if he lost everything and had nothing to offer. That his role in his child's life wouldn't be limited to a financial one without being given a chance to be a real dad. And for some reason, Zuri's forgiveness mattered to him more than anything.

CHAPTER SEVEN

ZURI PUT ON a light jacket and started lacing her sneakers. The morning sun was a bit warmer today than it had been yesterday. There were fewer clouds in the sky. Caden and Sara were already outside, but instead of following them, Damon leaned against the wall in the front corridor and waited as Zuri got ready.

"Don't you have to work? You've probably already missed more time than you'd planned on, with our showing up in town. I'm sure we can find a tour guide for sightseeing on Roanoke Island. Melanie has brochures right here," Zuri said.

The Outer Banks had one main highway that ran from the north end of the barrier reef to the southern end with only a couple of ways to exit onto the mainland. The different islands making up the two hundred miles of reef were joined by bridges.

Turtleback Beach was on Hatteras Island, farther south and less populated. It was where that movie she'd seen, *Nights in Rodanthe*, was set. Other than famous lighthouses that ran all along the Outer Banks, many of the tourist attractions were farther north on Roanoke Island, such as the Wright Brothers museum in Kill Devil Hills or the Elizabethan gardens and the North Carolina Aquarium in Manteo. When she and Caden came down, the trip had consisted of flying to Norfolk, taking a shuttle to the Outer Banks and then hiring an Uber to get down to Hatteras Island.

In retrospect, she probably should have rented a car in lieu of using the private taxi service, but she hadn't planned on venturing far from town. Once she saw all the brochures Melanie had on hand, she realized seeing some of the sights would not only be good for Caden, it would be educational. Plus, it would keep him from getting bored. He tended to get more depressed when he wasn't doing things.

"I'm good," Damon said. He seemed extra relaxed today. Was he up to something? "I want to spend more time with my son. I made arrangements with everyone at the station. They've got things covered. And Faye—she's the sheriff's fiancée and Clara's twin I told you about—is going to take care of Duck for me. She owns a dog service place in Turtleback—grooming, training, walks and all. So, I'm all yours for the day."

Zuri tried not to read into that. He wanted to spend time with Caden. Not her. She finished with her shoes and slung her small purse across her chest.

"All right, then. Where to?"

He held the door open for her and she hurried past him, knowing she liked the scent of his aftershave way too much, and stumbled on a pair of pink galoshes that Sara must have forgotten by the door. Damon reacted in a flash, grabbing her arm and putting his other hand on her back until she regained her footing.

"Thanks," she said, acting like she wouldn't have actually fallen and wasn't really a klutz, but she knew her face probably looked like she'd tried applying blush in the dark. She didn't look at him. He let go and she headed down the wooden steps that led to the driveway.

The ride to Manteo was just over thirty minutes, most of it along the long stretch of Highway 12 with the ocean or marsh lands to either side of them. She focused on the stunning views while Caden and Sara told jokes and riddles in the back seat. Some were so funny in a slightly geeky, smart humor sort of way that she and Damon fell into a pattern of chuckling and grinning at each other, and it didn't occur to her that neither of them had snapped at the other or frowned or looked stressed until he mentioned that they were five minutes away from the aquarium.

"Have you been to any aquariums, Caden?" Damon asked, turning into the parking area.

"Nope. I did go to a zoo once for a school field trip, but that's it. I didn't really like it. Some of the exhibits were nice, but some didn't look natural. I'm not sure about aquariums either. I mean, shouldn't all those animals be free?"

"I hear ya. Living in captivity is inhumane. I'm absolutely against the old-style zoos where animals are trafficked just so people can gawk at them. It's awful. However, most modern zoos take part in breeding programs and animal studies geared toward trying to save species from extinction, whether they've been endangered because of disease, habitat loss or poaching," Damon said.

"You mean they're not there for just looking at? They're in aquariums and zoos so people can try and learn about them and help them?" Sara asked.

"Exactly. I mean, bad 'zoos' still exists around the world—too many of them—but the well-known, legitimate zoos aren't like that anymore."

"Caden docs really well in science," Zuri said.

"Me, too. I think I want to be a vet like Dr. Zale," Sara said, unbuckling as Damon turned off the engine.

"I can tell you like science from those jokes, Caden. Best ones I've heard in a long time," Damon said. She caught him glancing in the rearview mirror to check the boy's reaction. Zuri looked over her shoulder but she couldn't read the expression on her nephew's face.

"I thought they were hilarious. I'm going to use them when I go back to school. Yours were way funnier than mine," Sara said. Now *that* made the corner of Caden's mouth quirk up.

"Yeah?"

"Definitely."

Zuri's door flew open, catching her by surprise. She hadn't even realized he'd parked. Damon smiled.

"All set?" he asked.

She climbed out and adjusted her jacket as the kids joined them and Damon locked the doors. The pavilion-style entrance to the aquarium was lovely. The grounds included metal sculptures of fish and a sea turtle. There were models of sharks and even a T-Rex. Caden used to love dinosaurs and asked to have his picture taken. Zuri used her cell phone to get a photo of him and Sara standing in front of it.

Inside was amazing. There was a huge glass wall as part of an enclosure that housed every fish imaginable, including smaller sharks.

"Do we have to stick with you guys?" Caden asked.

"Nope. As long as you follow the rules and check back with us every twenty minutes," Damon said.

"Wait. I'm not sure. How big is this place?" Zuri didn't want them getting lost or kidnapped or something. Yes, she was a worrier, but Caden was her responsibility and, for the day, so was Sara. If anything happened to her, Melanie would never forgive them.

"Not big enough to lose them. It's fine. They can text us or call if they can't find us."

"Caden doesn't have a cell phone."

Her nephew made a face that had "whose fault is that" written all over it. Damon's expression was almost identical.

"Really? Isn't he old enough?"

"Yeah, Aunt Zuri. Aren't I old enough?"

"We're not getting into this now," Zuri said.

"I have mine on me." Sara held up her phone as proof, then tucked it back in her pocket.

"Fine." Zuri wanted them to have fun

and she was feeling put on the spot and like a stick-in-the-mud. "Go on. Just stay in touch. I don't want to have to call search and rescue."

"He *is* search and rescue," Caden said, waving his hand at Damon.

Zuri rolled her eyes as they went off. He had her there. The kid was getting cheeky. She wasn't sure if that was a good thing or bad. Was he getting bolder just because of age or because of Sara or was this defiance stemming from the trauma of losing his mother?

"I didn't mean to overstep. I know you're not used to me being around," Damon said, "but a little independence is good for him. And seriously, no phone?"

They started walking past the exhibits and stopping at each one to look at the marine life, both real and modeled.

"Vera had told him he could have one when he turned thirteen. I'm honoring that. And for the record, I give him independence."

"You sure about that? The Zuri Habib I knew liked to make sure everyone was taken care of. That's what made you the best tutor I ever had. You sure you don't coddle him? And I don't mean that in a bad way. It's just you seem very protective, and rightfully so, especially given the circumstances."

He thought she was his best tutor and caring?

"I don't coddle." She pursed her lips and sighed. "Okay, maybe a little, but like you said, with good reason."

"He's stronger than you think he is."

"You don't know him well enough to say that."

"Zuri, you don't always have to know someone a long time to *get* them. Sometimes people just connect and understand one another, like you and I did in high school. *Before* I proved I was a mindless jerk," he quickly interjected. "Plus, I studied a lot of psychology and learned how to read people as a matter of strategy and survival in the navy."

"Were you an interrogator?"

"No. At least not as my main duty, but everyone had some cross-training. Let's just say I pay attention to details in human behavior and leave it at that. But I must say, the phone thing…that's gotta be tough. I mean, I agree there has to be limits, but it can also be a way to keep him connected to friends."

They passed an exhibit full of turtles and another with jellyfish.

"Damon." Zuri lowered her voice so that other visitors wouldn't overhear. "He gets depressed as it is. Have you read the studies on how social media increases the risk of depression and suicide in children? Once they have a phone, that's it. I know there are parent spy programs and tracking and whatnot, but the reality is that it becomes harder and harder to control what they get into. He's a smart kid. Vera wanted him to focus on schoolwork, not social media."

"There are plenty of ways to keep an eye on things. Ground rules. But you have to consider safety. Having a phone on him means being able to call for help when needed. What if you're late picking him up from school or somewhere? Or there's an emergency at the school like a shooting or tornado? Times have changed. I live in a small town, but even Turtleback Beach has its dangers. I've been out there in the world. I've seen things firsthand most people can't imagine. So, I guess I'm just seeing the phone thing from a different angle."

Maybe he was right. There *were* times when she got caught in traffic between the lab and the school and he had to wait on her. Her anxiety always shot up, wondering if he was all right. But the factors she was worried about were valid, as well.

"I'll think about it. I hear what you're saying. I just need to think about it."

"Fair enough," Damon said.

They walked through the exhibits, from a round pool of stingrays to one about wetlands, finally meeting up with the kids at the one about sea turtle conservation. She remembered Damon warning Caden not to take Duck in the areas marked off on the beach. Melanie had also explained that the area was a known sea turtle breeding ground due to their migration route.

"Sea turtles are my favorite animal," Sara said. "What's yours?"

Caden's forehead wrinkled up.

"I don't know. Dogs, I guess. Yeah, Dogs. The animals here are cool, but you can't hug a shark or turtle or have one sleep at the foot of your bed."

"I can see that logic," Damon said.

"Maybe, one of these days, kiddo." Zuri might eventually give in. She wasn't making promises though. And it would have to be a small dog that didn't bite. No giants like Duck, although she had to admit, once she got past the fear of Duck jumping on her, she could see how cuddly Duck was. "These sea turtles…are these the kind that hatch down on the beach? The nests you pointed out and told us to be careful with?"

"There isn't just one kind. We get nests laid by loggerheads, leatherbacks, hawksbill, Kemp's ridley and others, but those are the most common. The Outer Banks are right along their annual migration path as they head north. They usually lay May through August, then when the eggs hatch, the babies make their way into the ocean guided by the light of the moon reflecting off the water. The problem is that artificial lights from towns along the shores can confuse them and if they head in the wrong direction, they risk getting eaten by a predator before they make it to water safely," Damon said.

"I was visiting my grandma over the summer once and saw some hatch. They were the cutest things I've ever seen. I've been in love with them ever since," Sara declared.

"They are cute," Caden admitted.

"I want to show you all another place in town, so when you've seen everything here let us know," Damon said. *Us.* The word made it sound like they were together. Like they were parents.

"Can we go to the gift shop first?" Caden asked.

"Sure. Go look and then we'll head to the car," Zuri said.

She browsed, too, but didn't plan on getting anything. Damon fiddled with some gadgets they had and spent some time looking at a telescope. The place was overpriced, as most gift shops were, but it was fun to look. They had every kind of stuffed animal you could think of, books, mugs and more. Caden came over and whispered in her ear. Zuri looked over to where Sara was looking through a bin with semiprecious stones, then at the stuffed animals.

"Okay. Which one? Point it out subtly and I'll get it." He did exactly what she said then returned to Sara. In the meantime, Zuri purchased the item he said he wanted to give to Sara for Christmas and tucked it deep in its bag so that the girl wouldn't see it. It was a super sweet gesture. Maybe the kid was going to be okay after all.

They headed to the car and within minutes they were driving through a picturesque town. Manteo was quaint, like Turtleback, but in a different way. The houses and shops had a seaside village flair, but were pristine looking, rather than weathered, since the town lay on the more protected sound side of the Outer Banks. There was obviously more tourist money that went into the local economy here. Everything was neat and inviting, from the town's iron clock standing on its pedestal to the boats anchored side by side in the marina. The sun was beginning to set. Damon parked again and they all got out.

"If it was summer, I'd take you to see this outdoor play they do here called *The*

Lost Colony and there's a festival where you can watch blacksmiths at work and such. A bunch of historical reenactments. But that'll have to be another time. For now, you've got to see this. You kids will love it. Follow me," Damon said, laying his hand gently on Zuri's back to keep her close, as a group of people passed by.

She recalled Caden's words. *He is search and rescue.* She liked that Damon was protective. He guided her to the other side of the street, Caden and Sara close beside them, and didn't break contact until they'd crossed. Her back felt cold when he did. She liked his arm around her and imagined what it would be like walking hand in hand with him. *Stop. You can't go thinking like that. It'll just get you in trouble.*

They passed more stores and holiday shoppers trying to tick off their lists before going home from work.

"We can stop for dinner before heading back, if you guys are hungry, or we can just get snacks. But first, over there. See that ship? It's a replica of the *Elizabeth II*, a sixteenth-century ship. I think we made it in time before tours close," Damon said.

A brown ship with a blue stripe running its length and white stripes near the bow was anchored close enough to land for folks to board it.

"You mean we can go on it?" Caden asked, his voice cracking in his excitement. He heard the crack and cleared his throat. The poor kid looked confused for a second. *Voice changes. He's growing up.* The boy was self-conscious as it was. She hoped this wasn't going to be a new problem.

"If we hurry."

"Way cool!"

"I've been on it once. It really is neat," Sara said, jogging ahead with him. Zuri waited until they were a good five yards away.

"Today has been great. More than great, Damon. Thank you for all of it. I mean, I've loved it, but I don't think that comes close to how much Caden has. It has been a long time since I've seen him letting loose," Zuri said, walking alongside Damon as they watched the kids run along.

Damon put his hands in his pockets and nodded with a bit of swagger that was incredibly attractive. She didn't want to be attracted to him. Part of her wanted to blare warning sirens but another part, her gut, wanted to take a chance again. Risk it. Let her guard down. She swallowed hard and increased the distance between them by at least a few inches. He glanced her way and she almost missed the twinge of his brow. He'd noticed. The town's Christmas lights came on and the place was turned into an instant wonderland. Even the ship lit up.

"I've enjoyed the day myself. Been here plenty of times, but I've never taken it in like today."

He looked at her again but he didn't smile. Instead, his eyes and lips softened with a sincerity that nearly stole her breath. Was he trying to tell her that he liked spending time with her? No. No way. She was reading into things again. She felt it— the signals and energy between them—but she had to be misinterpreting it all. *You're not his type.*

"It's really beautiful here," she said, not knowing what else to say.

"I agree." He was still glancing over at her every few seconds.

"Aunt Zuri, are you going on it? Can we go?" Caden called back at them.

"Yes. Wait up," Zuri said.

She and Damon picked up their pace and greeted the man who welcomed tourists onboard. He was dressed as though he was still in the sixteenth century and kept in character, too.

"No need to wait on us. You two explore," Damon said. He held out his hand to help Zuri onto the deck, then let go.

The ship was incredible. Caden and Sara had to be having a blast. It was like walking into a reenactment. The crew were in costume. The rooms below deck were set up as if they'd traveled back in time, from the hourglass, globe and time pieces on the small desk near a cot, to the ropes and supply bins and iron tools.

Caden and Sara checked out every nook and cranny, and Damon took the time to explain some of the history to them. The guy knew his maritime history. She was impressed and loved the way the kids, particularly Caden, really listened to him. Damon had a knack for making whatever he was talking about sound mesmerizing.

He was a good storyteller. Some of Zuri's favorite teachers had been that way.

The kids could have probably spent another thirty minutes on board, but the tours were shutting down for the night and they needed to feed the kids or at least get them something to tide them over for dinner at Melanie's.

"Why don't we just get a treat and head back. I don't want to stop for dinner if Melanie's gone out of her way to cook," Zuri said.

Damon glanced at his watch.

"I agree. That wouldn't be nice to her, but I'm guessing you kids are starving. How about some soft pretzels or kettle corn? You can eat in the car. Just don't make a mess," Damon said.

"Yes, please," Sara said.

"Sounds good to me. This place was fun," Caden added. The kid was softening up around his dad. This was good.

"You should thank him for bringing us here and for planning such a fun day," Zuri reminded.

"Thanks, Mr. Woods," Sara said, giving him a shy smile.

Caden dug the toe of his sneaker in the ground and stuffed his hands in his jeans.

"Yeah, thanks… Dad."

Zuri's heart nearly stopped and Sara's lips parted, but she quickly sealed them. Something shifted in Damon's face.

Caden had called him *Dad*.

HE HAD BEEN in Turtleback Beach for four days now and was sort of starting to like it. The truth was that he wasn't sure if he liked the town itself or hanging out with Sara. It mattered because she didn't live here all year. He still wasn't sure if his aunt was going to keep her promise and not leave him. A part of him didn't care so much anymore. He hadn't expected the word *Dad* to leave his mouth yesterday, but it just came out. And it felt okay. Better than okay. It felt good to be able to call someone that.

His dad was turning out to be all right. Sure, Caden knew he was cool and superhero-like when he first saw him, but now he knew that the guy was actually nice. They had fun yesterday. And his dad had been cool about letting him look around with Sara instead of asking them to stick next to the grown-ups like toddlers. His aunt wouldn't have, had it been up to her. His dad even seemed surprised that he didn't have a cell phone. Another point for him.

Caden was beginning to think that maybe quitting school in Boston and coming to live here wouldn't be so bad. It would be better than dealing with kids he hated up there or being in his house where everything he looked at reminded him that his mom was dead.

But you want to be close to her grave, don't you? You don't want to forget her, do you?

He was being a terrible person again. Betraying his mother. What kind of human being would leave their mom behind, even in her grave, and actually start to like being around a parent he barely knew, who'd never been around in his life? What kind of loyalty was that? Dogs were more loyal than he was. Braver, too. Maybe he needed to take a few lessons from Duck and Laddie.

He trudged through the sand, trailing

a few yards behind Sara as they collected sea glass and shells. What was he thinking? He'd make a terrible dog. He wasn't athletic—or apparently loyal—enough.

Sara wasn't saying much. He wasn't sure if that made him nervous—like, maybe she was getting bored with him because he was a boring person—or if he was relieved. He didn't really feel like talking. Yesterday had been super fun, but it sort of left him feeling drained and depleted, too. It made no sense, but he wasn't good at making sense of anything lately. Sara had pulled him aside to ask about Damon being his father, but she didn't press for details when his only answer was "yeah." How could he answer questions when the whole thing was new to him?

He picked up a sand dollar, but it was broken at the tip, so he tossed it as far as he could into the surf. And what was with the way his dad and aunt kept looking at each other and brushing up against each other? His aunt and his dad? Maybe he was imagining things.

"Hey, Caden, look. A conch shell. I don't see these that often. I think there are too many people shell hunting in the summer, but this time of year is great." She held the conch up to her ear and smiled. "Try it."

Caden took the shell and pressed it to the side of his head. He'd never done it before, though he'd heard about it plenty. He could hear the swooshing sound that he figured everyone talked about. Sure, it sounded like waves. But he could hear the real waves to the left of him, so he wasn't sure why listening to a shell was such a big deal. He handed the conch back.

"Don't you think it's cool?" Sara asked.

"I guess."

"You don't sound like you think it is."

"We've got the ocean right here."

"But for people who don't, they can hear it in a conch. It's like, if this shell left this beach and was taken to some city, it would be taking the sounds of the ocean with it and sharing it," Sara said.

"It's not really though. You know that, don't you? It's just physics. The shape of it makes air or any sound waves bounce around and sound louder. It's an amplifier. It's not really the sound of the ocean itself."

Sara's smile disappeared and she dropped

the shell back where she'd found it. Caden wanted to die. He'd let the nerd in him surface. He had been trying so hard to not be "that kid" since yesterday. Sara always looked so impressed with Damon and was totally into the kind of dude Chase Falcon was in the book series. Caden wasn't sure why, but he just really wanted to be a little bit like that. Especially around her.

"You're just being salty," she said.

"What? Salty?"

"Yeah. Like the ocean. As opposed to sweet."

"I'm not salty. Look, I'm sorry. You like the shell, take it."

"No. You ruined it for me."

"I said I'm sorry. I'm just…bored." There. Maybe if he claimed *being* bored, he wouldn't *be* the boring one. Sara's eyes lit up, then narrowed at him, like someone about to get involved in a conspiracy. He had definitely been reading too much Chase Falcon.

"Wanna do something fun, then? I know somewhere so quiet you can barely hear the ocean or anything else. And I know how to sneak in."

That sounded dangerous. Mysterious. Totally badass.

"I don't know…"

"Oh, come on. It's not scary. You said you were bored."

"I didn't say I was scared. I'm totally game."

"Good. Follow me."

She took off at a slow jog and he followed. Running through the sand was so much harder than doing required laps on the track at his school for PE class. He pushed himself to keep up her pace. They ran alongside the dunes that separated the cottages from the beach but rather than taking any of the wood plank walkways that led to each house and the main road, they crouched through the tall grasses and reeds that danced in the ocean breeze.

"I thought we were supposed to stay off the fenced nesting areas," Caden said.

"We're not crossing the fencing. Besides, there aren't going to be any turtle eggs this time of year. They just keep the main breeding areas undisturbed. Come on. Don't be a chicken."

"Where are we headed?"

"Right there." She pointed up at the Tur-tleback Lighthouse.

He wasn't a chicken. His face heated and he bypassed her, jogging straight for the lighthouse, but coming to a dead stop when he hit a marked off area with signs that said Private Property and No Trespassing.

There was a massive clearing with a small house to the left, closer to the road, and the lighthouse off to the right on the ocean side. The pillar towered above them with black and white diagonal stripes wind-ing up into the sky, ending with a lookout. The base was surrounded with thick stone walls and a massive door with iron trim. Sara caught up to him and crouched down, pulling him behind a clump of grass. A startled bird took off from behind them, scaring the bejeebers out of him, but he tried to make it look like he was just catch-ing his breath.

"That's the ranger cottage. Dr. Zale, the vet you met, used to live there. He still owns it, but he and Miss Mandi moved into her grandmother's house after they inher-ited it and got married. That place down there." She pointed to a white, two-story cottage with Victorian trim and a turret farther down the beach.

"It says no trespassing."

"He won't care. Besides, he's at the clinic this time of day and Laddie would be at reading time over at Castaway Books. Plus, there're only four days left to Christmas, not counting today. Everyone is working or getting last minute holiday shopping done. The coast is clear."

Caden knew right from wrong. His family had always drilled it into him. He knew better. But doing the right thing didn't always pay off, did it? He prayed and did everything he could to help around the house so that his mom could rest and made good grades so that she wouldn't be stressed about his schooling—he'd read that stress reduced a person's immune system—but she had died anyway. If he had learned anything from that, it was that life was short. If he was going to have fun or prove himself, there was no point in waiting or second-guessing everything. Following rules and doing what's right all the time? It wasn't worth it.

"Isn't it kept locked?" he asked.

"I saw Miss Mandi get their extra emergency key once. It's hidden behind the ranger cottage. Are you with me or what?"

"Yeah, I'm with." He stayed crouched behind her as they retrieved the key from a hidden box, then scurried through the surrounding dunes and reeds until they were close enough to the lighthouse door to make a run for it. Sara had them inside in a jiffy and they slammed the door behind them and started laughing.

Caden had heard about adrenaline rushes, but he'd never experienced one. This had to be it. His pulse pounded and blood rushed and a strange euphoria coursed through him. They both leaned back against the whitewashed masonry walls to catch their breaths.

The air was damp and salty and all sorts of wonderful. Or maybe the wonderful part was being here with Sara and sensing that she'd forgiven the conch shell incident and was seeing firsthand just how not boring he was.

The floor was made of black and white tiles that were chipped in a few places and an iron staircase spiraled around the tower's core, leading to the top.

"How many steps?"

"Two hundred and eight," Sara said. "Can you do it?"

"Piece of cake." He took a deep breath. His mile time at school was pitiful and he was feeling the ache in his thighs from running as far as they did through the sand. But no way was he going to fail now. Not in front of her. He knew adrenaline could make a person lift cars and all sorts of wack, superhuman stuff. He knew he wasn't close to that level, but maybe he was just hyped enough to make it. He bolted up the steps. "Meet you at the top."

"Hey, wait up!"

He could hear her climbing behind him, chasing him, but it only spurred him on. Something competitive and wild took over him. He took step after step, his lungs burning hotter and hotter with each one, the muscles in his legs stinging like the time he'd inadvertently picked a battle with a wasp while messing around in the yard. He held the railing to help hoist himself up, but he refused to stop.

Fifty. How many did she say there were? He counted and heaved as he went. The pain felt good in a twisted way. It was deserved. He deserved it for not being able to save his mother. For being angry at her for keeping his dad a secret. For not wanting to forgive her or his aunt.

One hundred. For not being cool at school. For hating himself for not being stronger. For life in general.

One-fifty. For hating Aunt Zuri for her role in all this and for not warning him about meeting his father. For having fun when it wasn't right to be happy with his mom gone. He didn't care if his therapist said it was okay to have fun and be happy…that his mom would want him to. Burning pain ate at him. Punishment for everything he was feeling.

Two hundred. Especially for…for actually liking his dad. *Traitor.*

He took the last couple of steps and collapsed at the landing. He rolled on his back and struggled to slow his breathing. But he'd made it. He made it to the top. He'd done something he didn't think he could…

something no one back at school would believe bookworm Caden could have done.

*I knew you could do it, Caden. You've
always had it in you. You're more like your
father than you'll ever know.*

He jolted up. He could have sworn he'd
heard his mother's voice. Her words were
crystal clear. Was the lighthouse haunted?
Or was it just high enough for him to skim
heaven?

He looked around. The lookout was
glass enclosed, giving him a panoramic
view of the Outer Banks, from the Atlantic
side in the east to the inland sound on the
west and the expanse north and south of
them. He could see the bed-and-breakfast,
his dad's place, the rescue station and the
town. A flock of birds dove past him,
flapping their winds like angels in flight.
Mom? He blinked and shook away the notion.

Sara made it to the top and gave him an
irritated look. What was that about? He'd
just proven to her that he wasn't a wimp.
He thought she'd be impressed.

"You could have waited for me," she
huffed.

"I thought getting here was the point."

"Getting here *together*. You took the fun out of it," she said. "What's with you today?"

"Nothing. Everything." He was confused. He didn't understand women.

"Yesterday and before that, you were being nice. Today, you're being... I don't know. Self-absorbed."

"You're kidding. Self-absorbed?"

"Yeah. I mean, I get that your mom passed away a few months ago and I'm so sorry for that. I really am. But—"

"But what? I'm supposed to pretend that everything is chill because if I get down about life, it makes you uncomfortable? I shouldn't be upset because it ruins everyone else's day?"

"That's not what I was about to say."

"Then what?" he snapped. "You don't know what it's like to feel alone. To have your mom die and feel like no one else really wants you. To miss her. To feel like you're drowning and not knowing if everything's ever going to be okay."

He was tired. The energy that had propelled him to the top was plummeting. His emotions were in free fall. He raked back his hair and looked outside the window—the only thing keeping him from soaring like those birds…from diving into the waters below…from reuniting with his mom. *Stop. Just stop.* He closed his eyes and rubbed his face. He dried his cheek on his sleeve and swallowed hard to keep more tears from falling.

No, he didn't want to join his mom. Maybe at one point after she'd died, he might have thought about it, but not anymore. He had been hating life, that was for sure, but the reality was that even if he hated therapy, some of the stuff he'd heard had stuck with him.

Focusing on hope and doing something to make a difference, like when he had donated his allowance to cancer research in his mother's name. And the books he started reading…the Falcon series. It would sound stupid to others, but not only had the stories been an escape, the hero had also faced the impossible and always made it through. Falcon had faced death and had been tortured by the enemy, but he always persevered and made life better for it. That message had really stuck with Caden and had gotten him through some dark nights. As depressed as he could get, he didn't really want to join his mom when it came down to it, because he knew he wasn't really alone. He had Aunt Zuri and his grandparents. He knew they loved him and cared. He did have some teachers who cared and made him feel good, and a few friends at school, too. And now he had his dad and…and a friend in Sara, unless he'd blown it.

"Maybe you should stop with the self-pity," Sara said, scattering his thoughts. "Maybe I do know what it's like. You're not the only person alive who has felt lost or like life was ruined. But I chose not to give up hope and to focus on all that was good and my life did get better and I'm grateful for that."

Caden turned to face her. Tears streamed down her face, but she tipped her chin up and held her shoulders high.

"I don't get it. You seem so happy all the time and you have your parents and your grandma and all the fun times you talk about."

"Yes, I do. But it wasn't always like that, Caden. I was adopted when I was eight. After both of my parents were killed in a crash. At least you still have your dad."

With that, she headed back down the stairs. Alone.

CHAPTER EIGHT

DAMON POURED A cup of coffee and took a scalding gulp. It was bitter. Kiko must have made it. She was great at water rescue, but awful at making coffee. She never made it unless she was the first one at the station this morning. He braved another sip, desperate for the caffeine, and set his mug aside.

He hardly slept last night. Spending the day on Roanoke with Zuri and Caden had him thinking about things he'd blocked for years…like the idea of ever having a family or kids. His parents hadn't been a great example. Witnessing evil in the world while working as a SEAL hadn't done much to make him want to have a family either. What if he couldn't protect them? He wasn't around for his brother, and Lucas's death hadn't even involved the kind of violence that ravaged the world. There were too many things in life—both man and nature related—that he couldn't control.

But the fact was that he was now a father whether he'd expected or planned to be or not. And yesterday that fact managed to seed itself deep in his psyche. Walking with Zuri and having other families mistake them as a couple—as parents— had awakened something raw and primal in him.

And then Caden had called him "Dad" for the first time and Damon had crumbled inside. It had taken everything in him not to fall to his knees and take the boy in his arms right then and there, but he didn't because he knew what it was like to be twelve and trying to figure himself out and prove himself to others. So, all he did was fist-bump the kid and gloss over the word instead, ushering them all to his truck for the ride home.

But that primal feeling? He wanted to protect his son…and Zuri. It was all he could think about last night. Knowing that he'd never be able to guarantee that no harm would ever come to them in life had kept him tossing and turning until he'd given up on sleep or even getting any work done in his office and sat with Duck watching documentaries instead.

He walked over to where Sanjay was reviewing weather forecast reports coming into their station and others along the coast.

"How's it looking for Christmas?" he asked. He hadn't shopped yet. He usually gave his team gift certificates, but he couldn't imagine not getting gifts for Caden and Zuri. He had no clue what they'd want though. He had also seen a weather report on TV last night indicating a winter storm headed their way.

Sanjay spun around in his chair and made clicking noises with his pen—a habit Damon couldn't stand. Damon snatched the pen from him.

"Someone didn't get enough sleep," Sanjay said.

"I slept fine. What's the forecast?"

"Christmas still looks all right, but I think it'll hit us by New Year's. They say the pressure is dropping with the system and tracks are looking like it'll come our way as opposed to making landfall further north. I'll stay on it. Maybe we'll get lucky and it'll stay far enough offshore."

Depending on how bad it would be, Damon didn't want Zuri or Caden on the road or on a plane headed north in the middle of bad weather. It wasn't a hurricane, but the effects of any major storm hitting the Banks could be just as devastating. The barrier reef was narrow and prone to flooding, beach erosion and structural damage. The worst part was that folks could get stuck in heavy traffic on evacuation routes. It was effectively a one-way-in and one-way-out scenario for most of the reef.

People who lived here accepted the risk just like folks who lived in the Caribbean or Florida did when it came to hurricanes. It was a small price to pay for living in heaven, much like west coasters were willing to risk earthquakes and Hawaii had volcanoes on top of it all. Don't even get him started on what climate change had done to make things worse. He'd seen the effects.

He was used to evacuations, as were the residents. They knew the protocol when a storm was headed their way. But Zuri didn't. He needed to spend more time with them and didn't want their trip ruined, but he absolutely didn't want to put them at risk. He needed to keep a close eye on weather developments as Christmas approached.

"Let me know if you hear the forecast change," he told Sanjay. "Kiko, Mark, keep an eye on the south beach. Brad and I will cover the north side. Make sure the red flags go up. We're still days away, but the second that water gets rough, no surfing."

"Got it," Mark said.

There were always a few people who were drawn to the rough waves, even in winter, sometimes without common sense. Some people didn't understand mortality. That or they had no respect for the power of the seas and nature.

During summers, they had plenty of college-aged lifeguards stationed along the Outer Banks beaches, but during the winter months, particularly on less crowded beaches like in this town, the Ocean Rescue and Beach Patrol team covered the terrain.

"Duck."

His dog got off her bed and wagged her tail. She knew their schedule. She knew what was coming and craved getting out there. She wanted the water, the waves and the sand. She needed to swim.

She was a surfer dog. One who risked her life to save others. Just like a SEAL. Plus, she understood what it was like to come from a broken family. But she'd found a new one in Damon and learned to trust again. Maybe—just maybe—he'd found his, too. And not just with Caden, but Zuri.

He stepped outside and scanned the horizon. The wind kicked up a notch and filled his lungs. He'd braved rough waters before, figuratively and literally, so why did he feel like a coward when it came to Zuri or even parenthood? And why did he feel like he was standing at the edge of a storm that had nothing to do with the weather?

Zuri popped into The Saltwater Sweetery and just about melted on the spot. The aroma of freshly baked bread, pastries and taffy filled the place and the delectable display of different flavors of saltwater taffy drew her like a magnet. Holiday music played in the background and the woman behind the counter wore her blond hair in a thick braid and a headband with deer antlers on top of her head. She also had the tip of her nose colored red like Rudolf.

The place was busy. A few people sat at bistro tables and others waited in line then carried away boxes of goodies. Zuri looked over the flavors of taffy. A variety box would make a good gift to mail to her parents and colleagues at the lab. They'd make good stocking stuffers for Caden and Sara, too. *Stockings.* He didn't have a stocking here in Turtleback. She'd planned on bringing his with them and hanging it in their room, but she had totally forgotten. How could she? Had he noticed? What if he thought she didn't care enough?

She went to stand in line and waited her turn while checking emails on her phone. There was another from work. Why did her chest clench whenever she saw an email from work? She opened it up and started to read, but the chime for the bakery door and her name rang out at the same time. She had stood in coffee lines back home for a good ten minutes where everyone in line had their noses buried in their phones and no one paid attention to who was ahead of them or behind them and the cashier looked wiped out. Here, on the other hand, everyone ahead of her was chitchatting, the cashier was a bubbly Rudolf and within two minutes of getting in line she had someone she'd met only once giving her a hug.

It was nice. So much nicer than the underlying competitive attitude of people at her work. So much more relaxed. She slipped her phone in her pocket as she reciprocated the quick hug from Eve. Her pixie-cut hair peeked out from under a green beanie hat and little candy cane earrings dangled from her ears. She kind of liked Eve's whimsical, boho-chic style.

"I saw you coming in here and was ready for a cup of tea, so I thought I'd say hi. How are you enjoying your trip so far? Faye told me she watched Damon's dog yesterday, so that you could all go up to Manteo. Did you have fun?" Eve asked.

"Yes. It's a beautiful town. I mean, so is

Turtleback Beach, of course, but yes, we had a great time. We went to the aquarium and that boat…the old replica."

"The *Elizabeth II*. Caden must have loved that."

"He did. Sara came along, so they had fun. How are things at your bookstore today?" Zuri asked, wanting to change subjects. Word traveled fast and she didn't want anyone making assumptions about her and Damon.

"Christmas shopping has been good this year. Reading time was extra busy because of parents wanting to buy gifts for their kids without their kids seeing what they got."

"That makes sense." Zuri glanced over to make sure she wasn't holding up the line. She and Eve took a few steps forward. "Oh, you'd probably know. Where would I find a Christmas stocking around here? I forgot Caden's back home."

"Just go three doors down to the store that's purple on the outside. It's called the SEAmstress. Get it? Holly Mann owns it and sells everything for sewing and knitting projects and crafts, including material and yarn. She does alterations when needed, but this time of year she makes things like stockings, Santa hats, elf costumes and such and sells them. Her stockings are really cute and if there's a specific design or theme you want that shc doesn't have, she'll make it for you."

"That's perfect. Thank you. I panicked when I realized I didn't bring his. I'll go there next."

"Any idea what he wants for Christmas?"

That was a loaded question. Caden had wanted his mother to be okay and Zuri had thought his top wish was to find his father, but he had lost his mother and when he found out Damon was his father, the boy fell apart instead of being happy. But he seemed to be coming around quickly. Almost too quickly.

She hadn't expected Caden to go along with their outing yesterday, but not only did he go, he had called Damon "Dad." He'd taken her by surprise. It was all good. It's why she had told Damon the truth about having a son in the first placc. She wanted them to have a connection. It was just that when she heard him say "Dad" a part of her got scared. What if Caden liked it so much here that he wouldn't want to come home? What if he didn't want her to have any say in his life, as guardian or aunt?

She could see why a teen boy would find a guy like Damon to be much cooler and more fun to hang around than an overly cautious aunt. The older teenagers got, the more defiant they could be, and she was starting to see his attitude toward her changing. She could already hear future Caden refusing to listen to her and telling her she wasn't his mother. She loved that boy and she was going to lose him. And losing him would be like losing a part of her sister all over again.

Damon is his father. You're only his aunt.

What did he want for Christmas? The problem was that what her nephew really wanted wasn't anything she could buy or stick under a tree. She smiled at Eve.

"Honestly? I'm still trying to figure it out," she said.

"Tweens and teens are hard. So many

end up just getting money so they can get whatever they want, but I don't think there's any fun in that. Books are always a good gift, and no, I'm not trying to make a sale, so don't take that the wrong way. Just trying to help."

"Books are one thing he's always loved, but I want to get him something unexpected."

As if meeting his dad wasn't, but that already happened.

An image of Damon sitting under her Christmas tree in his red ocean rescue swim trunks flashed in her mind. Talk about unexpected. Damon was *not* on her wish list. Well, maybe he used to be, and she had to admit he had been on her mind a lot lately, but no. No way. Picturing him that way was dangerous and would only lead to another crush, which would in turn lead to a crushed heart. She'd been down that road already. She was a scientist. If an experiment disproved a hypothesis, that was it. She wouldn't keep trying the same experiment hoping for different results. That, according to Einstein himself, would be the very definition of insanity. And being around Damon was doing enough of a number on her brain as it was.

"Can I help you?" The Rudolf lady grinned, then gave a small wave to Eve.

"Oh, yes. Hi," Zuri said, approaching the counter.

"Hey, Darla. This is Zuri. Damon's friend whose staying at Melanie's bed-and-breakfast," Eve said.

"Ah! *You're* Zuri. It's great to finally meet you."

Darla clearly already knew who she was. Boy, that saying about word traveling fast in small towns and everyone knowing everyone was obviously a scientifically proven fact.

"It's nice to meet you, too. I had some of your strawberry short—I mean, *sea*cakes and other confections and they were utterly amazing."

"Thank you!"

"She made my wedding cake—lemon chiffon and decorated with fresh lavender sprigs—and it was so good, Jordan and I ate the top the next day instead of saving it for our anniversary. I have no willpower when it comes to Darla's goods," Eve said.

"Um, my willpower wouldn't be any better. I heard you made your own wedding cake, too, and I heard from Melanie that it was stunning," Zuri said.

"Aw, you guys are really boosting my ego. Yes, I made mine, only Nora and I *do* have our top saved, but only because when you bake all day and live around all this butter and sugar, you become immune. Not entirely, but I've built some resistance to giving in. Now, what can I get you?"

That was her hint that a few more customers were waiting.

"I'll take five bags of assorted saltwater taffy."

"For gifts? I put them in cute bags if they are."

"Yes, please. And I'll also take a cup of coffee and a cream cheese Danish. Thanks. Oh, and can I treat you, Eve? You said you wanted tea, right?"

"Oh, you don't have to do that."

"I insist. You've been so helpful and nice. I'd really like to. Consider it my early Christmas gift. Darla, just add her order in."

"Well, then next time it's on me. Thank

you," Eve said. "I wish you weren't only here for a vacation. I like you."

Zuri pulled out her wallet and paid, while Darla's assistant helped her put the order together. She smiled at Eve.

"If I lived here, you might get tired of me. I'm a boring geek, I'm told."

"Damon told me you were an environmental chemist. And no, he wasn't gossiping. That's not his style. I asked him."

Eve took her tea and held Zuri's cup for her so that she could put her change away and carry the bag containing her order that Darla handed her. Eve carried the cups over to an empty table by the window. Zuri hadn't planned on staying but she figured that meant Eve wanted to sit a bit longer. She didn't mind, but the last thing she wanted was to get roped into talking about anything personal. She went ahead and sat. The aroma of baked treats made it hard to leave. She could always make excuses about needing to get errands done if the conversation veered in the wrong direction.

"Yep, that's me. I work in a lab analyzing water samples and data and such." She knew she was downplaying the fact that she was a successful researcher and professor at a university and on the brink of finding out if she'd get the tenure track position or not. The fewer people she told, the easier it would be on her if she didn't get the promotion.

"Wow. I wasn't very good at chemistry. I was a liberal arts major back in college."

"I'm a firm believer that one should pursue whatever makes them tick."

"And for you, that's water?" Eve teased.

"No one's ever put it that way." Zuri had to laugh. That really did make her sound boring. Bland like water. Funny, considering Damon's passion was water, but not in such a plain way. For some reason, she'd never seen them as interested in the same thing, but they were. The same passion expressed in different ways. She wanted to protect earth's water and he worked to protect those in it. Interesting. "I'm passionate about keeping contaminants out of the environment and water supply. I've been looking at rising levels of things like fertilizer in waterways."

"You must spend a lot of time in the field collecting samples, then."

"No. I used to, I guess, but after finishing my master's degree and then starting in on my PhD, I ended up sticking to the lab. Where I work now, there are others who get the samples. I do more on the analysis end and, of course, the writing up of research papers and results. Grant applications, etc...."

"Do you miss it? Being out in nature, collecting samples yourself?" Eve asked, sipping her herbal tea. The scent of mint and lemon zest wafted across the table.

Zuri glanced outside. Even from this vantage point, she could see past the restaurant on the boardwalk and to the beach and ocean beyond. No matter where you stood in Turtleback, there was water and nature all around you. That was a fact for the entire Outer Banks, for that matter. A person was literally surrounded by ocean on one side and marshes on the other. The place was teaming with wildlife. Would she miss it? Did she miss life before she had decided to stick to the lab?

"I suppose a little. But working in the

lab gave me more predictable hours when my sister was first diagnosed with cancer."

"I heard about Caden and your loss. I'm sorry."

"Thanks. Being here has helped, I think. I hope, in his case."

"Well, maybe you'll love it so much you'll never want to leave. If it's water you want to study, we have plenty of it. You can live the rest of your days in our lovely town and when you marry, Darla there can make your cake and *I'll* eat half of it."

Marry? Here in Turtleback Beach? She thought of Damon and how it almost felt like they were a family at the aquarium yesterday. But marriage? No. She'd never consider it. It didn't matter if she found him attractive. As a chemist, she understood that was just human nature. Hormones. Chemical reactions could change. It didn't mean they were destined to be together. Did it?

After all, here she was despite the fact that she thought she'd never see him again. She shook her head. Nope. The only relationship she'd ever have with him was that of being aunt to his son. And if Damon tried to take her nephew away from her, she'd never forgive him.

"I already love it here, but alas, there are no labs out here and I'm up for a tenure track position at the university where I work in Boston," she said.

She'd leave soon enough and, other than setting up visits for Caden with his dad, her and her nephew's lives would go back to normal or some sort of post-funeral normal. She downed the rest of her coffee and pastry and pushed her chair back. "I'm so sorry to run, but I need to finish shopping and get back. Caden's probably wondering what took me so long."

Eve picked up her tea and followed her to the door.

"No worries. I need to get back to work. It was nice talking and thank you for the tea. Please, let me know if you need anything while you're here." Eve crossed the street and disappeared into Castaway Books.

You can live the rest of your days in our lovely town and when you marry...

Right. That sounded like a fairy tale. Eve was the kind of person who read, believed in and was probably living a fairy-tale life. However, Zuri knew life didn't always turn out like a fairy tale. Her sister's hadn't. Damon's parents' marriage hadn't worked out. There were so many other relationships and lives she knew weren't going well. Basically, if Zuri were to look at data and analyze her life, the results would show what she already knew. That not everyone was destined to have a happily-ever-after.

CHAPTER NINE

"I TOLD YOU, it's a surprise." Damon unlocked his door and greeted Duck with extra belly rubs. It was his way of rewarding her for not jumping up. Jumping and a dog her size did not typically go well for the person on the receiving end. Zuri's presence had emphasized that. He nudged Duck away from the door and stepped aside so Caden and Zuri could enter.

After their trip to Manteo, the tension levels between them all had dropped a few notches, at least he thought so, and he didn't want to lose that momentum. He was headed in the right direction with his kid and he had a feeling Zuri was beginning to see that he wasn't totally oblivious about children. He had, after all, grown up around younger siblings. *Lucas.* Damon shut the door a tad harder than necessary. He needed to stop all the negative, intrusive thoughts that crept up out of nowhere every time he tried to just be in the moment. His son was the one who was present in the here and now. Not Lucas. People learned from the past. History was full of lessons if one paid enough attention to them. He could do this. He could be a responsible dad. He'd use his history—from how he behaved in high school, to coping with loss, to all he'd learned in the navy— to teach his son and help him get through life.

"You got a tree?" Caden asked. He had seemed rather glum when Damon swung by Melanie's to pick them up. The boy had been a lot happier yesterday and Damon really hoped this would cheer him up again.

"I did. It's artificial, but it'll have to do for now. That box is full of decorations and I thought you guys could help me make this place more festive. Dinner, hot chocolate and marshmallows are on the house."

"Awesome," Caden said. He went straight for the box.

"Aren't you worried that Duck will knock over the tree like you said she did at the station last year?" Zuri asked.

"She hasn't bothered the one at the station so far this year, so I figured we'd give it a try."

He wasn't sure what had spurred him to do it, but right after his shift at the beach, when his team was going over plans for the town's holiday parade, he had decided that if his son was going to be here for Christmas, Damon needed to make it a memorable one. Decorating his place was the least he could do. And if that storm ended up getting forecast to arrive sooner and Caden and Zuri had to evacuate, then at least Damon would have had the chance to create some holiday memories with them.

"Lights go on first, right?" Caden asked.

"Yep." Damon went over and rummaged through the box with the ornaments, while Caden opened the one with lights. Zuri set her purse down, gave Duck a scratch, this time on the slobber-free top of her head, and joined them. She seemed to be getting more and more comfortable around Duck.

"Do you have a theme?" she asked.

"Theme? Are you kidding? I just bought whatever was left at the store. Which wasn't much. You do themes?"

"Aunt Zuri's tree is always organized."

Damon chuckled. "I don't doubt it. Your aunt was born organized."

"You said you were in the navy. Don't you have to be real organized for that? Like, bounce a penny or quarter off your bed and stuff?" Caden asked, as he started wrapping a string of lights around the tree.

Damon took the end from him and continued wrapping when it got too high for the kid to reach. Zuri started hanging ball ornaments, standing back every so often to judge placement. She looked so beautiful standing there. It felt so right having her around again, in his home…in his life.

He cursed himself silently for having blown their friendship apart when he was eighteen. What if he hadn't? What would his life be like right now if he had accepted when she'd asked him out? Would they still be together? Would he have ever joined the navy and become a SEAL? Probably not.

Guilt settled like ice-cold snow on his chest because as much as he regretted their blowout, he didn't regret his years as a SEAL. It had made him who he was today. Stronger. More resilient.

Zuri brushed her long hair over her shoulder then hung another ornament. She was different, too. She'd also grown into a more confident individual. She had done well for herself.

Everything happens for a reason. Maybe their time apart allowed him to appreciate her so much more now. Maybe he had needed that time in the navy to build enough courage to face the fact that Zuri had always been special to him…had always filled a special place in his heart. A fact he wasn't afraid of anymore. The only thing he was beginning to fear was losing her again. Losing them both.

He looked over at Caden, realizing he'd been lost in thought and hadn't answered the coin bounce question.

"Yep. You do, at the beginning. It's all about discipline and training."

"You have to be smart to be a navy SEAL, don't you? That's what Chase Falcon says in that book series I'm reading. The character has this super high IQ."

The book series, again. The one his aunt didn't approve of. The one Damon wrote. *Tell her. Trust her. It'll be fine.* Fine wasn't good enough. Courage or not, he couldn't handle Zuri being disapproving. Maybe if they didn't have a past where he'd disappointed her so ruthlessly it would be different, but they did, so her approval meant a lot to him. While he trusted her on one level, the cynic in him, who'd learned enough from growing up in a lawyer family, had to consider that if she ever thought about suing him for custody, knowing he was a bestselling author with deep pockets might tip the scales against him. He'd heard plenty of stories where individuals sold information to the press. Media loved gossip about famous people—secret babies, surprise weddings and such. Zuri wasn't greedy though. At least the girl he used to know hadn't been. Not that he'd hold back from supporting his son. On the contrary, he wanted to give him everything and more. But he'd seen celebrities getting made out to be the bad guys and taken for every last dime. Sure, he had a private lawyer and a family of them, but he didn't want to deal with that kind of chaos and he needed to protect his son from it, too. What if his name got out there? Zuri wouldn't do that to him, would she?

Okay, so maybe he shouldn't tell Zuri yet. He wasn't sure. He cranked his neck to the left and right to unkink the knot that was forming in his muscles.

"Um, yes. You do. Same for marines and most special ops."

"That must mean you made good grades in school. Right?"

"Caden, I don't think you like the water enough to join the navy, if that's where this is going," Zuri said.

Is that what the line of questioning was about? His kid wanted to follow in his footsteps? Damon's chest swelled. They were going to have to get Caden in swim lessons first thing after the holidays and even then, only time would tell. The swimming endurance tests used to weed out applicants were brutal when he went through the process. Did Caden have it in him?

"He's twelve. I'm sure he has a long time to think about it."

Damon wanted to ask when his birthday was, but not in front of Caden. He didn't want to highlight the fact that he didn't know his own son's birthday. He made a mental note to ask Zuri later. He took one of the decorative balls and hung it on a branch.

"That can't go there, Damon. You put two balls of the same color next to each other. The reds and golds should be spread out," Zuri said.

"I told you," Caden said, rolling his eyes at Damon.

"Your aunt's methodical approach helped me in school, so we'll give her a pass on the tree."

"How'd she help *you*?" Caden asked.

"I survived my science class because of her tutoring."

"You struggled in school?"

No, he didn't in general. At least not until senior year. He had always had a high GPA prior to that, but Zuri didn't know that and this was a chance to prove he wasn't trying to come between her and her nephew. He wanted Caden to respect her. He wished his parents had focused more on teaching their kids to respect the other parent, rather than bringing each other down in front of their children. He'd learn from history all right.

"I struggled a lot my senior year," he said, evading how he'd done prior to that. He didn't give details about why he struggled. The homework help with Zuri started when his grades started dropping because tension between his parents at home had become too distracting. It was hard to study around parents who argued all the time, and those disagreements about the most mundane things made them both irritable. Irritable parents had a way of snapping at everything their kids did.

As the oldest, that left Damon feeling like he'd never be good enough. He was expected to be an example for his brothers. The burden was on him, and every time his siblings messed up, their parents had a tendency to blame him or look in his direction. He loved his mom and dad and now knew that his mother had been doing the best she could at the time, but that fact didn't change the past or what he went through. How it had affected his focus and will. He simply didn't care about how well he did in school or college applications anymore. None of it seemed to matter.

His parents had also tended to unconsciously draw their kids into the relationship battle, complaining about each other to them, making them feel caught in a tug-of-war and forced to take sides. It wasn't healthy.

God, he didn't want his son to get caught in a custody battle between him and Zuri. *Don't let history repeat itself. Just don't.* His mother was wonderful. She really was. His dad was a good man, too. They both were when they weren't together. His parents had simply gotten lost in their relationship, a fact that his mother realized and apologized for after Damon had reconnected, about a year into the navy. She had been trying to make up for it since then.

"You struggled in school? Like bad grades?" Caden asked.

"Yeah, for one semester my senior year."

"Why only senior year?

"Senioritis," Damon said. "Spring fever." He wasn't about to tell Caden about how his parents had been. "But I got back in gear and worked hard after that."

Caden nodded.

The truth was, all it had taken was a

few study sessions with Zuri and he had pulled his act together at school because, for some reason he couldn't put his finger on at the time, he didn't want her to think he was stupid.

She had intrigued him with her matter-of-fact, down-to-earth way of looking at things. She had been quiet and caring and he had needed that to balance him against the arguments at home. She didn't judge. So even when his grades improved, he said he still needed help. He kept going to the tutoring clinic and they kept meeting at the library on their own time so that she could give him extra help. He just wanted to spend more time with her but needed an excuse because she didn't fit his image. She didn't fit in with his cool crowd.

He hadn't realized at the time that he was leading her on. It hadn't occurred to him that someone like Zuri would actually fall for him. That she'd ever see him as more than the school jock who wasn't her type. On some level, he must have thought he was safe, enjoying her company and their connection without the responsibility of it ever becoming more.

Until the day she had asked him out.

And as if that hadn't caught him off guard and scared him enough, others had overheard. People he didn't want to share anything about his private life or thoughts with. Just like now. *Haven't changed much, have you? D. L. Dylan*. Hiding behind a name. He put his hands in his back pockets and pretended to inspect how the tree was coming along.

"But I thought you said you had to be smart to become a navy SEAL," Caden pointed out.

Checkmate. Not much got past the kid. Damon looked over to gauge Zuri's expression. She pretended not to pay attention, but he saw her drying the corner of her eyes before continuing to decorate. This conversation was bringing back a bad memory for her, but he couldn't ignore Caden. He needed to make things right.

"True." He sat down on an armchair near the tree and leaned forward. "But nothing in life is unforgivable or the end of the world, if a person can prove themselves. If you bomb a quiz or test, you study harder for the next one. If you can only do five push-ups, you practice daily until you can do more. And if you ever say or do something that hurts someone's feelings, you apologize sincerely, and prove you can do better. Life's never perfect, but when you fall, you get up again and again and keep walking. Being smart isn't only about information or facts, it has to do with doing what's right and doing it with heart and soul."

Zuri was now staring at him, her eyes watering and her hand holding a decoration but stalling in front of the tree. The second his eyes met hers, she ducked behind a branch and pretending to be looking for a better spot to hang the ornament. He hoped she understood that he was truly sorry. So much so that he couldn't find the right words to do it justice.

"Are you hungry yet, Caden?" Zuri asked. "Or do you want to finish the tree first?" She was trying to change the subject. He couldn't blame her. He was grateful for it.

"We can finish first," Caden said. His brow furrowed and he hung another ornament but with much less excitement.

Damon pulled a stocking hook out from the box and set it on the table, then rummaged for the Newfoundland dog ornament he'd seen in the gift shop.

"You don't have a fireplace," Caden said, when he saw the holder. Zuri, face dried, came around to get another ornament and to see what Caden was talking about. Damon thumbed at the roughhewn, wooden shelf that hung over his television.

"I have that. It'll work for stocking hanging. Only, I didn't get a stocking for you yet."

"I did," Zuri said. She bit her lower lip and came around to the couch for a break. "I forgot yours in Boston, but I bought one today and was going to surprise you and hang it at the foot of your bed. If you'd like to hang it here, I'm okay with that. Unless, you want to get one yourself," she said, looking at Damon.

"The one you got works for me. Bring it over anytime," he said. Her gaze lingered on him a few seconds, then she cleared her throat and got up.

"Uh, I'm going to borrow your restroom," she said.

"Don't forget to give it back," Caden quipped with a lopsided grin.

"Huh?" Zuri didn't get it.

Damon chuckled and stood to work on the tree.

"You don't *borrow* a bathroom. You use it, Aunt Zuri."

"Oh. Okay, smarty-pants. I'll be right back."

"She's really gullible when it comes to jokes by the way," Caden said.

"I'll remember that."

Her nephew had her pegged. Damon used to get a kick out of teasing her in a friendly way. She always fell for his jokes. Caden's face turned serious again. He glanced over toward the hallway where his aunt disappeared, then fiddled with the stocking hook.

"Can I ask you something man to man?" His voice was lowered so that Zuri wouldn't hear.

Man to man. Damon's chest pinched at how sincere Caden sounded.

"You bet. What is it?"

"Woman problems."

Damon kept a straight face. He rubbed his chin.

"I see. Woman problems can be the worst. This have anything to do with Sara?"

"Yeah. I guess. I think she's mad at me. I might have said the wrong thing. I didn't know she was adopted."

"I see." Damon didn't either. This was the first he'd heard of it. "Well. The fact that you recognize that you may have upset her means you're a good guy who pays attention. Being a good listener is important. Just say sorry and be honest about how you feel. Sometimes the stuff we worry about gets worse when we let it fester in our heads. Don't keep it bottled up. Make sure she gets the message."

"Like those ships they stick in bottles I saw at the gift shop, except some people stick notes in them and toss them out to sea? That happened in a story I read once when the main character was shipwrecked on an island."

"Sort of like that. Why don't you tell her that her friendship is important to you, then hear her out without getting defensive and, come to think of it, since Christmas is around the corner, you could make or give her something as a gesture."

"I could do that. I already got her a stuffed turtle yesterday and had Aunt Zuri hide it, for Christmas, because Sara loves turtles. But I know something else she'd want that doesn't cost anything." His face brightened. "Thanks for the advice."

"Anytime, kiddo."

Zuri reappeared and they both smiled up at her.

"What?" She looked down to make sure she was zipped and buttoned and they started laughing. Gullible indeed.

"Can I plug it in?" Caden asked.

"Light her up," Damon said. Caden stuck the cord in the nearest outlet and the tree came to life. Caden sat on the floor and leaned back onto Duck, who curled around him like a pillow.

"It's beautiful," Zuri said. "It makes the place feel like h—Christmassy."

She was going to say home. He was sure of it. She was right. It did. But it wasn't just about the decorations. It was the fact that his dog, son and Zuri were here. Family.

They weren't exactly a family, but he… wished…

He moved the box and set it by the door and brushed his hands together.

"Let's eat," Damon said.

He stood there and watched Zuri and Caden head to the kitchen with Duck at their heels. *Family.* Was it possible? Could he build one that was strong, loving and right that would last forever? He scrubbed the stubble along his jaw and rubbed at the pounding in his chest. He was a dad. He'd just had his first father-son talk and he had quite possibly learned more from it than his son had. Maybe it was time he listened to his own advice. Maybe all he had to do was tell Zuri the truth and say he was sorry. Maybe it was time to uncork the bottle and set his feelings for her free.

ZURI CURLED UP on the chair in the corner of the bedroom and turned on the small bedside lamp. She didn't want to wake Caden up, but she couldn't sleep and figured she could read the copy of the science journal she'd brought along. This time, dinner at Damon's had been wonderful. She didn't know how else to describe it. Decorating for the holidays like an ordinary family who wasn't suffering, watching Damon and Caden connect in a way that seemed to infuse her nephew with a level of confidence she hadn't seen in him before and doing mundane, normal things like washing and drying dishes with Damon as Caden played in the living room with Duck was…indescribable. It was as if she and Damon had recaptured the comfortable, unguarded feeling and dynamic between them that they used to have.

The only problem was that she liked it too much. And that scared her a little. Hoping for more was asking too much.

The rhythmic sound of waves crashing on the shore had lulled Caden to sleep pretty quickly. He'd had a long day and was exhausted. He had complained a little about his leg muscles aching, but he didn't have a fever earlier. She hoped he wasn't coming down with anything. They had been doing a lot of walking that he wasn't used to, so that was likely all it was.

She got up and tiptoed over to his bed and touched his forehead gently, just to be sure. Nope. No fever. The book he'd fallen asleep reading was slipping from his fingers and half-covering his face. She picked it up slowly, so as not to wake him, and almost set it on his nightstand.

Chase Falcon: A Spy Amongst Us by D. L. Dylan. She was curious. If she hoped to understand her nephew better and if she wanted to keep from losing the relationship they'd had since he was born, she needed to make an effort to get where he was coming from.

Look at Eve and how she seemed to understand kids. She gave off a Peter Pan vibe that Zuri never could, but there was something to be said about grown-ups not losing their inner child. She had always been the responsible one and she saw so much of that in her nephew. Children who suffered trauma, like losing a parent, tended to grow up far too quickly. She didn't want him jaded. She wanted him to embrace life.

Was Damon right? Was she partly at fault for being overprotective? She needed to give him some space to grow up or she was going to lose him altogether, whether it was to his father or not.

She read the blurb on the back of the cover. Interesting. It wasn't the first book, but it was in her hands. If Caden knew she jumped into a series out of order he would go ballistic. To him, spoilers were criminal. But she just wanted to know why he loved the series so much.

She took the book, went back to the chair, and pulled the afghan around her shoulders. The wind picked up, rattling the screen on the window as it did every night. The rumble, smash, swoosh of the waves attacking the shore, only to retreat in defeat, added to the ambience. And less than one page in, she was swept away.

CADEN TRUDGED BACK from the beach with his prize in hand. He'd gotten up before his aunt and the only person awake downstairs had been Mrs. Biddle. He'd almost called her Grandma Mel, because he'd heard Sara say it so much, but caught himself just in time. He told her he was going for a walk on the beach and she made him promise not to go near the water's edge and to be back within ten minutes or she'd start worrying. She also made him put a jacket on because the windchill that morning had dipped into the upper forties. It still felt like early spring up north to him and he didn't get cold easily, but he obeyed anyway and put his jacket on. He didn't zip it up though.

He had hoped he'd run into his dad walking Duck or even that veterinarian walking his dog, Laddie, the one who had been at Castaway Books, or even Duck's son, Shamu, but no one was out other than two guys he could see with surfboards much farther down the beach—too far to see details—and someone in red from the patrol team talking to them. He couldn't tell if it was his dad, though he assumed it wasn't since Duck wasn't in sight.

He made his way up to the low dune that shielded the cottage from the beach and took the pier-style walkway past the firepit, then jogged up the steps to the deck. He could see Sara walking into the kitchen. She yawned and accepted a cup of juice from her grandmother.

He held his hands behind his back. He

needed to talk to Sara, but not in front of anyone. He looked around. Maybe he could hide what he'd gotten her and give it to her later. He started for a ceramic pot in the corner of the deck but the glass door opened and Sara stepped out, closing it behind her. Her expression was neutral. He wasn't sure if that was good or bad.

"I was told to let you know that breakfast is ready if you want some."

He nodded.

"Okay."

Come on, man. Say something that isn't stupid. She's gonna go back inside and you'll lose your chance. Channel your inner Falcon. Better yet, be brave like your dad.

Sara started to reach for the patio door handle.

"Wait," Caden said. Words turned on his tongue and he struggled to set them straight. He was feeling really hot and wished he hadn't put the jacket on after all. "I, um, I have something for you."

Sara cocked her head at him.

"Why?"

Why? He tried to recall every word of his dad's advice.

...if you ever say or do something that hurts someone's feelings, you apologize and prove you can do better.

His dad was right. He needed to tell Sara he was sorry. He needed to get up and keep walking instead of giving up, so to speak. He remembered the scene in book one of the Falcon series where Chase had admitted he'd made a critical mistake and everyone thought it would put the world in danger, but in the end, his being humble enough to admit when he was wrong led to him working with others and discovering a truth that saved them all.

"Because I was a jerk and I'm sorry."

"I'm listening."

He took the conch shell out from behind his back—the exact one she'd found and tossed back into the sand—and handed it to her.

"I'm the one who is ready to listen."

ZURI WAS EXHAUSTED from sheer lack of sleep. That book had kept her up most of the night. It was a page-turner and pretty intense, but Eve and Damon were right. Given the kind of books her nephew had been reading and some of the movies he'd seen, the Falcon books were fine for him. Even good for him, given their positive message. They were kind of like taking Indiana Jones and Han Solo, blending them and putting them in a modern setting. It wasn't what she usually read, but she had to admit she was hooked. She had even looked up the author but his bio was pretty generic and there weren't any photos of him anywhere. The book website seemed to focus on the hero of the books, rather than the author. Hmm.

She filled her mug with a second cup of coffee and dug into her Strawberry Seacake, which was becoming a really bad breakfast habit. Her doctor parents would have heart attacks if they knew how many she'd eaten since arriving at Turtle-back Beach. *They'll have heart attacks if you tell them about Damon*. She took the last bite unapologetically and swallowed away that thought. She'd eat healthy after the holidays. It would be easier once she was miles and miles away from The Salt-water Sweetery.

"Are you sure you don't want eggs?" Melanie asked.

"No thank you. I'm stuffed. I need to walk this off. Fresh air might wake me up," Zuri said. She pushed her chair back and took her plate to the kitchen.

"I'll take that," Melanie said. "You're a guest here. You're not supposed to clean up."

"I really don't mind."

"No, no. You go take a walk. Might as well take advantage of the nice weather we've been having before it changes."

"I have noticed it getting breezier."

"There's a low-pressure system building in the Atlantic further south. Those usually make their way up the coastline and either fizzle out, head back to sea or come right at us. If this one builds, it'll get to us right after Christmas."

"Oh. Like a hurricane? I thought hurricane season was in the summer and ended by fall."

"That's the height of it, but there are always exceptions. This is just a winter storm, but they can get rough with high tides, flooding and the fact that we basically live on a sandbar. But don't worry. We're used to it. You'll be fine. You're scheduled to leave the thirtieth and I don't think it'll hit until right after that."

"Right. I hope it won't be bad for your sake."

"Don't worry. This old house has survived many a storm. And the town usually pulls together to help each other with repairs and cleanup. But, you know? Life here is worth it. I wouldn't have it any other way."

Zuri cradled her mug, then took the last sip. Damon was busy today. He said he had work to catch up on. She wasn't sure if he just needed a break from them, but either way she understood. She hated to admit it, but she already missed having him around.

"This town does grow on a person. I can see why you love it so much. I'm thinking of walking to the sound side. Is there a path I should take? I read on the brochure that the wetlands are beautiful, and I thought the kids might enjoy spotting wildlife."

"Yes, just leave from the front of the

cottage, cross the road and follow it down a quarter of a mile, passing the Zale Veterinary Clinic, then take the trail by the dead cedar tree and you'll end up at a pier and shed where kayaks get rented out for wetland tours in the summer. They're not open now but there are safe trails around there. Just keep the kids out of the water. Most of the area is a refuge and we do get alligators."

Gators? Zuri wasn't as afraid of wildlife as she was of dogs. She used to spend plenty of time in the field collecting water samples when she was working on her masters, then doctoral thesis. It was having kids near alligators that had her worried.

"Maybe we shouldn't go, then."

"You'll be fine. Just stay on the wooden walkway and don't venture beyond it. Call me on your cell if you run into a problem. Unless it's really an emergency, then call 9-1-1 and Sheriff Ryker will get to you in a flash."

"You're not instilling confidence."

Melanie laughed.

"I wouldn't send you if I thought it was that dangerous. Just follow the park signs and rules. Visitors walk the nature trail there all the time. The gate further in is closed this time of year to protect avian nesting areas, so just stay on the right side of it." Melanie raised a brow and looked pointedly at her. "You'll want to remind Caden and my granddaughter that no-trespassing signs are to be heeded."

"Is there something I should know?"

"Nope. Just saying. Kids get curious and think they're invincible." Melanie shook her head and turned on the faucet. "You'll want to use your phone to take pictures if you don't have a regular camera. We get tons of migratory birds this time of year."

"Okay. I will." She used to be so much more in touch with nature. A walk on a trail wasn't a big deal. She really needed to start getting out more. She was becoming a lab rat instead of a field mouse.

She went over to the patio door and paused before tapping it. Caden and Sara were in deep conversation down at the firepit and she didn't want them to think she was spying on them. They looked up when she knocked and she opened the door.

"How about a walk over to the marsh?"

"Sure," Sara said. She looked over at Caden for approval.

"Sure," he agreed. They waited for Sara as she ran upstairs to put a conch shell in her room, then headed out.

They were at the trail within twenty minutes and she must have warned the kids to stay clear of the water and muddy areas a zillion times because Caden was making an annoyed face at her when Sara wasn't looking.

The coastal habitat was stunning, and she could only imagine how full of life it must be, with dragonflies, skippers, basking turtles, during the warmer months. But Melanie was right, both the marsh and surrounding woodland were teeming with birds. A pair of mallard ducks flew overhead, landing in secret grass-enclosed coves, and the sounds of nature danced on the wind. A grove of massive black gum trees guarded the pond near the kayak shack and the pier stretched out over the rippling water where more waterfowl could be observed, from black-colored ducks to egrets and one with vibrant teal on its wings that she'd never seen before.

"Is that a swan?" Caden asked, standing on the pier and pointing out over the water.

"Oh my gosh, it is." Zuri took a photo. "You two, turn around and let me take a picture of you with this backdrop."

They turned to pose next to each other and Caden, to her surprise, put his arm around Sara. The girl didn't seem to mind one bit. So adorable. Zuri took the picture.

"Hey there. We meet again."

Zuri looked behind her and waved as Laddie, wagging his tail, jogged right past her and onto the pier to greet Caden and Sara. Gray, the vet she'd met outside the bookstore, took his time walking over with a woman at his side.

"Hi."

"Zuri, this is my wife, Mandi."

"Hi, Zuri. I've heard a lot about you."

"Small towns."

"You get used to it after a while." Mandi grinned and gave Gray's back a rub.

"Do you walk here often?" It was a silly question. His clinic wasn't that far away. She had never been good at small talk. Gray nodded as he scanned the marsh.

"Pretty often, I'd say. I'm a big nature

buff, so I'm either on the beach or here. I usually help local groups during sea turtle nesting season with nest marking. It helps keep track of hatching numbers, species, and keeps tourists and pets from damaging the nests. But this time of year, I take Laddie on more walks on this side of town. Fewer mosquitos in this cooler weather."

"That makes sense. This is all protected area, right? No waste dumping or runoff?" Zuri asked, going into scientist mode.

"Ah, yes. Zuri is an environmental chemist," he explained to Mandi.

"That sounds super interesting," Mandi said.

The lab results were, but she realized that the lab itself wasn't. It didn't come close to where she was standing right now and the work she used to do.

"It has its moments. I've been looking at the link between water pollution, climate change and the impact on the environment. Habitat and wildlife." It sounded so much better when she put it that way. Then why was the reality that she spent the bulk of her time with test tubes, assays and computerized data analysis?

"You know, come to think of it, there's a researcher who has been working on similar stuff out here. The wetlands around here, and hence the wildlife, are subjected to toxins from runoff. Sometimes it's from high-tide flooding and water contamination during storms. Runoff from asphalt on the roads, roofs, cars and such also ends up right here in these ponds. I've seen him and his team wading around taking samples for things like mercury testing. I think it's fascinating stuff."

"Really? Hmm. Maybe I'll look up his work and read about it," Zuri said. She meant it.

"Come on, Laddie!" Gray called out. The dog rounded up Caden and Sara and ushered them over to the adults. "Good girl. I'm afraid we have to head back. I have furry patients midmorning."

"Nice to meet you, Zuri. I hope you enjoy your stay," Mandi said.

"Thanks. Nice to see you both. We'll be walking back ourselves, shortly."

"We'll see you around. I'm sure you've heard that the town's annual Christmas parade is tomorrow. Trust me. You won't want to miss it," Gray said.

Melanie had mentioned something briefly about it. Zuri wasn't that into parades, so she was going to let Caden decide if he wanted to go. She wasn't sure if he'd think it was too babyish for him and Sara or not.

Mandi and Gray waved and headed back down the path. Zuri took a deep breath and closed her eyes for a second. The sounds and scent of brackish water and algae and moss enveloped her. It was grounding and calming. Rejuvenating and recharging. This was as close to feeling Zen as she'd come in years. She hoped it was having the same effect on her nephew.

"Laddie's such a great dog. Did you see him trying to herd us?" Caden asked.

"I did. Smart dog," Zuri said, opening her eyes slowly and taking in the view again.

"I wish I had a dog at home," Sara said.

"Me, too," Caden added, giving his aunt a sad puppy face.

Back to reality.

"You two ready to go or do you want to

stay longer?" Zuri asked. She wasn't falling for it.

"Are you kidding? This place is rad, Aunt Zuri. The town is totally awesome. I could stay here forever."

And just like that, any Zen she'd been feeling was gone.

CHAPTER TEN

DAMON READ HIS email and muttered a curse. He had enough going on. He didn't need to deal with deadline pressures right now. There was the town parade today, on top of it all, and the latest weather report indicated the storm would track toward the Outer Banks, rather than veer off to sea. They'd know soon if landfall at Turtleback Beach was likely and, if so, that meant having Zuri and Caden leave sooner than planned.

He and Zuri hadn't even gotten into legalities over Caden yet. They needed to. Caden had been through a lot with his mother's death and the last thing he wanted was to make life harder on him—Zuri had been right about that—but they needed to at least talk about it seriously. He had every right to be on that boy's birth certificate and to have his rights back as a father.

He stared at the computer screen. How was he supposed to be able to focus on writing when his reality was—as the saying went—stranger than fiction?

The talk would happen. The book would happen. He just needed to pace things and take it slow on both. He needed to be able to think, but so much had happened in such a short time. He scrubbed his face then answered the message from The General.

Buy me more time, Scarlett. I have some—

He mulled over how to phrase it without giving more personal information than necessary. *Visitors* didn't seem like a good enough excuse to be too preoccupied to meet a deadline. *Family...* Well, family was more of a priority but Scarlett already knew that his immediate family were aware he was Dylan. He tapped the keyboard then typed.

I have unexpected relatives in town for the holidays who don't know about my books. No time to write this week. I'll catch up soon.

He hit Send.

"It is what it is, Duck."

The fact was that he'd ignored her previous two emails, which was totally unprofessional of him. He needed to be more gracious. Scarlett had done a lot for him. She was his rock when he needed it. She'd covered for him plenty of times.

He really did need more time for family though. That was the truth. He needed to bond with his son. It wasn't enough that his kid thought that Damon's ocean rescue career was cool. He needed his son to accept him for who he was—his dad. If Caden knew right now that he wrote the Chase series, Damon would never know if the kid would have fully accepted him without that incentive. Sure, he'd called him dad, but that was just a label because he'd been told Damon was his father. He needed to earn his boy's respect before truly deserving that title. He wanted the fact that he was D. L. Dylan to be the icing on the cake, not the batter itself. He logged out of his email and turned off his computer.

"Let's go before we're late." He slapped his leg and Duck joined him. If he could just survive the holidays, then maybe he and Zuri could sort things out. But if things went south in terms of name changes and custody versus guardianship rights, he'd do what he needed to do to keep his son.

He hadn't told his family yet. He never involved family in matters unless he needed to. They complicated things. The only person who knew what was in his bank, his will, his contracts and took care of legal matters for him was Joel Burkitt.

Joel knew where Damon stood and had advised him on steps he could take when they were drawing up his will. He was just hoping Zuri wouldn't force him down that path. Zuri had caught him leaving Joel's office the other day and she had assumed the worse. That was exactly why he hadn't told her yet about his pseudonym. He didn't want her changing her mind about him because he was a celebrity. Zuri knew the person he had been long before fame. He hadn't been the nicest high schooler, but at the same time he hoped she'd be able to see and like the person he was beneath the surface, the same way she had done back then.

CADEN WATCHED IN wonder as the parade started down the street. The floats and marchers had all gathered down by the beach boardwalk and were marching through the town, then taking a left down the side road that led to his dad's place. According to Sara, it was supposed to end just beyond that, near the ocean rescue headquarters. She was with him in front of Castaway Books, where they stood on the bench near the shop for a better view. His aunt Zuri was standing with Miss Eve and the lady with the toddler and another woman who looked identical to her. Sometimes he wished he had a twin. Then he'd never be alone. He hated being an only child.

Music blared, courtesy of the local high school band. They were good. Caden had performed piano a few times onstage during assemblies with his school's orchestra, but otherwise he didn't play as part of a group. He was impressed with the drummers in particular and liked the elf costumes they wore. This was so different compared to the Boston parades he'd been to. The floats here were based on boats hitched on their wheeled carriers. Each was decorated uniquely, some in traditional holiday stuff and some with odd additions like a shark in a Santa hat or the one that looked like a boat-sleigh being led by a team of sea turtles with red noses. It was pretty silly but funny, too. His mom used to say dare to be different. Well, this was different all right.

Sara ran up and got a few candy canes that were being handed out by a snowman on another float. She gave one to the toddler they'd seen around with the bookshop owner's friend. Nim…that was the kid's name. Sara walked over and gave him one, as well.

"Thanks. These floats are wild."

"Yeah, they're pretty neat. Wait until you see the next one. Santa's on it."

"Is this where those gifts we donated get handed out?"

"No, that's not for this. The Santa float crew usually hands out candy. Those gifts that were being collected go to shelters or to families who need them. If he handed them out here anyone would grab them."

"You're right. Who plays Santa?"

"Take a look. There he is. I've been waiting for this surprise," Sara squealed, squeezing his arm.

Caden caught the shocked look on his aunt's face before he located Old St. Nick. Sitting on the float right by Santa in a matching hat was none other than Duck.

"My dad plays Santa?"

"Every year."

Zuri spewed hot chocolate and had to apologize to everyone in the group. They just laughed and admitted that they'd promised Damon not to say a word.

The man didn't even light up his cottage or have a wreath on his door and he didn't even have a tree inside until recently, and only then because of Caden. He played Santa *every* year?

He caught her gaze and gave her a wink that had the ladies whispering. Eve waggled her brows at her.

"Santa, baby," she said with exaggerated breathlessness, eliciting more laughs. Zuri felt her cheeks heat up.

"That's a song and nothing else."

"If you say so," Darla added, stealing

Nora's cup of cocoa and taking a sip, then giving it back.

"I do. Now, where does everyone go once the floats pass by?" Zuri asked.

"Some folks follow them then hang out on the beach where the parade ends. Others scramble to finish Christmas shopping or call it a day," Faye said, taking her niece, Nim, from Clara to give her identical twin sister a break.

"Hey, Caden," Zuri said. "Do you want to follow or stay here?"

"Let's follow," he said. "If you want to," he added to Sara.

"Absolutely. One should always follow the candy trail," Sara said. The two jumped off the bench and joined the tail end of the parade.

"I better catch up. I'll see you all later," Zuri said.

She didn't really want to stand out, so she walked closer to the edge of the pack. She still couldn't believe that Damon was the town Santa. Was that why he couldn't hang out yesterday? He must have been prepping for this.

The crowd thinned more and more the

closer they got to the beach. They passed the yellow cottage with the blue door and the white one farther down and across from it, both with holiday wreaths on their front doors. Eve had told her that the yellow one used to be her place and the white one was Sheriff Ryker's. They passed Damon's beach house next and it stood plain and gray as ever. Zero curb appeal or holiday spirit, except on the inside. Something about that made her feel special. Like she was privy to a part of him that no one else was allowed to see.

She lingered with the kids and forced herself through all the small talk with residents as the floats were dismantled and the majority of folks headed down the beach toward the boardwalk, just as she'd been told. Caden and Sara had checked with her before running ahead with the group. They wanted to get back to the bed-and-breakfast.

Zuri looked around for Damon but couldn't find him. He had to be busy taking off his Santa suit and he was probably hanging out with his crew or friends. He'd mentioned that the sheriff—Carlos—and

Gray and Jordan were his close friends. She didn't want to interfere with his plans.

Nerves suddenly rattled her stomach and high school flashbacks hit her. Damon hanging out with his cool friends and only spending time with her when it served a purpose. As teens it had been the tutoring he needed and now it was making sure he was a part of his son's life.

She rubbed her arms and swallowed hard. *You're not the same insecure girl anymore. Stop thinking like her.* Maybe so. But things were even more complicated now than they'd been in high school. She was still book smart, but she was also people smart now.

She gave up on waiting. The last thing she wanted was for Damon to think she was hanging around like a groupie. She started down the beach, unable to shake from her mind that wink he'd sent. There were plenty of cheesy or unwelcome winks out in the world but this one was different. Oh, so different. It was soft and warm and conveyed in no uncertain terms that out of the entire parade crowd, he had his eyes on her.

She thought she knew what stomach butterflies felt like before. If those had been butterflies, what she felt today was like an entire monarch migration.

"Zuri. Leaving without letting me know if I should quit this gig and head to the North Pole?"

She spun around at the sound of his voice and nearly lost her equilibrium. A smile she couldn't stop spread across her face. She lowered her chin and narrowed her eyes at him.

"That's a hard call. Both jobs require red uniforms and I must say it's a good color on you." Oh, gosh. She was flirting. Was that considered flirting? Maybe not. Or maybe it was. *You know what? You're a grown woman. Flirt if you want to. It's harmless. It doesn't mean anything beyond the moment.*

Damon cleared the last step from the ORBP headquarters and walked over with Duck at his heels. There was a bit of a swagger in his step and a look in his eyes that was making the sand shift out from under her feet even more. Duck came up to her without jumping. The girl was a quick learner. Zuri gave her a good pet.

She avoided any drool because she was a fast learner, too.

"Walk with me. I'm headed home. I'll drop off Duck and see you back to the bed-and-breakfast," he said. She fell into step with him and blamed the occasional brushing of arms on the sand and breeze throwing her balance off. Damon picked up a piece of driftwood and tossed it for Duck to fetch. For a minute, they walked in easy silence. She'd never been able to do that with anyone else…to just be with someone without expectation. No pressure to find the right thing to say or do. Someone you could enjoy silence with. It was meditative and calming, but a tiny part of her still wondered if she was imagining it. She believed in science and facts, and the data still indicated that they were too different and his life was here and hers was in Boston. The only thing tying them together was Caden. Would Damon be spending time with her if it weren't for that connection? They would still be a part of each other's history and would never have crossed paths again if it weren't for her nephew.

"I can see why you picked this town and job. It's gorgeous. Relatively private. A part of me hates living in the city and dealing with crowds and people all the time. I used to love the 'field' part of my research. Disappearing in nature. I suppose it wouldn't surprise you. I was never the super social extroverted type. I never understood why anyone would want to live in the limelight—and no I don't mean that as a dig into you being the popular kid at school. I'm referring more to celebrities and politicians and the like. You're pretty lucky to live out here with peace and quiet."

"That I am."

"Have you told your parents yet?" she finally asked.

"No. I should at some point but I don't want to put that kind of pressure on him."

"I haven't either."

Thirty seconds of silence passed.

"Wouldn't you love to be a fly on the wall?" he asked. They both laughed. She knew exactly what he meant. Just to see the looks on their mothers' faces when they found out they shared a grandson would be priceless.

"I never thought I'd ever see the humor in that," Zuri said. "To tell you the truth, the idea of telling them is downright frightening, but maybe it'll be all right."

"Who knows? He could end up being the magic ingredient for peace between them. Not that he needs that pressure on him either."

"Or he could end up being the spark that reignites the wildfire."

Duck came around her and nuzzled her hand as they walked. She looked down at the drool trail on the back of her hand, but it didn't really bother her this time. She was getting used to dogs and Duck was truly a sweet bear.

"Here." Damon noticed and whipped out a small cloth from his pocket and gave it to her. She dried her hand and passed it back. Damon stuffed it in his pocket. "For the record, I do keep in touch with my family. I don't visit more than once or twice a year, but I call every week or two, including birthdays and special occasions. So what I can't figure out is why my parents didn't tell me that they'd gone to your sister's funeral. That she'd passed away. They had plenty of opportunity to say something over the phone. I guess they never mention stuff like that to me because it always leads back to my brother and an argument breaks out."

"I don't know. Maybe they didn't think it mattered. You don't live there anymore. They didn't know any of us hung around at school. They had no idea you were Vera's prom date, since she had insisted on meeting you at school. She told me that you two had agreed not to tell my parents. She told my parents that she and a few other girls were promoting female independence by going as a group without dates. They fell for it."

"You mean being gullible is genetic?" he teased.

"Stop that," she said, elbowing him gently in the arm.

"Maybe they thought I wouldn't give a darn about the death of a classmate. What's that say about me?"

She reached over and rubbed his arm reassuringly.

"Don't read into it." Funny that he was

the one who always told her not to over-think things.

"Oh, boy, Zuri. What if my mom suspected? Obviously Caden was at his mother's funeral. My parents would have seen him. They had to have noticed his resemblance to me or Lucas. My mother wouldn't have missed it. I mean, I *knew* the minute I saw him. How could they not have?"

"I really don't know. It was a funeral and that would have been the last thing on their minds. Unless…maybe that's why your mom volunteered so much information about where you now lived and what you had been doing with your life. She was talking to my parents to pay her condolences, but she knew I was standing close enough to hear the conversation. Perhaps she suspected, but wasn't sure, but wanted to sort of let me know just in case. She was the one who mentioned that you had been a navy SEAL and were now living on the beach in North Carolina. In fact, come to think of it, my mom told me she saw Mary in a grocery store recently and that Mary seemed to ignore her. If she suspected something, it would explain why she tried extra hard to avoid my mother. Maybe the lawyer in her was playing it cool until she could find out more."

"Sounds like something my mom, and dad for that matter, would do. They were never straightforward when it came to communicating. I think that's why they fought so much. Neither could ever say what they really meant, which only led to frustration."

"You're not like that, though, are you? The Damon I always knew was always straightforward. Honest. Even bluntly so sometimes. Obviously, way too blunt on one particular occasion." She kind of regretted bringing up "the incident" right now. It was like the proverbial elephant or a dark cloud that lingered between them. She wished it would just burst open and disappear.

He didn't respond right away. He tossed another stick for Duck and put his hands in his pockets.

"I wasn't as straightforward as you think, Zuri. I regret that."

Her hair blew across her face and she

brushed it away, as they turned to cross over the sand dune to his place.

"What do you mean?"

"I mean that I never told you back then how much you really meant to me. And I haven't been entirely honest with you now either."

DAMON HELD HIS breath after the words left his mouth. Her lips parted and she avoided looking at him. He messed up. He shouldn't have said anything. *Wading is for babies. You're all in or all out. Take the dive.*

He looked around, not wanting any on-lookers, and took her hand. She didn't re-sist when he led her to a secluded spot under his deck. The dunes and beach grasses to either side of his house and be-tween them and the beach shielded them from prying eyes.

"Zuri, I was an idiot back then and I hung with kids who put popularity and being cool ahead of kindness and sincer-ity. It was hard not to care what everyone thought of me, peer pressure and all. You know how it was. Athletes hung out with athletes and cheerleaders. The theater kids stuck together. The—"

"Nerds? Geeks?"

"I was going to say the bookworms. Anyway, everyone had their groups and cliques. I shouldn't have listened to them or cared what they thought. The truth was, I really did like you. I started liking you even more the more we spent time together. For real. But I knew it wouldn't work because my friends weren't the kids you enjoyed being around. I don't think I'd ever seen you at a school sports event like Homecoming, let alone at parties. Plus, I didn't dare let you know how I felt because I knew your parents wouldn't approve and you were such a rule follower. I didn't want to put you in that position. I thought we had a connection. Something special. I messed that up. But there's more. That day, when you asked me out? I was upset and scared and confused. Angry, even. My mom had told me that she wanted to leave my dad. Their marriage was ending, graduation was around the corner and I had no clue what I was going to do with my life or where home base would be if our family fell apart. I was lost. But I take full responsibility for what happened, between us and with your sister."

Zuri pressed a finger to his lips.

"I know. I get it. I love my sister, but Vera was a rebel before motherhood slapped her with a good dose of reality. I was the realist and she was the risk taker."

Damon shook his head.

"It's not on her. I take responsibility."

"You're a good guy, Damon." Zuri put her hand on his arm. "She liked you a lot. She had been begging me to set the two of you up because she knew I was helping you with homework. She'd bragged to her friends that you were going to be her date. And she was absolutely livid and bitter when you told her it wasn't going anywhere and that what happened between you had been a mistake. The fact is you were both eighteen and not the first high school seniors on earth to do something without thinking. You left town not long after that. She swore she never wanted to see you again. I'm so sorry for all that happened, Damon."

"I'm not fishing for an apology. My

point is that I didn't deserve you," he said. "I still don't."

She frowned and licked her lips.

"You don't? Am I not understanding what's happening here?" she asked.

Damon rubbed his head.

"I don't know." He was saying too much. Or perhaps not enough. He felt something between them, but what if he was reading her signals wrong? What if he was setting himself up for getting rejected by her? *Karma.*

"I need to know one more thing. Do you hate me?" he asked.

"I did. I swore I'd never speak to you again. I felt like dying when you took Vera to prom and then what happened afterward… It took me years to recover from that. I never thought I could forgive you, but then every time I look at or hug Caden, I realize that he's a precious gift I wouldn't return for the world. It just wasn't our time."

Our time? Was she saying that now was? That she still felt something for him? He studied her face and brushed his finger under her chin. He wished he'd handled things differently back in school.

What if he'd never left Boston? What if they'd stayed in touch? All those times he lay on the cold ground or in bunkers in places so far from home on SEAL missions where the possibility of no return was very real, at least he'd have known that he had someone who wanted him to survive. Someone who was waiting. But instead, he had been just like his parents. Bad at communication. Ironically, keeping things to himself was probably why he'd done well in special ops. He knew how to keep secrets.

Secrets. Just like Zuri had kept. Granted, it wasn't hers to tell and he understood loyalty, but the fact remained that she had known about Caden all these years. It was complicated. God help him, they were just like his parents. And that relationship had gone downhill fast.

"There's something else I need to tell you," Damon said. *Tell her the truth. Tell her.*

Being part of a military team had required almost intuitive communication between members. When it came to each other, they had to be clear for the sake of their safety and success of the mission. The men and women on his team had been like brothers and sisters. They were a special kind of family with an unbreakable level of trust. Was he capable of having that now? Building a family with Zuri and Caden? Was trust all that was needed? Could he earn it?

"Tell me what?" she asked. Her hair blew across her face. He reached out and brushed it aside for her. It was silky and smelled of…he had no clue but it made him want to close his eyes and dream.

"I never want to lie to you again. I want us to be honest. Trust each other," he said, taking a step closer. She leaned back against one of the wooden stilts that held the deck and house above ground. "I don't want to be a coward when it comes to you. Not anymore." *Careful, man. She said she hates the limelight and doesn't understand celebrities. She'll run.*

Her eyes darkened and lips parted ever so slightly.

"What do you mean? What are you saying, Damon? We're adults now. Not schoolkids with crushes. Don't confuse me. I used to be confused around you and I don't want to be that again."

"Then let me be very clear." He brought his face close enough for the tips of their noses to touch. "Very, very clear."

With that, he brushed his lips against hers and kissed her gently before pulling back ever so slightly, waiting to see if she wanted more, hoping that she felt the same way. She leaned into him and he lost all reservations. He held her face and kissed her like he'd always wanted and had always dreamed of doing. He wrapped his arms around her and promised himself he'd never let her go.

He had meant to tell her everything. And he would. He'd show her his office and tell her the truth, but first he needed her to know how he felt about her. That she mattered more than any woman ever had in his life. The touch of her lips melted through him like a promise. Hope for a future. One touch and he knew he'd never be able to leave her again. But he couldn't help the nagging feeling in the pit of his stomach that warned she'd be the one to leave him this time.

Zuri could feel the cool plastic of the high school chair she was sitting on and she could taste the strawberry-flavored candy and chocolate bar Damon had snuck into the school library for her. She felt emboldened. More sure of herself than she'd ever been. Confidence coursed through her veins. She could feel the buzz and the way her heart seemed to swell when she thought of how Damon Woods, captain of the cross country team, looked at her. She smelled the cheap aroma of cafeteria food wafting through the school hallways. The chaotic chatter of student voices filled her ears, although their faces were all blurred.

Damon's was the only face she could see. There was a sparkle in his eyes and he gave her that to-die-for lopsided grin of his and those dimples. Then his expression suddenly switched from charming to appalled. And there was snickering and laughter and the faces of his buddies suddenly appeared clear as daylight. One of them fist-bumped Damon and another high-fived him. He'd gotten her to ask him out. The geeky girl. He'd gotten her to think she had a chance.

She could feel her throat closing and stomach sinking far beneath her feet. Eyes were on her and she wanted to hide. Then Damon's friends disappeared, and his expression changed again. For a fleeting moment, he looked upset and she saw his lips move. He was saying something she couldn't make out. Sorry? Was he sorry? No, that didn't make sense. She ran harder and harder. She needed to get out of there.

Zuri shot up in bed and tried to catch her breath. Her pulse skittered and chest pounded, and it took a minute for her to register where she was. She could hear Caden breathing in his sleep across the room. The waves crashing outside. She pulled her knees to her chest and pressed her forehead against them. *You were dreaming. Just a memory. It was in the past. You're awake now.* But it felt like the present. It felt so real.

Dreams dredged up fragments of memories and emotions, but this one felt more like a warning. As if her mind was trying to remind her of what happened so that she wouldn't make the same mistake again.

She slipped out of bed, tiptoed to the

bathroom and tried to close the door without waking up her nephew. She flipped on the light and splashed cold water on her face before sitting on the edge of the tub. She was overreacting. It was a dream about the past, not the present. Damon wasn't the same anymore. Neither of them were. He had apologized more than once. What was it going to take for her to trust him? Not with Caden, but with her heart.

She touched her lips. That kiss. It had been everything she'd ever imagined and then some. It had been heady and magical, and it warmed every cell in her body. The touch of his hands caressing her back, holding her desperately, had made her want to lose her soul in his. That had all been more real than her dream. That had happened in the present, not the past. There was nothing fake about that kiss or the emotion behind it. She would have sensed it. She wasn't naive anymore. Right? He wasn't leading her on. Not like before.

You're just scared to put your heart out there again. You know he won't hurt you again, don't you? She'd seen how he behaved around the townsfolk and how helpful and caring he was now. She was just being paranoid.

She got up and took a few sips of water, then returned to her bed. Her phone screen read four-fifty in the morning. She'd never be able to fall back asleep. She unlocked it to check emails and noticed a message from Damon last night. She had silenced her phone so it wouldn't wake Caden up. She opened it.

We need to talk. There's something I need to clear up. You deserve the truth.

Zuri's stomach knotted. Maybe her dream had been more than a reminder of the past. It had been a premonition. Damon was already regretting that kiss.

CHAPTER ELEVEN

DAMON WAS GETTING NERVOUS. He hadn't heard back from Zuri since last night. He should have told her the truth yesterday. He'd planned to, but Sanjay and Kiko had come jogging down the steps and Zuri had quickly pulled away from him. His teammates ended up walking back to town with them because Kiko wanted to go to the boardwalk restaurant to eat.

He checked his phone messages again. Nothing. What if he had moved too fast for her? What if he had scared her off?

"Come on, man. It's only six in the morning. Right, Duck?" The dog lifted her head then got up and walked over to her food bowl and looked at him again. "Right."

He filled her bowl, topped off her water and went to pour himself a second cup of coffee.

His phone pinged and he rushed over to the table where he'd left it. Zuri.

Don't worry. We can pretend it never happened.

Aw, geez. No, no, no. This was why he hated technology sometimes. You couldn't convey the right tone or emotions sometimes.

I'm coming over now. Walk Duck with me. We'll talk.

His finger hovered over the heart emoji. Nah. It might scare her. Or she might interpret it wrong. He just wasn't an emoji kind of guy. He'd see her in a few minutes and clarify things in person. So much better than texts. She replied saying Caden was still asleep and he told her to leave him and let Mel know she'd be back. This wouldn't take long. He was on shift this morning for work.

"Hurry up, Duck." Damon put on his sneakers and grabbed some dog treats just in case. Duck wagged her tail and followed him out the door and onto the beach. They jogged the half mile toward the other side of town until he was close enough to see Zuri emerging from the dunes in front of the B and B with her jacket on and a cup of coffee warming her hands. She looked serious. Worried.

"Hey. Good morning," he said, catching up to her. Duck ran a circle around her, as if looking for Caden, then galloped toward the water to splash in the surf.

"Hey." Zuri glanced at him from beneath her lashes as she took a sip of her drink. "So, um. Like I said—"

"Hold up. Don't say a thing. Walk with me." They started down the beach, accompanied only by his dog and a smattering of seagulls. "You misunderstood my text. It wasn't anything bad. For God's sake, Zuri, I don't want to forget kissing you. I don't regret yesterday for a second. I hope you don't either."

She licked her lips and frowned.

"I don't. I mean it was wonderful, Damon, but I don't know. I once swore I'd never fall for you again."

He put his hand on her shoulder and

stopped walking. He linked his fingers in her free hand and held it to his chest.

"I'd give anything to change the past. I have a lot of regrets. But my son isn't one and nor is falling for you. I don't regret that kiss, but I should have told you the truth about myself before it. I want whatever is between us to be built on truth. No more lies."

"You've been lying about something?" She narrowed her eyes at him. "You're still working as a SEAL? As in going overseas and possibly never returning?"

"No. Zuri… I'm D. L. Dylan."

He could tell by the way her brows lifted that it sunk in.

"The author?"

He nodded.

"Very few people know. Immediate family and one or two close friends. Around here, only Carlos, Gray, Jordan and my lawyer. It needs to stay that way for safety reasons because of my time in the navy."

Zuri was dumbfounded. She wasn't sure what to think. She wasn't sure if this made things better or worse.

"You're Dylan? It's a pseudonym? You're him?"

"Yeah. The initials were for my name and Lucas, to honor him, and Dylan is my middle name."

Damon Dylan Woods. She'd seen that before in the school yearbook. But it wasn't that uncommon a name. Damon was D. L. Dylan? The *New York Times* bestselling author? She was pretty sure a curse word passed her lips, but her head was pounding so loudly she couldn't hear her own voice. She closed her eyes, realizing what she looked like at the moment.

"Zuri, I would have told you eventually. It's just that you've not been here that long, and we were still trying to process and figure out Caden being in my life. *You* being in my life again. I wanted you to like me for me."

"You thought I'd be after your celebrity status or money? Me?"

"Not you. Not really. But I had a serious relationship once and she made it clear that she was disappointed and dissatisfied. She said that she'd expected a different lifestyle from an ex-SEAL who had a well-to-do family. She topped that with some choice words about my personality and how she hated brooding— Let's just say her next word started with a *b*. This was right before I started writing. I took it as both karma—heaven knows I had it coming—and a lesson. An early warning."

"I see."

"You need to keep this to yourself."

"What about Caden? He loves your books."

"I can't tell him yet. Zuri, I don't want him accepting me just because I write those books. I want him to get to know the real me. I need to know my son accepts me for who I am, not for some idea he has of what the Chase Falcon author would be like."

Zuri looked up at the sky then let out a sigh.

"Okay. For now. Although for the record, I think he has already warmed up to you."

"Thank you for that. I don't know though. The minute the newness wears off and I start enforcing rules, or he gets to be a couple of years older—because we all know how stubborn teenagers get—he could hate me. I also don't want him thinking he has to impress me, Zuri. He's a good kid. I just want him to understand that I like him for who *he* is, too. That he doesn't have to change for anyone. I just want him safe, you know? I don't want him doing anything he's not comfortable with, like my brother did."

Zuri wrapped her arms around Damon and pressed her cheek to his heart.

"Thank you, Damon. You're going to make a wonderful dad."

Zuri set the two gift bags she'd gotten for Sara and Melanie under the tree. Caden had already tucked the one he'd gotten for Sara with the pile of elaborately wrapped boxes all with her name on them but from her grandmother and parents, who had just arrived that morning. Zuri didn't want to impose on the family for Christmas Eve and Damon had wanted her and Caden to spend it at his place, but Melanie insisted they all join the Biddles for a late lunch/ early dinner before going to Damon's.

The entire house smelled heavenly. The aroma of biscuits fresh out of the oven, orange-glazed baked salmon and roasted potatoes infused the air. Melanie set a grilled pear and gorgonzola salad on the table along with a green bean casserole. Sara and her mom set the table while Caden helped with taking out the trash and Sara's dad kept pots and pans washed and put away as his mom cooked. Damon went to pick up Melanie's dessert order at the bakery and Zuri set up drinks on the buffet near the table. She kept insisting on helping with the dishes and cooking, but Melanie wouldn't let her and there really wasn't room in the kitchen for more bodies.

"This all smells so good and really looks amazing. Like a meal photographed in a culinary magazine. You should post it to your website," Zuri said.

"I hope it tastes as good as it looks."

"I'm sure it does," Sara's mom said.

She could hear the door open and close. Damon appeared with pastry boxes from the bakery.

"Here's the yule log and pie you ordered. Darla says Merry Christmas," Damon said.

Melanie took the boxes from him.

"Thank you so much. I think everything

is ready. Everyone take a seat before it gets cold."

They all found places around the table and after Melanie said a prayer, they ate until it simply wasn't possible to eat any more. Even then, Zuri wished she had room for another bite because everything tasted so good.

"Can I open a gift? Just one?" Sara asked. "I made something that I want to give Caden since he'll be at Mr. Woods's house in the morning."

Caden looked surprised and a little mortified that Sara's parents were smiling at them.

"Sure. Have at it. Just one," her dad said. "Mom, you did all this cooking so you're not touching the cleanup."

"We've got this, Mel. You go take a nap or watch a movie and we'll clear this all up," Sara's mom said.

"We'll help, too," Zuri said, and Damon agreed.

They helped clear the table and put leftovers into containers, while the Biddles worked in the kitchen. Melanie went upstairs for a cat nap, and Sara and Caden were huddled around the tree. Zuri glanced over her shoulder as she gathered dishes. Caden handed Sara his gift. She pulled the plush turtle he'd asked Zuri to buy using his allowance when they were at the aquarium.

"Oh! I love it! I didn't even see you getting this." Sara gave it a big squeeze.

"You said you really liked sea turtles," Caden said sheepishly.

"I do. I've always wanted one of these. Thank you, thank you, thank you. Oh, and here. I made something for you."

"Really? Thanks." He took the small bag from her and shook it out. A woven friendship bracelet fell onto his palm. "You made this? Cool. It's awesome. I saw some of the guys my dad works with at the station wearing them." He tried laying it over his wrist, but it needed tying.

"Here." Sara reached over and tied it to his wrist.

"I'm never taking this off."

"Good. That way you'll always remember me and the fun we had this vacation," she said. Then she leaned over and gave him a kiss on the cheek.

And the look on his face? Zuri would never forget it and she was pretty sure the moment would be engraved in his memory forever. He just needed the good moments to keep coming so that, someday, they'd outnumber the bad.

Damon filled Duck's food and water bowl, then set a pot on the stove for hot apple cider.

"You have three stockings up. I only gave you the one I bought for Caden," Zuri said. He could hear the surprise in her voice.

"You noticed," he said, raising his voice so that she'd hear him in the kitchen.

"Are you planning to put coal in mine?" she asked. She appeared around the corner, double-checked to make sure Caden was busy putting on music and stole a kiss from Damon.

"I think one more and maybe I'll reconsider the coal," he said, kissing her again.

"Why doesn't Duck have a present under the tree?" Caden asked. They put distance between them just in time. Caden plopped down on a stool near the end of the kitchen counter.

"Because if I put a bone under there, even wrapped up, she'd sniff it out and get to it before tomorrow."

"How about you let her open one gift tonight?" Caden said. "She won't care."

"Hmm. Are you trying to pave the way for yourself? You already got one today. From Sara." Damon gave him a good job signal when Zuri turned her face away to sneeze.

"Yeah, did you see how many she had under there? It was unreal," Caden said.

"Caden," Zuri admonished.

The tree at Damon's only had two gifts under it for Caden and two for Zuri and one for him from both of them. What the kid didn't know was that Damon had gotten six other gifts but had them hidden in a closet. He was planning to put them out during the night to surprise Caden in the morning.

"No, I didn't mean it that way. I don't need anything. This trip was supposed to be part of my gift. I just meant that it was good to see that her parents were nice people."

"I think it's nice of you to care," Zuri said.

"Agreed," Damon added. He poured hot cider into mugs and handed them each one. "So, do you really want to open gifts now?"

"Oh, my gosh, you're terrible," Zuri said. "What happened to waiting until morning?"

"I have a confession. I've never, ever been good at that," Damon said.

"You mean you literally never waited?" Caden asked.

"Literally. When I was your age, I'd take advantage of the open one gift option, but then, when everyone was asleep, I would carefully peel the tape off one end of any gift that had my name on them so that I could see what it was. Then I'd seal it back up and no one knew."

Zuri and Caden stared at him with open mouths. He just splayed his hands.

"What can I say? I had a knack for sneaking into things unnoticed."

"That's dishonest, but spies do that. Chase Falcon does it all the time to find and save people, so I guess if it's for a good cause, it can be forgiven," Caden said.

"You're being a bad influence," Zuri said, but the twinkle in her eyes made it clear she was kidding. The last thing he wanted was for her to think he wasn't a good role model or father material.

"One gift or all?" Caden asked.

"Zuri?"

"Fine. Whatever."

"Oooh, you're becoming a rule breaker," Damon teased. Zuri made a face at him.

"Where's Duck's, then? I'm not leaving her out," Caden said.

"All right, all right. Hang on." Damon went to the closet and got the bone. "Here you go." He handed it to Caden so that the boy could earn brownie points with Duck.

"She likes it," Caden said.

"I've never seen her drool that much and I've seen and touched my share of it," Zuri said.

"Here, open yours." Caden handed Damon a box. "It's from both of us."

"It's not much," Zuri said.

"I already got the best gift in the world, so this is just icing," he said, scruffing the top of Caden's head and smiling at Zuri to let her know he meant both of them.

He opened the gift and held it up. It was a framed photo of him standing with Caden on the beach, both facing the water and unaware that Zuri captured the moment on her phone. "Man. I don't know what to say."

"I decorated the frame, gluing the shells on a plain one," Caden said.

Damon nodded and swallowed hard. The rims of his eyes stung, and he could barely get his words out. "Come here, son."

He wrapped him in a hug. He hadn't called him son before. He didn't realize it until the word left his lips. It felt good. He felt whole. He felt like he had a family and his place wasn't just a house but a home.

"You like it?" Caden asked, when Damon finally set him free.

"I love it. Thanks. Both of you." Zuri would be getting a thank-you kiss later.

"I made this for you, Aunt Zuri." It was a small box from a craft store with shells glued all over it. "I thought you could use it for jewelry."

"It's wonderful, Caden! Thank you." She gave him a huge hug.

"My gift to you works well with his

and we didn't even plan it. Here." Damon handed her a box. She opened it and looked at him like it was her turn to cry. She lifted the necklace out and held it up to her neck. He knew she'd understand. It was a small, silver ocean wave. Nothing fancy or gaudy because that wasn't her style. But it represented water—a passion that connected them—and her visit here, so that she'd never forget.

"I have no words." Her voice hitched and she cleared her throat.

"Here, I'll clasp it for you." He scooted closer and she pulled her hair to the side. He worked the clasp at the back of her neck. Her skin was soft and warm as it brushed his knuckles and he could see goose bumps trail along her skin from his touch. He sat back a few feet away from her and she let go of her hair.

"It's really nice," Caden said, leaning in to get a closer look.

"Thank you. It's perfect."

"That leaves two for you. Which one do you want to open first?" Damon asked Caden.

"Um. I'll do Aunt Zuri's first." He ripped

open the snowman wrapping paper and his eyes widened. "No way! Are you serious? But I'm not thirteen yet."

"I think you've earned it and I'm convinced you shouldn't have to wait." She glanced over at Damon. She had listened to him and trusted his opinion and judgment about getting Caden a cell phone. That meant everything to him. "There will be rules of course, for safety reasons."

Caden almost knocked her backward with his hug. She laughed and hugged him back.

"You're pulling a Duck on me," she said.

"This is awesome. Thanks, Aunt Zuri. Okay, last one."

"Careful how you open it. It might rip with the wrapping," Damon warned. Caden slowed down and peeled the tape off the ends and middle, then unfolded the wrapping paper. He froze. He didn't move at all. Damon started to worry. Maybe he'd guessed wrong when it came to what his kid would like.

Caden let out a breath that sounded more like he was going to hyperventilate. He looked stunned.

"Hold it up," Zuri said, trying to figure out why he was speechless.

Caden held the book up in what seemed like slow motion. A round, gold signed-by-the-author sticker glistened in the light from the Christmas tree.

"I... I don't get it. I don't believe it. This isn't supposed to release for at least another month. Like, it's not out yet." His voice cracked as he got louder. He angled it for his aunt to see. "It's the next Chase Falcon book." He flipped open the front cover. "It's signed. With my name! Look. 'Caden, Merry Christmas and Happy New Year. D. L. Dylan.' How'd you get this?"

"I'm wondering the same thing. How'd you get a book that hasn't been released yet?" Zuri asked. Sarcasm at its best.

"I know someone who knows the author's agent and when I found out that you liked the series so much, I made a call and got an advanced release copy signed for you. They usually only give those to reviewers, but an exception was made for you. Sometimes it's good to have connections," Damon said, giving her a side look.

Caden pulled a Duck, as Zuri put it, on him, as well.

"I hope you like it."

"Are you kidding me? I don't think I'll be able to sleep tonight."

"That's an incredible gift," Zuri said. "Thanks for going out of your way to get that for him. I actually read the one you brought on the trip and it was really, really good."

"You read it before the first ones? Aw, man, Aunt Zuri. That's worse than scraping your fingernails on a chalkboard."

"Yeah, that's pretty bad. You are really getting carried away with the rule breaking. Reading books out of order? I'm sorry but your stocking is getting stuffed with coal."

"Come on, guys. What happened to forgiveness as a virtue?" Zuri gave them a sad puppy face.

"We'll think about it," Caden said. "I finished the last one, so I'm allowed to start reading this one right this minute. I can't wait. Do you guys care?"

The plan was for them to stay the night so that Melanie could spend time with her family and, well, Caden could spend time with his. Damon had two bedrooms other than his office, so he was going to let Zuri use the extra room and Caden would sleep on the couch.

"I'm actually feeling really tired. I wouldn't mind going to bed early," Zuri said.

Damon had wanted to stay up longer with them, but he understood.

"Let me get a blanket for Caden. Follow me, Zuri, and I'll show you the spare room."

She did follow him, and he pointed out the bathroom on the way. He took down two extra blankets from the closet and put one on her bed.

"I'll take this to Caden. If you need anything else in here, just let me know."

"Thanks. I'm good. And thank you for this." She touched the necklace. Damon lifted her chin and pressed his lips to hers. He wanted it to be a promise that every evening would be like this—the three of them together like a family—but she did look tired and he didn't want to scare her with too much too soon.

"I'm glad you like it. Get some rest."

He closed the door and took the extra cover to Caden. Duck was already taking up half of the couch next to him.

"You can use this if you get cold, but my guess is that Duck's going to keep that from happening. I'm in the room at the end of the hall and Zuri's in the one on the right, next to the bathroom. Okay?"

"Yeah, I'm good."

Damon turned off the kitchen light. He'd need to remember to wake up before Caden to sneak the other presents under the tree.

"Dad…" God, he'd never get tired of hearing his son call him that "…thanks."

"You bet. Good night."

Two hours into reading and Caden needed to pee really badly, but it was so hard to put the book down. He also had to figure out how to get up when Duck was half covering his right leg.

He managed to get off the couch and he set the book carefully on the table. On second thought, what if Duck slobbered on it…or worse, chewed it up? He moved it over to the shelf where the stockings hung, then went down the hall to use the bathroom. He tried to be quiet and made quick time of his business. He really was getting sleepy, but he wanted to read more. Maybe he should just finish the book tomorrow. No, he needed to at least finish the chapter he was on. Chase Falcon was in the middle of a covert operation, sneaking through the house of a government traitor in search of evidence. From the way it read, he was about to get caught.

Caden left the bathroom but looked to his right when he heard a cough. It came from the room next to him. Was his aunt getting sick? The other door at the end of the hall was his dad's room. Then what was the room across from him?

It wasn't his business. His mom and his aunt taught him never to snoop. He was supposed to respect rules and people's privacy, but it wasn't like she'd never broken rules before. Surely she had. Besides, checking out a room was harmless. Breaking into the lighthouse with Sara had been more daring than this. He was just curious. He touched the doorknob. It wasn't like he was going to steal anything. He just felt like he was channeling his inner Falcon. *Be gutsy like him. Adventurous.* He turned the knob.

The door opened and he stepped in, hoping Duck wouldn't come and bark or knock something over and wake everyone up. He flicked on a lamp and looked around. Two big computer screens, that were turned off, sat on a desk near a window. A shelf of books and...what?

He looked closer. The entire Chase Falcon series was there. But not only one copy of each. There were multiple copies. There was a box next to the shelf with the upcoming release stacked in it. His pulse started racing. No, it couldn't be. He went over to the piles of notes on the desk near the computers. Handwritten notes. Some were printouts. Some were sticky notes. He couldn't believe it. It wasn't possible.

His dad wrote the Chase Falcon series? But wouldn't he have said something earlier? Why didn't he? Did everyone else know? Did Sara?

It didn't make sense. His aunt had been worried about the books. Did his father not think that Caden was worth sharing this with? He'd given him a signed book and everything and flat out lied about how he'd gotten the autograph. Did Aunt Zuri know the truth and go along with the lie… just like before?

He hated this. He hated being treated like a baby. Sara was the only person he could trust around here. He needed to ask her if she knew Damon was D. L. Dylan. He really hoped she didn't know about this. Because if she did, that would mean that she had lied to him, too. And he wouldn't be able to handle that. It would be too much.

CHAPTER TWELVE

ZURI WASN'T FEELING so hot. She really hoped it wasn't a cold. Maybe she was just suffering from holiday exhaustion. On the surface, Caden seemed to have had a great Christmas morning yesterday. Damon had surprised him by piling unexpected presents under the tree. She hadn't bought nearly as many and felt a bit inadequate, but she understood Damon's need to try and make up for lost time. As long as Caden was happy that was all that mattered. But something about her nephew was off. He had been quieter and a tad moody yesterday. When she had tried to put her hand against his forehead to check for fever, he swatted her away and told her to stop hovering. He insisted he was fine and just hadn't slept well because he'd stayed up reading. But he was still irritable today. Maybe it was nothing more than a Christmas crash. Lots of people experienced it.

He'd spoken to his grandparents—her parents—to say Merry Christmas, but only after Zuri explained that they didn't know about his dad and that they should wait to tell them in person. Luckily, he understood. He had sounded peppier talking to them, but then his tone had changed as soon as they hung up. She really hoped he wasn't getting sick. Unless it wasn't that at all. She closed her eyes and dried the corners with her hands. This was his first Christmas without his mom. Sobs tangled in her chest and she couldn't get them out. She breathed through the pressure and blinked away the sting in her eyes.

I wish you were here, Vera.

That had to be it. Caden needed space and time. Except he was also invited to lunch at the boardwalk restaurant with Sara and her parents today and he hadn't hesitated to accept. It was like he couldn't wait to get away from Zuri. Was this about the Christmas gifts? Had he faked liking his presents just to be polite? Was he disappointed? Zuri scrunched her nose. Was this about a puppy? Oh God. When he first met Duck he had said he'd take a puppy any day over a cell phone. She didn't think he was being serious at the time. He had Duck to play with and getting a pup was a huge deal. She wiped her palm across her eyes and sighed. Well, she'd have a talk with him later to get to the bottom of it.

Zuri walked along the beach toward Damon's place. She was carrying the used copy of Damon's—Dylan's—book that Caden had bought and had promised him she'd get Damon to see if he could get it autographed by the author for him, like he did with the advanced copy. But she had forgotten her phone at the bed-and-breakfast, right where she'd plugged it in to charge that morning. Still, she didn't feel the panicked need to retrieve it the way she always felt back home. This was a small town. A person didn't need to go far to talk to another or to find out everyone's news.

She and Caden hadn't seen Damon since leaving his place after a pancake breakfast yesterday. He had told her he was going to be busy working. With the wind picking up again and the sky on the horizon looking overcast, she knew he had his hands full with ocean patrol duties.

They didn't have much time before she was scheduled to head back to Boston, and she wanted to spend as much of it as possible with him. She also needed to know that he'd be okay with leaving things as they were with Caden. She didn't mind him having rights, she just didn't want him physically taking the boy away from everyone he knew up north, including herself.

But what if you became a family? What if this thing between you and Damon is more? Then everything else would be moot because you'd all be together no matter what.

Was that possible? She couldn't make that assumption. Going from a few kisses to being a family...as in marriage...was a huge leap. They weren't there yet. Were they? He hadn't said anything to that effect. Not specifically.

Why was she so darn awkward and clueless when it came to relationship issues? She really needed to see him and talk to him. She didn't want to interrupt his workday, but it was lunchtime, so she was hoping to catch him either at home or at the station. She knew he wouldn't have much time to talk, but seeing him, hugging him, would be a reassurance and they could decide on when he'd have time for just the two of them.

Sand filled her sneakers as she trudged along the edge of where beach met dunes. The sounds of the sea and the life that depended upon it were becoming such a part of her. The scent of saltwater air and the seaweed and shells that lay listless along the shore filled her. She looked toward the horizon.

"In one drop of water are found all the secrets of all the oceans." It was her father's favorite quote by the famous poet Khalil Gibran. Was the secret to finding happiness right here in Turtleback? Water droplets traveled and connected ocean to river to pond and every molecule that rained upon them. Had one of those drops led her here? Was this her destiny? How could it be? This would all be gone once she returned to Boston.

The sounds and smells of city traffic and restless people, of chemicals and restaurants and muddy snow piling along the roads rushed through her mind. Did she miss it? Or would she miss this? What about Caden? How would he react in a few days when she reminded him it was time to leave? How often would they be able to return to visit? There would be school and work schedules and the splitting of time between both sets of grandparents and relatives once they all found out.

The ocean was angry and petulant today, reaching higher onto the shoreline as the waves slapped and clawed in her direction. She turned her face away from the wind that shoved against her back and made her way through the dunes in front of Damon's place. The clumps of reeds swaying to either side of her slashed their blades against her hands and jeans as she approached his house from the beach. The beam she'd leaned against when he'd first kissed her looked barren. Lonely. She touched her fingers to her lips then hugged her arms around herself. The temperature seemed to have dropped a little today.

She walked past the beam and other stilts that lifted the house above potential storm tides and made her way toward the front. She didn't want to use the deck, since he wasn't expecting her. She almost made it to the front but stopped when she saw the silver luxury car pulling into his gravel parking area. It wasn't his. It looked out of place for Turtleback. Too shiny and new. A tall, gorgeous woman got out of the car, first unfolding long slender legs that were barely covered by her skirt, then the rest of her. She was dressed like she'd stepped off the runway of a Paris fashion show.

The old Zuri would have hidden behind the front steps. But she wasn't that shy, timid girl anymore. She marched forward. Whoever this person was, they were on private property. Damon had told her he used a pseudonym for a reason. For protection. As she got closer, she was struck again by how beautiful the woman was. Zuri shook her head, confident in the blossoming relationship between her and Damon. He had made his feelings clear. He had assured her she mattered. She trusted him.

She just hated how jealous she was feeling, how her old insecurities edged back.

She looked down at her jeans and old sweatshirt, then at the supermodel-like woman, who was fumbling in her purse for something. Yep, jealous and insecure. Just as she used to feel sitting in the lunchroom at school. *You're not a kid anymore. Stand your ground.*

She hugged the book she was carrying to her chest and headed right for the car. The woman looked up and narrowed her eyes. Zuri could see her gaze flit from her sneakers and jeans to her sweatshirt.

"Hi. Can I help you?" she asked. Her tone sounded as if Zuri was the one intruding in her space.

"I was wondering the same."

"I haven't seen you before around here," the woman said.

"I'm not from here, but—"

"Ah, I see. Well, you're trespassing on private property. So, if you don't mind, you'll need to get back to the beach."

"I'm actually here to see the owner of the house. Who are you?" Zuri asked.

"Scarlett. His girlfriend. He's expecting me, so I know he's not expecting you and he doesn't take kindly to trespassers, so if you don't want me calling the sheriff, you should go."

Girlfriend?

Zuri kept as straight a face as possible. She forced a smile.

"No problem. My mistake." Her stomach felt like it had been sucked out to sea by a riptide.

She spun on her heel and walked back in the direction she'd come from. She felt sick. Confused. Stupid. She marched over the first dune pausing only when she heard a door open and Damon's voice. *Keep walking. Don't stop.* She stopped and crouched behind some reeds and, against her better judgment, looked over to where Scarlett parked. Damon was walking toward the woman.

"What are you doing here? I told you this was a bad time and that I'd call you soon." Damon sounded nervous.

Scarlett hugged him and planted a kiss on his face, then looped her arm in his. "Come on. You know why I'm here and I'm not leaving until I'm satisfied that I'll be getting what I want."

Zuri covered her face and retreated farther past the dunes. Everything from the past assaulted her—the dare, Damon's rejection, the heartbreak she'd suffered the night he'd taken Vera to prom and, later, the news her sister was carrying his child. Tears streamed down her face. *You two-timing, lying—*

She rushed down the beach but not so fast that anyone would wonder what was wrong. She bounded up the back steps to the bed-and-breakfast, grabbing the box of tissues Melanie had on the console behind her sofa.

"Everything all right?" Melanie asked, peeking out from the pantry.

"Yes. It's just a cold. I'm going to go lie down."

"I can make you soup or tea."

"No, don't worry about me. I'll be fine. I just need a little sleep." She hurried upstairs, collapsed on her bed and let the hurricane of tears she'd been holding back loose.

DAMON WAS FURIOUS that Scarlett had shown up in town. The reality was that he couldn't stop her. Turtleback Beach was open to tourists and she could come there if she wanted. Especially since he was late on his deadline and had been brushing her off. He had that problem. Avoiding people when life got overwhelming.

He locked the door as Scarlett walked back to her car. They had gone over what he had for his next deadline and agreed to buy him a little more time with the publisher. He then warned her not to stay in the Outer Banks because word was the storm had picked up speed and was coming ashore a day sooner than expected. She didn't need to get stuck with flooded roadways or any potential evacuations. Everything was still fluid with the situation. He needed to let Zuri know, too.

Duck followed him through the house. She sensed he was on edge. He knew she did because dogs were uncanny that way. He locked the door to his office, so he wouldn't forget if Caden came over again. He'd forgotten on Christmas Eve, and had tensed when he went to get Caden's gifts where he had them hidden in his office closet, but then he realized everything was fine. Nothing was touched or moved.

Zuri was still asleep in the guest room and Caden was out cold on the couch with his book on his face. He was in the same position, with Duck draped over him, that Damon had left him in the night before. He needed to be careful though.

He pinched the bridge of his nose and leaned against the glass of his deck door. The sea was already showing signs of the storm coming in. He needed to get over to the station for his shift. They needed to communicate with the fire department and sheriff's office to coordinate efforts depending on how severe the storm was predicted to be at landfall. There would likely be power outages and possible water supply contamination and closed roads. They'd been waiting on any state warnings or closures to come through so they could act on them. His team needed to clear and patrol the beach regardless. The riptides and undertow were extra vicious in this kind of weather.

Scarlett said she had been in Charlotte, so she had decided to just drive over when she got word his publisher needed material by New Year's Day and signatures before a filming date could be set. He looked at the time. Had Scarlet not shown up, he would have been able to go and make Zuri pack up an hour ago. She and Caden needed to leave ASAP.

ZURI ROLLED OVER and pulled the covers to her chin. She had mild shivers and wasn't feeling well, but she wasn't sure if stress had lowered her immune system or if what happened had rattled her to the point of shaking. She wasn't sure if she was more angry at Damon or disappointed in herself for not being more careful. How could she have let this happen again? How?

Her phone charging on the nightstand lit up. She hoisted herself up and checked the screen. There were two texts. One from her boss and one was from Damon. She tossed the phone on the bed. Dr. Farthan was probably just thanking her for the taffy and wishing her happy holidays. Nothing happy about it.

And Damon…she willed herself to ignore him. It didn't work. She could always check the text and not answer it if she didn't feel like getting into it with him. She opened the message from work first and all it said was for her to check her emails. She opened Damon's.

I think you should leave town sooner than planned. Things are not looking good. On my way.

She sat up and threw off the covers. Her temples pounded and she squeezed her eyes, but she was not going to cry. Not this time. She'd been through this before. The whole history repeats itself? She'd show history what she was made of. She blew her nose, then checked her email. *No way. Seriously?*

She got it. She was being offered ten-ure track. Her pulse raced. It was a sign. Both texts coming together like that. The universe was telling her she didn't need him. That she'd be all right. That her parents had been right about making sure their daughters got college educations so they could always stand on their own two feet. They were thinking financially, not emotionally, but it was all a matter of survival at the moment.

"That's what Damon wants, that's what he'll get." She got up, pausing for a second to steady herself when the room spun, then grabbed her small suitcase. She threw Caden's onto his bed as well, so he could pack as soon as he got back from lunch with Sara and her parents. She emptied her sweaters and underwear from the dresser drawer and the items she'd hung in the closet to keep them from wrinkling. She grabbed her phone charger and threw it in the suitcase. "A ride. You need to change your Uber reservation."

She sat down and dialed. No luck. She even tried a few local shuttle companies but either there were no drivers available until the one she'd prearranged for the thirtieth because they themselves were on vacation, or they were all booked up because of the holidays.

She held her head in her hand, then went to the bathroom and splashed cold water on her face. It didn't really help.

There was a rap at the door. Ugh. She knew Melanie meant well and probably went and made soup and tea even if Zuri had told her not to bother, but she really didn't want to be seen this way. There was another knock. *You know hot tea would make you feel better.* It would. She pushed her hair back and opened the door, then slammed it, but Damon caught it with his leg. He was holding a tray in his hands.

"Whoa, you don't look so good."

"Why thank you, Damon. I have a mirror," she snapped. *Don't cry. He's not worth it.*

Damon set the tray at the foot of the second bed and put his hand to her head. She pulled away but his touch felt good even if she didn't want it to.

"Melanie said you weren't feeling well. I think you might have a low-grade fever."

"I'm fine. And we'll be leaving as soon as I arrange transportation. I got your message loud and clear. We won't cramp your style."

"What in the world are you—"

She held up a finger.

"Don't worry, we can talk about visitation and what's best for Caden, but he needs to finish his school year. I'm sure you can agree with that."

Damon's face scrunched and he shook his head.

"What are you talking about, Zuri? I was talking about the weather. The storm that's coming. Cramping my style? Visitation? What about us?"

"Us? What about your girlfriend? The babe who had her arms around you earlier?"

God, she hated how she sounded. Like she cared. Like she was jealous and petty. *Petty.* She'd used that word on her mother regarding Damon's mother. It was genetic. She was turning into her mother. Now she and Damon could join the family war. Man, her head hurt. Maybe she did have a fever and it was frying her brain cells.

Damon sat on the edge of her bed and scrubbed his hands across his head, then took a deep breath.

"Zuri. That woman you saw wasn't what you think. She's not someone I'm interested in. She's someone I work with. Scarlett is my agent."

"Right. That's why, in her own words, she told me she was your girlfriend."

"That's our agreed MO if anyone who

doesn't know who I am around here sees her and asks questions. She must have thought she needed to shield me from you. She said my publisher was pushing for more publicity because the series has been optioned for movies and she knows I don't want fans around here."

"Fans. Oh, gosh. I was carrying your book because Caden wanted the older copy he has signed."

"That explains a lot. I'm sorry, Zuri. I didn't mean to hurt you. I want you happy and in my life."

She snorted and it wasn't because of her stuffy nose.

"I was considering leaving my position in Boston for you and so that Caden could be with us both. You know me, Damon. I'm not the kind of person who wants to be in the spotlight and if this ever does get out—because I believe in Murphy's Law and chaos and you won't be able to hide forever—then I'm not going to be that girl on the sidelines while you're surrounded by groupies and fans and media. It'll be high school all over again. I don't want Caden subjected to that either."

"That's not going to happen. I won't let it because I won't put you or him or anyone I love at risk."

Love? He was referring to his son. Not her. Of that much, she was sure.

"You can't predict the future, Damon. You couldn't have predicted becoming a father senior year or your parents divorcing or Vera dying from cancer or your brother drowning. You can't tell me that everything will be okay and that you can protect us or keep your life sane and simple. Things happen, Damon. Life is unpredictable. That's reality. Not fiction."

His eyes darkened and the creases that ran along his forehead and framed his lips and tugged at the corners of his eyes twitched with the pain she knew her words inflicted. She didn't want to hurt him. She really didn't, but she was hurting and confused and…scared. Scared of losing everything all over again. Scared of not being able to protect Caden from any more upheaval in his life.

"I've seen and felt more reality in this world than you'll ever understand."

He started slowly for the door but was at

it in one long stride when Melanie called his name. There was no mistaking the worry in her voice. Damon looked back at Zuri and he didn't need to say a word to know the same terrifying thought came to mind. She jumped from the bed and hurried after him.

"Damon!" Footsteps pounded the stairs before he reached the landing. Melanie sounded breathless. "Damon. Sara's parents just got back and thought the kids would be here. They wanted to check out the shops after lunch and the kids said they were going to Castaway Books, but Eve said they never showed up there. They walked around for thirty minutes and haven't found them. And Sara hasn't answered her cell phone. That's what has them worried. I know they have to be somewhere, but the weather is changing fast and I don't know if maybe they went hiking inland again or if they're on the beach somewhere. I looked from the deck and can't see them."

"It's all right. I'll find them," Damon reassured. "Kids explore around here all the time. Sara knows the area."

He followed her downstairs, keeping his cool, but Zuri could see the tension in his shoulders. She speed-dialed Caden's new cell number but there wasn't an answer. Damon looked at her and she shook her head.

"Don't worry," he told Sara's parents. "We'll track them down. They'll probably show up here any minute. I'll call around and let you know where they are." He dialed a number on his cell.

"Hey, Carlos, I know they've only been missing an hour or so, but if you see Sara and Caden, could you or whoever's on duty pick them up? I'm about to check the beach area. They may have gone toward the marsh. Parents are worried…yeah…thanks." He dialed again. "Mark, we have a couple of ducklings on the loose and the tide is coming in…thanks…take Duck with you. I'll be there in a second."

"I'm coming with you," Sara's dad insisted. Damon nodded.

"So am I," Zuri said.

"You're not feeling well. I'll find them," Damon said.

"I'm coming whether you like it or not." The throbbing in her head had suddenly cleared and felt like it had traveled to her chest instead. Kids explored. It wasn't the first time. It hadn't been that long. But then why was her gut telling her something wasn't right? Parental instinct? What happened to Caden having a cell phone to make him safer? She should have turned on his tracking. They'd barely set up a few phone numbers. This was all her fault.

"Sara's phone," Zuri said. "Can you track her location?"

"Yes, I forgot. We've never needed to but yes," her mother said, searching her phone. "Here."

Damon looked at her screen and Zuri could tell from the way his mouth flattened that he didn't like it.

"They're on the beach beyond the pier."

Damon called in the location to his team. They were by the water. Zuri touched her necklace and the pulse in her chest thrummed against her hand. She took off after Damon, but he was so much faster than she was. The wind surged and the waves got louder. They had to be safe. They had to be.

CADEN LAUGHED AS he and Sara ditched the waves. They'd taken off their sneakers and socks and he didn't care if it was cold or not. He was having a blast. This was the best day ever. He hadn't told anyone about who his dad really was, not even Sara yet, but he had wanted to. He didn't, though, because he realized this gave him an edge. He felt empowered and special. Bolder.

His dad wasn't just D. L. Dylan. His dad was basically Chase Falcon himself. The character who'd given Caden hope and helped him escape when school sucked and made him see what it meant to be fearless and brave. That's who he wanted to be like.

He didn't care if he'd always been the very opposite…a geek like his aunt. He didn't want to be that person. People could change. Sara made him want to change. Meeting his father made him want to change. And thinking of his mom made him want to, as well. She had liked his dad at one point in time. That meant she liked the kind of guy he was, and Caden wanted his mom, even in spirit, to be proud of him.

They ran back onto the cold wet sand,

right to where the water had pulled away, drawing the sand out from under their feet.

The shock of cold water helped him forget that his mom wasn't here. That Christmas wasn't the same without her. He just wanted to run and be with Sara and forget how much he was hurting inside. Being around Sara kept him from crying because he didn't dare let her see him break down. He didn't want to cry. He wanted to be strong. Invincible. Immune to pain.

"Ready? It's coming," Sara said. She grinned at him, challenged him. He thought she was really pretty. He was so glad she'd forgiven him.

He fiddled with the bracelet she'd tied to his wrist as he stood, ready to run. He looked over his shoulder.

"Now!"

They raced up the beach, missing all but the mist that sprayed them from the crashing wave and laughed hysterically.

"Oh, geez. Did you see that? It was huge!" Caden said.

"Gargantuan!" Sara said. She spread her arms out and faced the ocean. "'I know not all that may be coming, but be it what it will, I'll go to it laughing.'"

"Hey that's from *Moby Dick*! I read that this year." He loved that she read as much as he did and loved books like he did. He wanted to be great like his dad, but he didn't think Sara cared that much about it. Not after the lighthouse. He could be himself around her and it was okay. But that only made him want to be braver even more.

"Hurry, another is coming." Sara ran to the wet sand again and he followed. "Wait, see that? Oh, my God, that shell is huge! I can reach it. I have time."

It was huge, but it was half-sunken in the wet sand and way too close to where the earth disappeared beneath water.

"Sara, don't. That's not a good idea. Get back."

"Don't be like that. I can reach it easily."

The next wave was still rolling in. Maybe she did have time, but he was getting nervous.

"Leave it. It's not worth it. Come on. We should head back. Your parents will be wondering where you are."

He walked toward her, the sand slipping and sucking at him, making it harder to move fast.

"Sara, don't be like Elsa in *Indiana Jones and the Last Crusade.* It's not the Holy Grail. It's not worth it. Leave it."

She didn't listen. She grabbed the shell and lost her footing. Caden lunged and held onto her arm. It happened all at once. He heard the lifeguard whistle. He heard the dog barking. He heard their names and the horror in his aunt's voice. But the wave caught Sara first, then him and the ground disappeared. He found his footing, barely, and came up for air. Sara. She was only a few feet from him, gasping and flailing.

He could reach her. He had to. *Swimming in the ocean isn't like a pool.* His aunt's warning filled his ears. It didn't matter. Sara was now a little farther. He could get to her before it was too late. He swam toward her, fast and furious, struggling to keep afloat. He touched her but her hand slipped from his. He reached again and had her, but the current sucked them out much farther from shore than they had been when the wave first hit.

"Hold on!" He held her from behind because he remembered Chase Falcon doing that so that the person he was saving wouldn't pull him under. But they were both getting hammered by the waves and farther from shore by the second. He thought he heard a motor then saw something red bopping in the water. Then something dark…like a seal…or a shark. Panic zipped through him and water filled his mouth. Then another wave covered them. Sara slipped away from him and he couldn't swim anymore.

DAMON SWAM LIKE he had hellfire behind him, fueled by terror and adrenaline and something he'd never felt before in all the rescues he'd ever done. Duck was just ahead of him. She had reached and entered the water faster than he could. He couldn't wait for the boat or backup. He'd grabbed Mark's buoy and ran with it.

He dove under every wave and beat the water behind him. He couldn't let them die. He couldn't fail this time.

You've got this.

It wasn't his voice in his head. It was

Lucas, urging him on. Damon swam harder, his muscles burning while the cold waters numbed his skin. He could see Duck reaching Sara and holding on to her.

"Good girl! Take her in!" He looked around but couldn't spot Caden. Sanjay and Kiko were intercepting Duck and helped her haul Sara to safety.

"Caden!" The wind blew harder and the whitecaps bigger. Then a head came up feet away. He swam toward his son. He couldn't tell if he was too late. "Caden!"

He reached for him and put the buoy around him and started swimming parallel to the shoreline to escape the riptide. He could see the patrol boat heading their way. The boy coughed and sputtered up water. "Hang on. I've got you."

Then he saw it coming. The driftwood riding the next wave. And everything went black.

CHAPTER THIRTEEN

ZURI NEVER THOUGHT it was possible to be alive and dead at the same time, but that's exactly what she was experiencing. She couldn't breathe or swallow or feel her body, but she was running and she could hear herself screaming.

Sara was going to be all right. Duck had saved her, along with some help. Paramedics were on the beach giving her first aid and her parents were going to ride to the hospital with her. And Zuri thought she'd see Damon bringing Caden in next, but instead she saw him disappear just as Caden was pulled out of the water and onto a boat. Then she saw Mark dive in and the minutes it took before she saw him reemerge with Damon seemed like an eternity.

She paced in the sand, frantically waiting for them to make it ashore, and ran like mad when the second team of paramedics helped pull Damon's listless body from the boat. They lifted Caden, wrapped him for warmth and put him on a stretcher.

"He's alive."

That's all she heard but she didn't know who said the words. Caden whimpered and she wanted to hold him, but the emergency crew ordered her to let them stabilize him first.

"He'll be okay. Just hold on."

But Damon…they were pressing down on his chest, yelling at him, telling him he wasn't allowed to give up. Zuri's life flashed before her…all that was important and all that wasn't.

Then ocean water spewed from him and there was movement and cheers. But she wasn't cheering yet. He had to be okay.

"Let's go."

They were leaving for the hospital. She climbed in with her nephew and held his hand. And all she could do was swear that she loved them both and promise that she'd never leave them if only they could both be okay.

DAMON WALKED UP the steps to his house, wincing when he moved his shoulder the wrong way. He had dislocated it and had to keep it in the sling until his follow-up visit. He was lucky that he wasn't killed and luckier that his son was going to be okay. Caden had a busted eardrum that would take a few weeks to heal. Zuri had been given antibiotic drops to use on him.

All three of them, and Sara and her family, ended up riding out the storm at the hospital. He hadn't seen the aftermath— the littered road and broken shingles and a few windows—until they were headed home. Zuri had driven his truck and Duck had stayed with Faye and Carlos down the street. They said they'd bring her by later.

He looked behind him as Zuri helped Caden up the steps. The boy was still washed-out and weak. It would take time. That kid had gone above and beyond. He had seen Caden making that split-second decision to go after his friend, which spoke to his bravery, but Damon had given him a lecture. He'd put both kids on the spot in front of his crew when they visited them at the hospital, not to shame anyone, but to drive a point home. There was something to be said for rules and thinking before doing. Caden may have helped save Sara by keeping her afloat a few minutes longer, but he created a situation where more people had to be saved.

Damon wasn't happy that they had been playing dangerously close to the water during a red flag either. In fact, he was pretty mad. They had endangered themselves and his rescue team. He knew kids, especially as they entered the teenage years, were prone to risky behavior—heck, he knew that firsthand—but that didn't make it okay. Zuri had told him he couldn't predict the future, but he was predicting a lot of father-son talks in Caden's.

"You need to lie down. The doctor said you need a lot of rest. I'll make you something to eat," Zuri said, ushering Caden down the hall and into the spare room she had used just days before. She returned as Damon lowered himself gingerly onto the couch.

"Do you need pain meds? I have your prescription in my purse," she said, grabbing a throw pillow and trying to help him get comfortable. He shook his head. Pain meds messed with his head. He wanted to be able to think straight. She touched his cheek and inspected the blue welt on the side of his forehead.

"Are you sure? Between your head and shoulder, you've got to be miserable."

He used his good hand to guide her onto the couch next to him. He laced his fingers in hers.

"Thank you for being here," he said. It wasn't enough.

"Thank you, for saving Caden and Sara and for not dying on me." Tears welled in her eyes.

He lifted her hand and kissed it, letting his lips linger as he closed his eyes and tried to find the right words to apologize and make up for the secrets he kept and for all she'd been through. But with all he could try to say, he realized there were only three words that mattered. He moved her hand to his chest and held it right where his heart beat…for her, for Caden, for family…and said the one thing he meant more than anything else in the world. Just three words that held the power of the world, much like a drop of water could hold the spirit of the seas.

"I love you."

She covered her mouth and tried to dry her eyes but it wasn't happening. He wiped his thumb across her cheek.

"I mean it. I love you and always have. And I love Caden and can't imagine life without us as a family. The three of us, Zuri." The corner of his mouth quirked up. "Unless Caden wants a sibling. Didn't he say something about not wanting to be an only child?"

Zuri pursed her lips.

"Did he now? I'm not sure I recall that."

"I'm sure he did. We could ask Duck. Maybe he mentioned it to her."

Zuri chuckled then gave him a long sobering look.

"Damon, I love you, too. And life's too short to waste it apart any longer. We both know that. We've been given a second chance…third, really, after nearly losing you both…and I want to take it. With every cell of my body and breath I take, I want us to be a family, too."

"We'll figure it out. So long as we're together, we'll figure out how."

"While you were sleeping, in the hospital,

I made a call. I was offered the kind of next step in my career that I always thought I wanted. But I realized it wasn't. At least, not as it stands. I've scheduled a meeting to see if they'll be willing to have me work from here, but still in connection to the university and with the tenure track I was offered. Gray is going to put me in touch with a local scientist he said was studying water contamination and I'm going to see if we can get a joint grant and maybe set up a satellite research lab. My department in Boston could even send students to me for field study experience. Either way, I'll find a way to make it work because I've decided to move to Turtleback Beach. For Caden. For *us*. We can talk to Caden about it to be sure he transitions smoothly and is okay with it all, but I know my heart is here."

"But what if they don't agree? You can't give up a career move like that."

"The truth is I wasn't really happy. I miss field work and being outdoors. If they don't agree to a satellite site out here, then I'll get a grant and do it myself. I can always work with this guy Gray knows or affiliate myself with a North Carolina university. I'll make it work."

Damon kissed her and the way she kissed him back was better than any pain prescription a guy could ever take. She kissed him with promises and love and trust.

"Are you sure? Because I'd give this all up for you," he said.

"I know. But I don't want you to. This town is home in ways I never felt before. I want to be a part of it and I'm sure Caden will, too."

"You got that right! So, this means we're staying forever? I can go to school down here and Duck will be my dog, too?" Caden appeared from the hallway where he'd been eavesdropping. So much for getting that boy to rest. Zuri and Damon laughed.

"Yes, she's your dog, too. I'm pretty sure she already decided that when you two first met. And this is your home. *Our* home."

A *real* home for the first time. And a family forever.

EPILOGUE

New Year's Eve, one year later...

CADEN FILLED A second glass of fruit punch and carried it over to where Sara was standing watching the bride and groom dance. She looked really pretty tonight in her wine-red bridesmaid dress. She had told him that he looked good in a tuxedo, as well. The suit wasn't comfortable, but he liked that she liked him in it. Sara's grandmother, Miss Melanie, had gone overboard with taking photos of the two of them and commenting on how cute they looked. His dad helped him pick out the tux. Damon wore his formal navy attire and his aunt Zuri had on a white dress. Sara kept saying that it was the prettiest dress she'd ever seen, but most wedding dresses looked the same to Caden. They were all white so why did the rest matter?

Damon and Zuri finished their dance and raised their glasses to the room, which was basically a bunch of fancy tables, chairs, flowers and desserts all set up under the protection of a giant, heated party tent. They had planned to have the wedding outdoors, but winter weather came into play.

"Happy New Year! Here's to hope and new beginnings. May this next year bring happiness, good health and love to all," Damon said. He turned to his bride and kissed Zuri. *Again*. Caden had never seen his aunt so happy. It was nice. It made him happy. His dad and his aunt together were the best thing that had happened to him for as long as he could remember. Well, getting to know Sara, too.

She had returned to Turtleback Beach last summer and they had spent most of it together. His dad made sure that they were both strong swimmers by the end of summer and, the best part, Caden asked Sara to be his girlfriend—he didn't really mind that she was an older woman, having just turned fourteen while he was still thirteen—and she said yes.

Best. Moment. Ever.

Caden and Sara raised their juice glasses to the toast.

"Let's dance," Sara said. Thank goodness his dad had given him lessons in that department, as well. The entire dance floor filled with everyone they knew in town.

He took Sara's hand and led her into the middle, not far from the bride and groom. His dad had been huge about rules on how to treat women. He had drilled in proper behavior and respect for women so many times that Caden wondered where it had all come from.

Sara rested her cheek on his shoulder and Caden felt his cheeks heat up when he caught his aunt and dad smiling over at them. Whatever. Grown-ups made things weird.

His grandmothers had been making things extra weird, talking about babies all the time. Funny thing was that his parents—he liked calling his dad and aunt that—told him that Caden's grandmas used to hate each other. Now the two finally had a common goal that they couldn't stop trying to plan for. Another grandchild.

It wouldn't be so bad. Caden kind of liked the idea of someday being a big brother and showing a younger bro or sis the ropes. Kind of like Duck had been doing since Christmas.

Caden couldn't believe that he actually got a puppy for Christmas this year. The fluffiest, cutest golden retriever ever. He named him Chase, after the book hero… and because he liked to run after the birds on the beach. Damon said he'd teach Caden how to train him. His aunt was extra fond of the puppy. Especially since it was still small, though she had gotten pretty used to dogs. Her department back in Boston had agreed to give her tenure track while also allowing her to set up and pursue her research in the Outer Banks. In fact, she had just gotten another grant with a local scientist. She was spending more time outdoors than she ever did back in Boston. She smiled a lot more, though that probably had a lot to do with his dad, too.

Caden was definitely happier. He missed his mom, but he knew she'd be happy that he was in a good place.

The music stopped and Sara gave him a

peck on the cheek. It always made him feel taller when she did that. He really wished he'd have another growth spurt so that he could catch up to her. She didn't seem to care though. She was the coolest girl ever.

"I see my mom waving me over. I'm going to go see what she wants and I'll be back," Sara said.

"Okay. I'll get us more cake," Caden said.

Damon and Zuri came over and his aunt wrapped her arms around him and gave him a huge hug. His dad put his arms around them both.

"Thank you for being such an awesome kid," Zuri said.

"Ditto that," Damon added.

"Aw seriously, guys. You're gonna embarrass me. But I guess I'll let it pass, it being your wedding and all. And New Year's."

"Happy New Year to you," Damon said.

"I hope it's full of good luck for you," Zuri added.

"Are you kidding me?" Caden looked up at the two of them. "I'm the luckiest kid on earth. Sure, I'll always miss Mom, but right now I have the two of you, a new puppy and Duck, and a great girlfriend. And double the grandparents than I used to have. Not to mention, I get to read every future Chase Falcon book before it's ever released. What more could a kid want?" He headed toward Sara but glanced over his shoulder at them and grinned.

Damon had his arms wrapped around Zuri and they were kissing again. He could tell that his dad was head over heels in love because his latest Falcon book ended up having Chase fall in love. Damon's sales had skyrocketed because of it. There was something about this romance stuff. He was going to have to get used to Damon and Zuri being all lovey-dovey. Maybe he'd spend more time outside with Duck and Chase…and Sara. He didn't mind one bit.

Sara smiled at him from across the room. Life was good.

* * * * *

Get 4 **FREE REWARDS!**

We'll send you 2 FREE Books plus 2 FREE Mystery Gifts.

Love Inspired books feature uplifting stories where faith helps guide you through life's challenges and discover the promise of a new beginning.

FREE Value Over **$20**

THE 2020 CHRISTMAS ROMANCE COLLECTION!

5 FREE TRADE-SIZE BOOKS IN ALL!

'Tis the season for romance!
You're sure to fall in love with these tenderhearted love stories from some of your favorite bestselling authors!

YES! Please send me the first shipment of **The 2020 Christmas Romance Collection**. This collection begins with 1 FREE TRADE SIZE BOOK and 2 FREE gifts in the first shipment (approx. retail value of the gifts is $7.99 each). Along with my free book, I'll also get **2** additional mass-market paperback books. If I do not cancel, I will continue to receive three books a month for four additional months. My first four shipments will be billed at the discount price of $19.98 U.S./$25.98 CAN., plus $1.99 U.S./$3.99 CAN. for shipping and handling*. My fifth and final shipment will be billed at the discount price of $18.98 U.S./$23.98 CAN., plus $1.99 U.S./$3.99 CAN. for shipping and handling*. I understand that accepting the free books and gifts places me under no obligation to buy anything. I can always return a shipment and cancel at any time. My free books and gifts are mine to keep no matter what I decide.

☐ 260 HCN 5449   ☐ 460 HCN 5449

Name (please print)

Address   Apt. #

City   State/Province   Zip/Postal Code

Mail to the Harlequin Reader Service:
IN U.S.A.: P.O. Box 1341, Buffalo, NY, 14240-8531
IN CANADA: P.O. Box 603, Fort Erie, Ontario L2A 5X3

---

*Terms and prices subject to change without notice. Prices do not include sales taxes which will be charged (if applicable) based on your state or country of residence. Offer not valid in Quebec. All orders subject to approval. Credit or debit balances in a customer's account(s) may be offset by any other outstanding balance owed by or to the customer. Please allow 3 to 4 weeks for delivery. Offer available while quantities last. © 2020 Harlequin Enterprises ULC.

Your Privacy—Your information is being collected by Harlequin Enterprises ULC, operating as Harlequin Reader Service. To see how we collect and use this information visit https://corporate.harlequin.com/privacy-notice. From time to time we may also exchange your personal information with reputable third parties. If you wish to opt out of this sharing of your personal information, please visit www.readerservice.com/consumerschoice or call 1-800-873-8635. Notice to California Residents—Under California law, you have specific rights to control and access your data. For more information visit https://corporate.harlequin.com/california-privacy.

XMASR20

COMING NEXT MONTH FROM

HEARTWARMING

Available February 9, 2021

#363 CATCHING MR. RIGHT

Seasons of Alaska • by Carol Ross

Pro angler Victoria Thibodeaux is this close to landing the industry's top spokesperson contract. Then she meets Seth James, the smooth-talking finalist who is looking to both outfish and outcharm her!

#364 THE LITTLEST COWGIRLS

The Mountain Monroes • by Melinda Curtis

Former child actress Ashley Monroe needs Wyatt Halford as the star in her Western movie, not as her wedding date! That is until a mix-up ties them together in a way they never could have expected.

#365 A VALENTINE'S PROPOSAL

Cupid's Crossing • by Kim Findlay

The future of Carter's Crossing hinges on a Valentine's Day proposal between Nelson and Mariah. Will the reformed groomzilla and wedding planner make this a night to remember, or jeopardize the whole town?

#366 COMING HOME TO TEXAS

Truly Texas • by Kit Hawthorne

A reckless mistake drove Dalia Ramirez away from the Texas ranch she loves and the boy who broke her heart. Is a disaster enough for her to return to her hometown and face Tony Reyes?

HWCNM0121

Visit ReaderService.com Today!

As a valued member of the Harlequin Reader Service, you'll find these benefits and more at ReaderService.com:

- Try 2 free books from any series
- Access risk-free special offers
- View your account history & manage payments
- Browse the latest Bonus Bucks catalog

Don't miss out!

If you want to stay up-to-date on the latest at the Harlequin Reader Service and enjoy more content, make sure you've signed up for our monthly News & Notes email newsletter. Sign up online at ReaderService.com or by calling Customer Service at 1-800-873-8635.